A
WEB
OF LIES

A Dark Mafia Anastasia Romance

BEENA KHAN

A Beena Khan Book

Book 3 of Black Widow Series
Genre: Dark Mafia
July 2022

Cover design: Ms. Betty
Cover Photographs: DepositPhotos
Editor: L.L Lily
Proofreaders: Evelyn at Pinpoint Editing, Zainab M

Come say hi on Beena's Beastlys!

Reading Order

RED SERIES

Book #1: The Name of Red
(Kabir & Red)

A mysterious woman in that red dress seeking shelter came inside the restaurant he was busy working in—primarily the bar. So, he decided to leave her books anonymously with notes in them. He just didn't expect to get caught so soon.

Book #2: The Weight on Skin

The wealthy playboy has gone rogue because of a woman. Eight months have gone by, and Kabir still hasn't moved on from the woman he still loves.

Book #3: Color Me Red
(Red's Standalone: Prequel)

Red was always taught by her parents that she will meet 'the one'. Torn between two men, she must choose between right and wrong before each man takes a piece of her and never returns it.

Book #4: The Whispers of Rifts
(Aryan's Standalone)

To the world, he's the secret keeper, but no one knows his secrets. Aryan Singh is a bartender at the restaurant and bar of his best friend Kabir. While homeless, Aryan had met a girl, a college student named Aanaah.

FORBIDDEN SERIES: SPIN OFF OF RED SERIES
Book #1: The Flame Must Burn
(Cyrah & Ryder)
From a traditional Middle Eastern family, Cyrah is a young
foreign-exchange student studying abroad in a summer program
whose path crosses with the small-town's local biker from a
different culture.

Book #2: The Deepest Cut
(Ismat & Dara)
Dark and dangerous Dara is the brother of her father's sworn
enemy. He's the vicious villain and handsome as sin.
His brother is in jail. He sets out to find the sister of the woman
responsible, make her his bride and pay the price.

BEAUTY AND THE BEAST SERIES

Book #1: A Beauty So Cruel
I was a beauty, a stray orphan until the beast took me as his
hostage. Dahlia was the wrong person at the wrong time. To save
her life, she made a deal with the beast the mafia don. He didn't
know by taking her, he sealed his own fate.

Book #2: A Beast So Cold
(Sequel)
Vlad made Dahlia his queen. The reason behind his smile. Then,
she set his world on fire. Nobody takes away what he wants. A
beast is no man, and he's going to prove it by dragging her from
hell.

Book#3: A King Of Beasts
(Interconnected standalone)

A rival Italian mob set my world on fire by destroying everything I love. The people around me look away as my innocence is shed by the Mad King until one stare lingers. Bodyguards are meant to be protectors, not lovers.

Book #4: A Beauty So Cursed
(Interconnected Standalone)

Lada Sokolova, a noble Bratva Princess was supposed to be betrothed to my family. I'm twelve years her senior so I reject her. Now, she's getting married to a brutal *Vor* who's more than *twice* her age. I do the one thing I shouldn't have, causing my life on the line. I take her. I kidnap a bride in her wedding dress.

BLACK WIDOW SERIES

Book #1: A Kiss Of Venom
(Complete Standalone)

I've been in a coma for the past three years after an accident has left me unconscious and widowed. I'm in a sleep so deep, it cannot be broken until feel a brush of soft lips against mine. In my groggy state, I wake up to a pair of dark eyes and a sinister smile. As an agent, I revisit one of the most treacherous cases of the most dangerous man in New York City, Alexander Nikolaev, the *Pakhan* of the Russian Bratva.

Book #2: A Lock Of Death
(Complete Standalone)

I was locked in a skyscraper in New York City with eight other girls. I can't belong to a single man because I've belonged to *all*. No identity, no friends, and no life outside the gilded door of this tower. One day, the Bratva Brotherhood comes for me. Imagine my surprise when Dimitri Nikolaev says," You're being delivered."

DEVIL'S LAIR SERIES

Book #1: The Blue-Eyed Devil
(Salvi & Ehva)
I'm a wealthy and privileged Catholic girl who's returned from studying law abroad. It was a night out with my boyfriend, Adamo, when everything descended into chaos at the casino. He lost and gambled me away. Years ago, I took a vow of celibacy, but now a sadistic man tempts me with the dark side.

Book#2: The Fallen Angel
(The Sequel)
I considered Salvi Moretti my God, but he turned out to be the Devil in disguise. He can break my wings, but he may have forgotten my claws will always come out.

Book #3: The Night Thief
(Complete Standalone)
I'm a woman on a run. A con artist, scamming my way into the rich. I set my eyes on one of the most popular casinos in New York posing as a royal princess. Everything was going well until a pair of harsh blue eyes catch me red-handed.

HADES & PERSEPHONE DUET

Book #1: A Beautiful Liar

AUTHOR'S NOTE

This is a dark book revolving around the mafia and reader discretion is advised for sensitive readers. The author's books aren't light, nor safe, and meant for fictional reading for feeding the dark souls. While this has dark romance elements, it is *not* the main focus of the story. This is a complete standalone.

The book focuses on Anastasia, her life, her family, assassins, and the syndicates. This is a story about a woman finding herself in the mafia, and it ends with new beginnings. This story is *loosely* based on the legend combined with the author's imagination.

For a list of TWs, click <u>HERE.</u>

I stepped toward him to lift my blade again, but then footsteps flooded the living room. The front door burst open, bringing with it unwanted gusts of wintry wind. My skin chilled under the frigid cold.

I stilled as his men, all in black attire, surrounded me.

Over fifteen of them outnumbered me. I swapped one of my blades for my revolver as I lifted it to aim at one of their faces.

My gaze flicked to the man who still drank without a care in the world.

He leaned against the bar, standing so casually, as if my assassination attempt had unfazed him. Black silk pajamas clung to his body like the outfit had been made for him, and the first three buttons of his shirt were open.

He wore a silver pendant around his neck. I caught a pair of reddish curls on his chest. It was more light brown than red. He'd probably slipped downstairs for a drink in the middle of the night. Perhaps, he couldn't sleep.

His tall, six-foot-five self blinked down at my five-foot-nine frame. He was a lean, well-muscled giant with long, reddish-brown locks that framed his face like a Greek god. His hair was more of the lightest brown than red. It was smooth and straight, but the ends slightly curled at the nape.

The man studied me carefully like someone assessing their prey. A grim line stretched across his freckled face as he shook his head at me like I was an idiot for invading his home. Little freckles dotted his skin. I knew because I'd memorized his face in the back of my mind. Carved cheekbones, trimmed beard, and emerald eyes. I waited for his skin to turn red and flare up any second now. But it didn't.

His eyes continued to peer into mine, but he would find nothing but hollowness.

An empty soul.

"Unmask his face," the sleepy-eyed man murmured.

His low voice was rich and sounded older than me—*much older than me.*

One of the made men reached out to unmask my face, but I lifted my blade and sliced his hand off. The dismembered body part dropped to the floor and rolled away. It left stains of red droplets behind. If I were normal, my stomach would've been churning and twisting this very second, but it didn't. Instead of retching my guts out, I stared straight ahead.

The handless man shrieked, and the others rushed toward me, pointing a gun right in my face.

"No. Do not shoot. I want him alive... for now."

His men paused.

My gaze flicked to him, still sipping his brandy.

Well, he isn't planning on killing me yet, so don't mind if I ...

I flicked my revolver up at hip level and popped the bullet right at the groin of the made man who held a gun to my face. Now, he was dickless, and he couldn't fuck ever again. It was a damn pity. I almost felt guilty for his girl... or guy.

He or she would find someone else, anyway.

Blood gurgled from his lips and his lower region, darkening his pants with his blood. His hand dropped from my face, but not before another hand reached out and punched me on the back of my head. I bit down on my lip to keep myself from hissing as stars filled my mind.

Through my starry-eyed vision, I glanced over my shoulder, lifted my elbow, and jabbed the man right on the nose. The satisfaction of a crunch and the blood gushing out of his nose pleased me. Not risking any more chances, I made my next move and swung my long blade in the air, slashing it across, and catching their hands.

Like the others before them, they were now dismembered as well. I must have looked like a sight with blood spattered around me and chopped-off hands at my feet. The blood hadn't touched me yet. I hated getting blood on me. Other people's blood, at least. It never washed off.

Screams cackled and filled the atmosphere.

Breathing through my nose, I took a defensive stance again and pressed the trigger.

I fired.

Again and again.

The made men were ready to shoot me again, but then they paused.

I held in a smile.

As per their Boss's command, they couldn't kill me yet.

One of them behind me kicked my leg out from under me.

Well, he hadn't stopped them from trying to beat me to a pulp at least.

Before I could fall, I caught myself halfway. I wondered if it was the one, whose nose I had broken, had just kicked me. I was just about to turn around and shoot to give him another bloody nose, but a blade came from my right and knocked my revolver from my hand. Hissing under my breath, my stunned eyes fell on the blade sticking out of my leather glove.

Shit. That didn't look good.

It. Was. *Still.* Stuck. In. My. Skin.

Fuck.

I hadn't expected that, nor was I prepared to be struck by it. It came out of nowhere.

An ache filled the pierced skin, and I held back a groan.

Caught off guard, I stilled and glanced to my right.

My gaze glided to the culprit.

The brandy sipper had stopped sipping.

Maybe this was who he truly was.

Violent, unpredictable, and insanely powerful.

I'd never killed one of his kind before.

Too late for regrets now.

Instead of eating my face, his teeth landed on the edge of my jawline as his mouth snatched my mask off.

My fingers halted.

I stilled.

Frozen in place by his sudden gesture, I stared up at him.

He stared down at me.

He wore a knowing look as his eyes lost their edge.

My heart hammered in my chest.

Shit... Shit... Shit.

Lightning bolts exploded in my soul and sizzled through my veins.

My breath caught in my chest as dread crawled over me.

He might as well have killed me sooner.

Every inch of the fight in me dissolved.

Fuck my life.

My mask hung from my face, still looped around one ear, but the other had become disheveled. Little pants of air came out of my lips, hitting him right on the mouth.

The movement had brought him much closer to me now, his muscled chest pressed against mine. My breasts shoved against him, my femininity clashing with his masculinity, even though I had hidden it.

Electric shivers ran down my spine, sending sizzles between my legs. My erratic heartbeat thumped, and his eyes narrowed as if he could hear it.

Our eyes held each other captive.

My wild, stormy eyes never looked away from him.

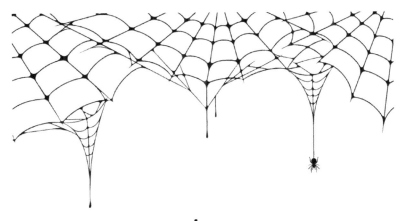

Ana

2

Don Surge Romano.

The Don to one of the Five Families of New York stared down at me.

His men no longer surrounded me, but they still stood a few feet away, like they were unwilling to let me leave. Even in his night clothes and the expensive silk clinging to his hips, he was still the most dangerous, violent, and trained man in this room.

My blade still poked out from his shoulder, too, and he hadn't bothered to remove it. Maybe because the wound was deeper than my hand injury, and if he pulled it out now, he would bleed out. My eyes darted to the wound again before I flicked my gaze to him. Keeping my face neutral, I reached out like lightning to draw the blade from his shoulder, hoping he would die, but he grabbed my injured, gloved hand instead.

I winced at the low blow. Well, I deserved it, since I was going to do the same to him, anyway. Hurting him in the same place he hurt, too.

I bit down on my lower full lip as I reached out to grab the handle of the blade. His hand still pressed against my hip, tightening against the flesh before slipping under my black shirt and resting against my bare skin. His hand was cool against me. My eyes widened as I glanced at the large hand under my shirt.

Flicking my gaze up, I shot him a deathly glare.

"You stupid shit," I muttered in my feminine voice.

Gasps of surprise filled the room from the back as I cussed.

I rolled my eyes, because I'd literally stabbed their precious Don, but that didn't seem to faze them. With my gleaming soul, I eyed the handle and twisted it deeper into his shoulder. His face contorted. More fresh blood gushed out of the wound.

His shirt was already stained. The red of it was invisible against the black fabric, but the fabric had darkened and looked soaked. Don Surge grabbed a hold of my hip skin with his thumb and forefinger and twisted it like I had done to him. I hissed under my breath before gripping the handle tighter.

His greens flared as he continued pinching and twisting my hip. He no longer pushed against my injured hand. I didn't understand why he didn't. Baffled at my thought, I gripped the handle and readied myself to yank it out. A twisted slyness fell over my soul, and I pulled out an inch. The Don winced, and I felt no ounce of pity for him. I was ready to complete the task until his hand left my poor, tingling flesh and now gripped my throat.

I stilled.

My hand halted as I met his dreadful eyes.

The glassiness in them had disappeared, and the narrowed coldness in them returned. His thumb found the center of my neck and pressed against it, cutting off my air.

My breath hitched that he might end me.

studied it, he'd never taken it out before. My blade was larger, but his smaller blade could cause some serious damage, too.

Don Surge studied my face before raising a light brown eyebrow. The cold metal held like a threat against my skin. Gulping, I met his eyes as he dug the sharp edge slightly deeper into my pale skin, nicking it. A trickle of warm blood trailed down from my neck. We both had our blades pressed to each other's necks and refused to look away. Our gazes battled for control, and his other sneaky hand captured my injured one. It rested just above the inflicted wound, like a threat that he would dig into my skin once again if I attacked him.

His much larger and rougher body pressed against mine. The man's chest was warm. The leather scent became more prominent. Our panting breaths came out rougher and mingled together, until I couldn't tell which breath was mine and which breath was his. I straightened my spine as I met his stare head-on. I was prepared to die in every mission.

Just like him.

It was what we were taught since we were children.

Breathe like it's your last.

If I had to die, I wouldn't die like a coward, and I would face my death head-on. Maybe we would both end up with decapitated bodies. Now, that would be a sight for people to find. Surge Romano's eyes grew colder, and they darkened as he leaned in closer. The blade glided across to the side of my skin where one of my carotid arteries rested. It seemed like he was playing with his food. Playing with me.

His voice was brutal as he spoke.

"I did mention earlier that I would slit your throat." His hand calmly rested on the artery. My pulse fluttered as he pressed the cool blade down on it. I shivered and tilted my neck.

"It would take only one nick and you would bleed out right before me."

His voice was low and seductive as he taunted me.

My stomach churned as I gritted my teeth.

"Perhaps, you're forgetting my blade is pressed against you?" I remarked as I calmed my breathing down. "You might not bleed out," I mentioned coyly, "but the kill will be messy, unclean, and you will suffer *painfully.*"

Don Surge only blinked, and his lip twitched. That wry smile of his sent chills down my spine. "You wanna know one thing?" he murmured as his breath fell on me again. His freckles were larger up close, like stars decorating the night sky. The blade he held was still steady against my skin. Our gazes locked on to each other. "Maybe I just might not kill you today. I like the color of your eyes. They match my carpet."

And with that, he pulled back and put a few feet between us, but not before snatching my blade from my grasp.

Dumbfounded at his backhanded compliment, I stared repulsively at him.

His jaw loosened, and it became less tense as he eyed me.

"You're in my home, Little Assassin, and my people are surrounding this mansion. *Run,*" he warned. The lethal warning raised the hairs on my nape. "You can run, but you might not get that far." His lip curled, like he enjoyed toying with me. I was pretty sure if I were a man, I would've been gutted already. "If you manage to escape without killing or harming more of my men, you are free to go, for now. If you harm my people yet again, I will bring you back myself, shackle you in the dungeon, and carve out your pretty little neck."

My breath hitched at the ultimatum.

It was impossible to escape and not kill.

He thought my neck was pretty.

My mind didn't pay attention to the fact that he'd also promised to carve it out.

The man had a blade sticking out from his shoulder, and half of his shirt was damp with blood, but right now, he was still playing with *my* blade. He ran his finger against the sharp silver edge of it like he was probably imagining it against my neck.

He continued to challenge me with no fear in his eyes.

I tilted my head as our gazes crashed and locked on to one another once again.

"Run." Don Surge's voice rumbled in the empty living room.

It echoed off the walls.

I took one glance at him still standing there before I ran out of the room.

As I escaped, I ended up killing two more of his people.

His challenge was impossible to resist.

If you harm my people yet again, I will bring you back myself.

That taunt haunted me.

It wouldn't be the last time I would see Don Surge Romano.

Later that night, when I returned home, Kirill was already sitting in our living room.

He was the *Brigadier* of the Bratva syndicate's Brotherhood.

The captain in charge that trained the assassins like me.

And he was also my husband.

Kirill Volkov.

"Is it done?" His deep, masculine voice came.

No hellos or greetings ever came from him, and I'd expected it. He wasn't the kind who was into small talk, even with his wife of two years. He'd found me when I was thirteen before recruiting me to work for him from the black market.

Everything in my memory was blank before that age. I had a bump on the back of my head, and I didn't know where I came from, much less who my family was.

Kirill was my family now.

I considered him my own, even though I was one of his soldiers.

During the day, I played the perfect role of a submissive wife.

During the night, I transformed into his assassin.

Everyone knew me as Anastasia Volkova, Kirill Volkov's wife, and only a few in our inner circle knew the double life I led. Most of Bratva soldiers didn't know, either.

Remembering his question, I sighed silently and shook my head.

He frowned, looking at me with disapproval written all over his face. The slight wrinkles around his eyes deepened as he waited for me to continue.

"Romano wasn't in his bedroom when I entered," I spoke softly. My voice always dropped low when it came to one of my leaders. "I can still do it, though."

He scoffed under his breath, and my heart sank lower into my chest.

I didn't like disappointing him.

I hadn't exactly lied, but I hadn't been fully truthful, either.

Surge Romano was the latest assignment given to me.

I didn't know why the Bratva wanted him dead. They had ordered his kill, and I had obeyed, not questioning them at all. It wasn't my place to.

This was the first time I'd returned without completing my mission.

I should have known better. The moment I realized Don Surge Romano wasn't in his room, I should have left and returned another night, or I should have waited for him to return. I acted a bit irrationally.

Fine, *much* more irrationally when I thought I could take everyone on. Not only had I jeopardized the mission, but the Don also knew what I looked like.

My breath caught in my throat as I stared at Kirill's cold, black eyes. I could never tell him that. He always reminded me I was the Bratva's chosen one, their secret weapon, because no one knew my identity, but the Don of the Romano family knew me *now*. Well, he knew that I was a female assassin and what I looked like. He still wasn't aware of what organization I belonged to or what my name was, but he expected me to make another assassination attempt now.

I still didn't know why he left me alive.

Jerking myself out of my thoughts, my eyes collided with Kirill's dark ones, and I knew he felt absolutely nothing for me.

No love, no intimacy, and definitely no comfort.

It was always business with him. I was surprised he'd married me when I'd turned eighteen. Kirill continued to glower at me. My heartbeat sped up as I remembered the Don's emerald green eyes. It thundered through my chest, and I was half afraid Kirill could hear it.

I took a seat across from him as I began removing my blades and hood. Luckily, the knives were clean. Otherwise, he would have questioned me as to whose blood it was. He didn't need to know I'd killed a few Italian soldiers and left some handless ones behind. Kirill's dry, invasive gaze stayed glued to me, and I couldn't avoid it much longer.

With my thundering heart, I met his desolate dark eyes.

He was in his mid-thirties compared to my twenties. His black hair was swept behind him, gelled, and neatly tucked behind his ears. His strong and well-defined features stood out, especially his chiseled and pale jawline. Kirill always had a clean-shaven face, but now he was sporting a shadow on his face.

He sat there casually in his black satin suit with one leg crossed over the other as his eyes continued to scrutinize me.

We'd touched once, though, in our two years of marriage, and it was on our wedding night. I remembered that giddiness I had felt, but then he'd avoided me like the plague after taking my virginity. I bit my tongue at what slipped out of my mouth about my leader. Sometimes I wondered if I'd stick around if he hadn't married me. I remembered that night even after these past years, and a part of me still craved it. Him.

I couldn't tell if it was because I had no other man around me but him. It didn't help that my lonely soul stared up at him, wanting to see the man I had married instead of the leader who expected me to fulfill my duties.

Love didn't exist in my life.

Marriage and duty did.

"Everything all right, Anastasia?" Kirill asked at last.

He bit down on his full lower lip as he waited for my answer, and my eyes went to his lips. The Don's lips were pinker than his. Kirill's were darker in color.

I snapped into focus, wondering why on earth I was comparing their mouths.

It's not like I'd felt the Don's lips before.

My cheeks warmed and my skin flushed.

Kirill noticed and raised an eyebrow.

"You're turning pink, *malyshka*."

Baby girl. He'd always called me that since I was young.

I almost laughed at the fact that he'd caught me.

"It's just hot in here," I said, waving a hand dramatically.

Kirill only stared, and I almost cowered under his gaze. It was like he could see right through me.

"*Ty vsegda v moikh meeslyah,*" he began. *I worry about you sometimes.* "You're always on my mind. You would let me know if something was wrong, correct?"

Something stirred in my soul that he cared about me.

I was the only female to fight in a New York mob. No one else was granted this permission. Then again, it wasn't the biggest achievement in the world. I was sure no one would look at it highly if I put *Assassin* on my resume.

Kirill had fought for me to reach this position, though.

He asked me to jump, and I jumped.

I would do anything for him, and he knew that.

I gave a tight-lipped smile. "Of course, Kirill. I'm fine."

I lied.

Another lie slipped past my disobedient mouth.

He never knew what laid in my soul.

Nor had he attempted to find out.

I searched his eyes and hoped he would discover the amount of love I wanted to give him. He was my husband, and I felt, as a wife, I should. Right? I didn't love Kirill. I didn't know what love was, nor did he allow me to show it to him. He was always distant and reserved. Sometimes we'd be in the same room, but it was like he was miles away from me. That he was physically present, but his mind was in another universe.

Kirill gave a curt nod as he stood up from his seat.

"I must give an update to *Pakhan*. Make sure the task is completed within two weeks, Anastasia," he commanded harshly.

I chewed on the inside of my lip as I replied softly, "Of course. I won't disappoint you again. *Ya vsyo sdeayu kak nado.*"

I'll do everything perfectly.

I stared up at him as he stood to his six-foot height and came around to stand next to me. I wondered for a second if he would let me hug him for once. I'd never hugged him or anyone. I didn't have any female friends. I wasn't exactly the friendliest person in the world. People thought I was too cold, too quiet, and extremely boring. Maybe I had friends in my childhood, but my mind always drew a blank.

How did one make friends, though?

I didn't remember how to.

Did they begin with introductions?

What did friends even do?

Instead of hugging me, Kirill swept past me to exit the room.

The tiny hope in my soul diminished, but I didn't feel as disappointed as I had been when I was younger. It was expected now. With a dimmed soul, I stared at his fading figure, hoping for once he would see me as his wife and not his soldier.

I wanted to tell him, *Vot moe serce. Ono polno lubvi.*

Here's my heart. It's full of love.

I caught a whiff of his lingering woodsmoke scent and his sharp cologne as he left. I slammed my eyes shut, and my hands clenched into fists. My knuckles turned white as I dug my sharp, burgundy-painted nails into my skin. It breached the softness, drawing blood from it. I still wore one of the good gloves and hid the injury from Kirill.

It was bandaged, and he would never know I'd been in battle. I'd burned the ripped glove on my way home. I'd cleaned my neck, too, before returning. He could never find out that I'd failed him and this mission.

I would make it up to him.

As I focused on his smell, I caught something else, too.

An unwanted scent that hadn't been there in the morning when I'd last seen him. A flowery, overwhelming scent like jasmine clung to him, too. I held in a sharp breath as I sighed and collapsed against the seat behind me.

I felt like a sore loser.

A sore loser who never had anything to claim as her own.

My husband never touched me after taking my virginity, but that didn't stop him from touching another woman.

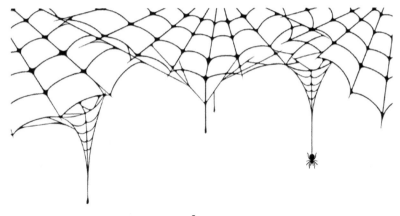

Ana

3

PAST
THIRTEEN YEARS OLD

My body jerked awake when the first bucket of ice-cold water splashed against my skin. My eyes snapped open as I laid in the middle of the dusty, brown ground. I groaned, my teeth clattering uncontrollably as I rendered myself awake.

Reaching up a hand, I rubbed the left side of my scalp. Hissing under my breath, through my blurry vision, I returned my hand in front of me again. It was covered in blood. I touched the bump again. As my crumpled body gathered itself, I tried to jerk myself up. Little pants of warm air left my throat as I shook my head slowly.

Vivid images of me on the metro played in my mind.

I remembered falling.

I didn't remember how I fell, though.

Maybe someone had pushed me accidentally? The metro had been crowded, though. I wondered why I was even there.

My mind drew a blank. I couldn't remember anything at all.

Running my cold hands over my face, I wiped away the remaining water from my face. Blood trickled down from the side of my forehead as it mingled with the water, creating an unpleasant metallic mixture. My limbs ached like they had run a marathon. I sat upright slowly, using my arms to drag myself up to my feet. The bright sunlight hit my sandpaper-like eyes.

Water invaded my eyes, and just the slightest liquid poked them. Sweat trickled down my nape, and I swept a hand through my matted, golden hair. Blinking, I stared straight ahead at the countless feet surrounding me. Awareness trickled in the back of my head. My pulse spiked. My scalp still ached, and I realized that the wound might leave a hidden scar behind. I didn't know where I was or what was happening.

I just wanted to return home.

My thoughts stopped.

Home? Where was my home?

I squeezed my eyes shut as I tried to remember something familiar, but nothing came up in my empty mind.

It was a haunting feeling. Something I'd never felt before.

I couldn't remember anything at all, as if my mind had been wiped.

"Five hundred dollars!" a voice shouted in the background.

My shoulders tensed, and my fleeting eyes jerked up.

"Seven hundred dollars."

The merchants all spoke over one another.

"Nine hundred dollars. And I want the necklace she's wearing on her neck."

Stunned, I clasped my hands around the blue necklace.

I didn't know where it came from. I just knew it was mine.

All I knew was that it belonged to me, and I wouldn't give it to these vultures.

"A thousand!" another voice competed.

Where was I?

My hands shook and I cowered.

I brought my knees to my chest as I stared up at the people surrounding me. Some were merchants while others were men in expensive suits.

I didn't recognize anyone around me.

They stared at me in such a way that made uncomfortable shivers run down my spine. I didn't recognize that look... I had nothing to compare it to.

I glanced down at my white dress, which had a stain of red on it. A big glob of scarlet on it marked me as the scarlet girl, and I didn't know what my crime was. Did I know anyone among this sea of men? I chewed on the inside of my cheek. Ignoring the pain on my scalp, I stared up at the strangers. One of the older men, in his fifties, wore a wicked glint in his eyes as he peered down at me. He moved toward me, and his musky, unpleasant scent filled my nostrils.

Why was he coming close to me?

I crawled away from him, but another pair of feet right behind me blocked me from escaping. My bewildered eyes searched my surroundings, hoping I could find a friend among foes, but all of them were strangers.

"I made the highest bid," the older man said as he stopped right before me.

Bid? What was this place?

His voice was harsh, and I didn't like how he stared at my girlish body.

I wanted to cover up from his disgusting stare.

"Fifteen thousand," a deeper, unfamiliar voice boomed out from the back.

The merchant looming in front of me paused and turned to look behind me.

Lifting my heavy-lidded eyes, I stared right at the man who had spoken. He was younger than the man, like he was in his mid-twenties.

I gulped at the sight of him.

My throat ran dry as my dreary eyes met his black ones.

The surrounding people parted as he moved through the circle like he was the leader of all of them. The baffled merchants scratched the back of their heads as they stared at one another.

The stranger was among a group of men in black suits. He was the man who hadn't spoken, like he wasn't part of this charade. As if he'd been walking past us and the commotion caught his attention. He stood right in front of me.

Lifting my head back and still leaning back against my elbows, I met his glassy eyes. His eyes were colder like the others, but the hunger in them was missing.

He looked kind of nicer than the others. More welcoming, even though his suit was intimidating to look at. He tilted his head as he stared down at me, and I caught a black marking on his neck. My eyes trailed from his fitted black suit before resting on his hand that hung limply by his side.

A spider's cobweb was imprinted on it.

Puzzled, I glanced at the men behind him and their hands.

They had a similar marking.

"She looks familiar… Is that—"

I gasped, and I looked at one man who had spoken.

A deeper and older voice.

As he looked at the desperation in my eyes, he went silent.

He had deep blue eyes and thick black hair. He looked like he was in his late forties. I glanced at his hand to see if he had a similar mark. He didn't have a cobweb tattooed on his skin, but the spider itself. A startling realization hit me that this older man was the leader among them. "Do you know me?" I choked out. "Do you know my family? I-I can't remember," I admitted as small whimpers escaped my mouth.

Black and blue eyes exchanged a look.

I didn't understand what passed between them.

Why weren't they telling me anything?

"Are you planning on selling her?"

Blue eyes' words changed.

Why didn't he finish his earlier sentence?

Sell? My heart stuttered.

I dry-heaved on the ground next to me as my frantic heartbeat pulsed uncontrollably. Tears filled my eyes. What were they planning on doing? This seemed like a nightmare come true. This couldn't be happening to me.

"We don't sell children. You're already aware of that," the older man continued. "If she was older, then sure, but she's a child."

I did not know what they were talking about.

The man with the cold, black eyes continued to stare at me before nodding.

"Yes, *Pakhan*, but she can be of value to us in other departments."

Pakhan? What did that mean?

I didn't understand the language they were speaking.

"We need to get moving. I have to head home for my son Zander's soccer game."

The man with black eyes only replied, "Yes, Boss."

The leader turned around, and, with the other men, they walked toward the door.

Now, there was only a pair of black eyes and me left.

He came toward me and crouched at eye level to look at me. My soul softened at the gesture. He didn't seem this scary up close. His eyes seemed to study me like I studied him. I hiccupped as his eyes stayed glued to my azure ones.

"What is your name, *malyshka?*"

Again, I didn't understand the poetic language coming from his mouth.

I understood English, but I wasn't sure if I spoke another language like him.

"What does that m-mean?" I stuttered, asking a question of my own.

His lips lifted a little as his hand rubbed the short, spiky beard growing on his chin.

His eyes grew darker by the second. They were black as the night sky. I could lose myself in them. The other merchants around him fell silent. No one else dared to interfere or challenge him now. His presence demanded attention and authority. Everyone listened to him like they were caught under a spider's web and spell.

"Well, you look like a baby. So that's what I called you. It means baby girl."

His voice was deep, and it was soft as he spoke.

I frowned. "I'm not a baby. I'm thirteen," I mumbled under my breath as I sat upright now. I winced as the pain on my scalp returned. I reached up to touch it again.

Black eyes caught my eyes again.

"How did you fall, *malyshka?*" He ignored the fact that I'd corrected him by saying I wasn't a baby.

I winced and pressed a hand against my bloody scalp.

"I was on the train, and I fell," I replied slowly. My eyes peered into his again. "I can't remember anything before that. Do you know who I am and where I came from?"

The stranger shook his head slowly.

My frown deepened.

"Do you remember your name?"

I searched through my empty mind until something familiar appeared.

"A-A..." I stuttered. "Ana... Ana..." My voice trailed off before I could finish.

I couldn't remember the rest of my name as I looked away from him and wiped my eyes with my bloody hand. I groaned at the mess I was making.

"Anastasia?" the stranger asked.

Anastasia. My wet eyes met his black ones again.

That seemed right, right? I slowly nodded. "I think."

The stranger's lips lifted again.

My soul turned soft.

No one had smiled at me like that.

"So, you must be Russian?"

He extended his hand toward me.

I only blinked. I didn't remember what that word meant.

"That fall must have affected your memory," he concluded. "No worries. I speak the language. I can teach it to you again. Baby steps."

Slowly, I bit down on my lip as I stared at his hand like it was poisonous. He still reminded me I was a baby to him, even though I'd clearly mentioned I was a teenager.

"Are you going to hurt me?" I questioned softly.

"No," he replied after a moment. "I don't harm babies."

His voice teased me.

And again, he was calling me a baby.

My drumming heart softened, and my tense shoulders relaxed.

I shouldn't trust him, but I didn't know who else to trust.

I didn't know where I was or who I was.

"W-what are you planning on doing, then?"

He shrugged. "Giving you a home."

I wanted to say I already had a home, but I said something else entirely. "The man with the spider marking said if I was older, he would sell me." I dry-heaved once again. "Is that why you're giving me a home?" I needed to know. I wasn't stupid.

A hand with a handkerchief pressed against my injured scalp.

A gasp left my lips as I met his cold eyes again.

My shaky hand reached up and pressed against his own. His hand was larger and rougher against mine. "No," he repeated slowly. His eyes seemed to laugh at me like I was a joke to him. "I'm Kirill."

Kirill. My breath hitched as my eyes fell on him again.

"Kirill Volkov."

I still stared at him as I rose to my feet slowly.

"Time to go home now, *malyshka.*"

Baby girl. It didn't sound that bad anymore.

He turned his back on me, and I silently followed behind his much larger frame.

A realization hammered in my mind.

If Kirill didn't know who I was, how did he know my name was Anastasia?

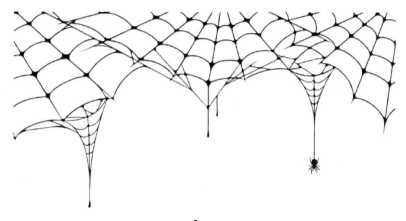

Ana

4

PAST

As I sat in the backseat of Kirill's car, he offered me a glass of water. I mumbled a thank you before grabbing the cup from him and gulping it down in three large mouthfuls. There was a strange taste in the water, but I was too thirsty to care. My stomach grumbled and my cheeks warmed.

I peeked at Kirill, who only raised an eyebrow at me.

"Hungry?"

I nodded.

"We'll be home soon," he replied as he glanced out the window.

I crossed my arms over my white crumpled dress before looking down at my bare feet. Brown, muddy stains clung to the bottoms of my feet, and I pulled the hem of the dress down to cover my dirtiness. A flush ran throughout my body. I hoped he wouldn't see how unclean I was compared to him.

A few seconds later, my vision blurred, and I tried to keep my eyes open, but they kept closing. My mind drifted away as I sank into a dreamless sleep.

The next time I woke up, I was in an unfamiliar room. As I pulled the comforter over myself, I blinked. I glanced down, thankful that I still wore the white dress I had on earlier. As my mind tried to wake me up, I sighed happily. It seemed like mission impossible as my eyes kept shutting. My stomach grumbled, and I willed it to shut up already. Sighing under my breath, I rose to my feet and wobbled like a sleepy penguin.

I must be in Kirill's home. Glancing at my surroundings, my gaze fell on the golden chandelier above me. Flicking my eyes downward, I noticed a soft and plush charcoal-colored rug spread underneath me. I poked my muddy feet out to touch it and sighed breathlessly. It was nice to touch.

I studied the room like an unwanted intruder. It was small and cozy with beige walls. Felt like a home. Kirill didn't seem that bad. Turning my head, I searched for the restroom, but then I caught my reflection in the mirror.

It wasn't my pale skin that looked translucent like a ghost, or the dark circles that hung underneath my eyes that caught my eye. My head was bandaged.

Someone must've bandaged it.

Was it Kirill?

My gaze fell on my hair.

My now jet-black hair.

Unease traveled through my spine.

I looked different.

I swore I had blonde hair a few hours ago.

Some strands of my hair were still blonde, but they were in streaks. *Oh.* That made sense. When I had touched my hair earlier, I had only looked at the blonde parts of my hair and not the black parts. Strange. I couldn't have highlights in my hair. I was kind of young. I tried to remember if I'd always had highlights or not, but I couldn't remember anything at all.

Was my hair black, golden, or both?

A drumming feeling began pounding in my forehead as my mind searched for answers. It had no reply to my questions, so I stopped thinking. The aching headache didn't help, either. I didn't even know what I had looked like before seeing myself in the mirror. Reaching up, I ran a hand through my long locks.

They were clean, and no longer covered with blood, like someone had rinsed them off with shampoo and water and brushed through them.

Frowning, I glanced down at my clothes. I still wore the same clothes I wore earlier. Maybe Kirill lived alone and had waited for me to wake up instead?

So many questions ran through my mind, and the man who could answer them was nowhere in sight.

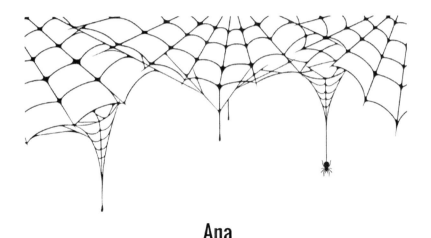

Ana

5

I had a mission to complete, and I wouldn't leave today without Surge Romano's head. I'd been tracking him for a week now. It had to be unexpected. I couldn't attack him soon, though. I had to wait it out. That was the strategy the Bratva Brotherhood had taught me. We waited. He still worked inside the warehouse— the same large warehouse he had inherited from the Senior Romano who had passed away years ago.

The Senior Romano had no other biological children that were male from his first wife. He had a daughter, though, but no one would let her rule. From what I'd heard, Annalisa Romano studied somewhere off in Paris.

Apparently, it was rumored that Mrs. Romano couldn't give him an heir, so he killed her and remarried another woman. That woman already had a child though, and that child was Surge. He was already one of the Romanos' young soldiers at that time.

The Senior Angelo Romano still had no biological male heirs when he adopted Surge, so I assumed it was him all along producing female babies and not his wife.

I shook my head slowly.

The idiot could have taken a test to figure that one out.

At least he had Surge to handle his business.

Surge Romano. No one knew his real name.

It wasn't an Italian first name.

It was past nine when I'd followed him into the warehouse. I couldn't slip into his mansion again. It was heavily guarded now. I knew because I'd checked. This seemed like a better option. Security was glued to his ass, and he never drove alone. He had chauffeurs, which made sense since he was their leader.

If he died, it would be the end of the Romano empire. I wondered if that was the reason the Bratva wanted to annihilate him...

Surge wasn't married yet. He had no heirs.

I paused. Well, maybe he had illegitimate kids.

Who knew? But he didn't have any children by marriage.

I rested my arm against the wall as I leaned in and peeked my head out. My eyes searched for the culprit who'd mercilessly stabbed my hand. My narrowed gaze landed on him as he examined the white substance in front of him.

Packets and packets of it.

The Bratva sold drugs too. I didn't take part in it, though. I wasn't allowed to partake in the drug deals since I put on a facade for the world. Few people knew the real me. Besides, I'd rather kill than sell drugs, no matter how fucked up that sounded. I'd gotten used to killing now. I made my first kill when I was initiated at fifteen. It was a part of me now, and I didn't know how to separate it from my identity.

I imagined Surge Romano dying in front of me, begging for mercy as he bled out. Blood would ooze out from every slice of flesh I carved out. My heartbeat quickened, and I could almost taste his blood on my lips. I wondered how he tasted, though… Sometimes, I tasted their blood. I decided the more bitter their blood tasted, the more wicked a person they were, and they deserved their death. Perhaps, it was just me trying to make myself feel better about the life I lived.

I focused on Surge Romano again.

He was no longer wearing silky pajamas but a black leather jacket with a white t-shirt and black fitted pants. He didn't wear a suit like other *famiglia* leaders. The leather was tight around his biceps, though, and his muscles flexed as he moved. He didn't wear his hair in a ponytail. It was loose, but it was styled neatly behind his head, and not a single hair was out of place. The gel had darkened his locks, and they looked deep brown under the artificial light over his head. I wondered if his shoulder had healed. He didn't wince as he moved his arms, though.

I glanced at my own bandaged hand, snugly covered with my leather glove. It would take a couple of months to heal completely, but it would leave a scar behind. Fucker had nicked me, but I had done the same to him.

I stared silently from the empty side of the warehouse I was in. One by one, each of his made men left until only two of them remained. I wanted to get him alone, since I hadn't planned on attacking him while his men were still around.

We all knew how last time went down…

I hid against the wall as Surge turned around and headed in my direction. The exit was behind me. I hid a coy smile as I rested my back against the wall. I slipped out a blade and began sharpening it. Once he was near me, I would stab it right in the artery he'd been threatening me with that night.

He came around the corner, unguarded, as he walked past me. He couldn't see me since I was pressed against the wall. I glanced behind me at where he'd been. Only one of his men was still there as he collected the white packets.

With my soundless boots, I crept right behind him and matched his footsteps. As he got closer to the door, I reached up, raised my sharpened blade, and pressed it against the side of his neck.

His feet halted and his body turned rigid.

I held in a pleased smile.

"One wrong move and an artery might just burst. Isn't that right, Surge?" I taunted under my breath. Clearly, I liked to play with my food before slaughtering it too. A new habit I had picked up just recently. I wondered who I'd learned it from.

I stared at the Don in front of me.

"So, you have finally returned." His deep voice thundered.

His magnetic voice resonated deep inside of me.

His scent was kind of nice, and I tried not to sniff him. He smelled of a clean shower, aftershave, and that leather aroma of his. My breasts pressed against his back, and I could feel his thumping heartbeat. My twisted insides were pleased.

"Surge," I deliberately repeated his name slowly. "You like to make people feel sudden and overwhelming emotions, do you not?" I didn't give him a chance to reply as I continued. "You're the poison they can't remove from their system. Your heart is racing, Mr. Romano." Sadly, the only time a man's heart raced around me was because I was about to kill them and never for me. "How does it feel to be on the other side today?"

I cocked my head to my right as I observed his carved jawline.

Light brown stubble stuck to his skin, even though I could smell the aftershave on him.

His jaw clenched as he shot me a death glare.

"Are you done with your threats, female?"

I blinked. Female? He did not just…

My eyebrows furrowed, and just to spite him, I nicked the side of his neck with my blade. A trickle of dark burgundy blood flowed down from the tip, just like he'd done the same to me.

Surge only raised his eyebrows as he murmured, "You really have a death wish, don't you?" I nodded fiercely just to taunt him some more. His cold eyes brightened for a second, and my heart skipped a beat. "Who are you?" he asked at last.

I clamped my mouth shut and refused to give him an answer.

"So fucking stubborn," he chided under his breath. "Didn't anyone teach you not to give your victim a moment of hesitation? I see you need more training."

I almost laughed.

"The notorious Don is calling himself a victim?"

He never answered, because he grabbed the blade I held against his neck and spun himself around. Now, his body faced me. My eyes widened—not because he'd snatched the blade from me, but because he had sliced the skin from his fingers when he'd yanked it.

Red liquid sputtered from his fingers, and my flailing hand almost reached out to touch his wound, but I stopped myself. Reaching out his free hand, he shoved my hood from my head, revealing my face.

"Stop hiding your face from me. I want to see you."

I gasped and reached out to punch him across the face, but in a lightning move, he had the blade pressed right against my mouth.

Not my neck, but my damn mouth.

My heart thundered and my pulse spiked.

He might just slice my lips right off.

Unease traveled through my spine.

I didn't even have my first kiss with him.

That was a stupid thought, though.

Maybe he was traumatizing me.

The tip of my silver blade was coated in his blood as he pressed it against my lips. His moss-green eyes taunted me as he smeared my lips with *him*.

His blood.

I stopped breathing for a second.

I hadn't expected that.

He leaned in closer, pressing the tip further against my lower lip. The threat of hacking it off lingered in the air, but he didn't move any further. The gold in his eyes shone as they glared down at me.

"You made this mess. Now lick it clean."

His voice dropped even lower, so seductively lower that my ears perked up.

My lips parted in surprise, and I wondered if I had heard him wrong.

He took my parted lips as an opportunity to smear my lips further with his blood. His warm and sticky blood. My treacherous tongue sneaked out and licked my lower lip. His blood didn't taste as bitter as I had imagined it to be.

Surge's eyes dilated, and he hummed in approval.

"See, you can be a sweet girl, too."

I swallowed at his praise and my chest trembled.

Why didn't Kirill praise me like that?

I wasn't sure if 'baby girl' even counted. He'd been calling me that since I was a child.

I frowned even with the blade pressed against my lips.

"A pretty girl..." Surge murmured under his breath like he didn't want me to hear.

Too late. I heard it.

My gaze flicked to his, still fixed on me.

My heart went in and out like a rapidly bouncing yo-yo.

I swallowed hard, and his eyes trailed the bobbing movement.

Looking for a distraction from his intense and intimidating gaze, my eyes fell on his bleeding fingers that held the handle. The top layers of skin were peeled as blood coated his hand. He must have cut himself deeply. I wanted to huff at him and breathed slowly through my nose as I peered up at him.

"Who told you to be some kind of hero and damage your fingers?"

Something unfamiliar stirred in my soul. I hadn't caused that wound. He had... and I kind of didn't like the fact that he'd harmed himself.

Surge's eyes dropped to my lips. His blood still coated them.

"Red is a nice color on you," he replied instead, ignoring my question completely.

I rolled my eyes, even though my heart flipflopped at the twisted compliment.

"Give me my blade," I demanded, glaring up at him.

He raised a refined brow. "No."

I frowned. "I'll stab you again."

Surge tilted his head. "Since when does an assassin threaten their target? Or is that something you began doing just recently?"

Stumped, I blinked rapidly before averting my gaze from his intense stare.

I didn't want him to figure me out. Figure anything out.

I had another blade hidden under my sleeve. I could easily pull it out since my arms were still free, but then my gaze fell on his bleeding fingers. He still bled. It was strange how it hadn't affected me that night when I'd stabbed his shoulder, but something unfamiliar in me stirred at him bleeding tonight.

"How come you haven't killed me by now?" I mumbled as I changed the topic.

"I can kill you easily," he simply stated with a nod.

He was right. I was in the den of a lion.

This was his turf yet again, and I was the unwelcome guest.

"Are you going to?" I whispered.

His long brown lashes touched the skin under his eyes as he blinked. I wondered what the point of his long lashes was. He would never wear mascara in his life.

I wondered for a second how he would look in makeup, but then I made a face, traumatizing myself this time.

"Do you want me to?" he challenged, his voice like silk.

I scowled instead, and his lip twitched.

I opened my mouth to cuss at him, but footsteps came from behind us.

"Boss," a masculine voice said. "Berlusconi is on the phone for you."

More footsteps came up next to that voice.

Familiar name.

It belonged to another ruling Family of New York.

The fifth Family.

One of the Bratva's rivals.

It must be about the drug deal they had planned.

I glanced behind me to cuss at his men instead, but Surge turned my face around and slammed his hand against my mouth. It muffled the cusses that I wanted to spit out of my mouth. Ignoring my muffled protests, his large body pushed against mine with astonishing strength, and my feet were dragged back as they hit the white wall behind me. We were hidden from his men now.

His hard chest pressed against my softness as my back dug further into the wall. His hand was rough and large as it covered my mouth. He seemed even taller up close. I hated how I was always forced to be this close to him. My bewildered eyes found his, and he only replied casually, "Be right there in a minute."

Now that his blade was no longer against my mouth, I bit down on his palm. I caught some skin and chewed on it like a maniac. The flat skin was harder to grasp, though. His lip twitched at my feeble attempt. He wouldn't be smiling if I slammed my blade right through his mouth. Footsteps moved away from us, and a moment later, Surge dropped his hand from my mouth.

I threw invisible sharp daggers through my eyes as I hissed, "What was that for? You might as well have let me slaughter your leftover soldiers as well."

He only blinked as he stepped away from me.

"Get out. Your presence is disturbing me now."

Baffled, I stared up at him. Now that was rude.

"Why do you keep letting me go?"

The Don's green eyes lit up as he studied his bleeding fingers. When he was done studying his fingers in fascination, his sharp gaze landed on me.

That cunning look in his eyes should have sent me shit-scared and running home, but I straightened my spine as I stood up straighter, my own fire challenging his.

I didn't understand what was between us. This back and forth pull. This game we played, wanting to end one another but couldn't do it at the same time.

His lips stretched in a charming yet wolfish grin. My stomach somersaulted at the unfamiliar expression on his face. I didn't know he could smile. The fine lines filled the corners of his mouth, reminding me that he was much older than me.

Twenty years.

He was forty and I was twenty.

He didn't look at me like I was a child, even though he had called me a girl. I couldn't exactly pinpoint what it was exactly when he looked at me.

Crinkles filled the corners of his eyes as he flashed his straight, white teeth at me. When he smiled, his entire face lit up. It was something that I hadn't seen him do before. Not even in the photographs that I'd spent hours studying.

My mouth almost dropped at his smile.

For a second, I wondered if I had just hallucinated.

"Little Assassin," he began as he continued to grin haughtily.

My spine tingled at the nickname.

"Why do you keep letting *me* go?"

I averted my eyes and stared at the ground instead.

I didn't want to see his smiling face anymore.

He didn't answer my question, nor did I have a reply to his.

And with that, Don Surge turned around to leave, but not before saying, "I look forward to seeing your stalkerish ass again. In fact, I'm counting on it."

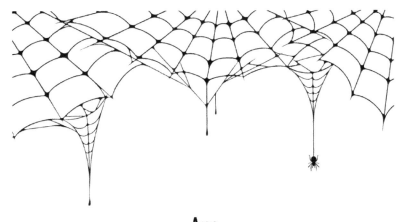

Ana

6

I had turned into Surge's Romano's stalker.

He'd been damn right about that. Blame it on my duty. Not that I enjoyed stalking him, though.

I didn't. I didn't. I did not…

My thoughts halted as he came into view.

I didn't know if he knew I still followed him around. Perhaps he did, and he waited for me to confront him. I had a million chances to complete my mission, and even with all my weapons on me every time, I still hadn't completed it.

He wore that familiar leather jacket again, zipped up to his neckline this time. As I studied him closer, I noticed little snowflakes falling on his silky locks. I wondered how his hair would feel under my fingers. Would it be soft? I hadn't thought about an assignment in such a way. I hadn't looked at a man in such a way either… It wasn't the same way I looked at my husband. If that marriage even counted.

I glanced down at my hand.

My bare ring finger. I didn't have a ring.

He never gave me one.

Loneliness stirred in my soul. I sighed under my breath as I focused on and ogled the Don privately. Maybe he liked having a secret admirer. I scoffed under my breath and rolled my eyes. He leaned casually against his Porsche as he chatted with some men outside the building he'd come out of. His corporate office. A cover-up to the police and the world that he was a decent man who had a decent livelihood.

Strange how we both led double lives.

Snapping out of my thoughts, I shoved my gloved hands into my pockets as I peered up at him. He raked a hand through his wet locks as he shoved the crystal-white flakes off his head. His pale skin had turned flush pink, and I wondered why he didn't wear a hat or carry an umbrella with him.

His lip curled up in that familiar grin as he spoke to the men. It was so easy to lose myself as I stared up at him. I wanted that smile to be in my direction. A dark feeling grew in the pit of my stomach. I *needed* his smile on me. It belonged to me. It wasn't fair that others could see it. When did I go from hating smiley people to liking them? Their smiles, I mean…

I waited until his men disappeared into their cars and Don Surge slipped into the driver's seat of his black Porsche. No chauffeur for him today.

My insides twisted and tingled at the fact that he would be alone today. His engine started, and that's when I pounced in his direction. Luckily, the blizzard fell heavily, and I could hide behind inches of snow, but I knew my black outfit stuck out like a sore thumb. He hadn't left yet. Maybe he was warming up his car. My breaths came out in white puffs amid crystallized air. My nose slowly turned pink and my kohled eyes had turned watery.

I wore makeup for the first time today. I didn't need to hide who I was anymore. Might as well make use of vanity.

The two cars of the men gained speed slowly and moved away from their parking spaces. Now, I crouched right below Don Surge's car. My gloved hand reached out for the handle before I flung it open to slip inside. I slammed the door behind me, not caring that it announced my arrival. The seats smelled like him. Sharp, clean, and strong.

The car radiated heat, and my popsicle-like body melted instantly. I sighed in relief as Surge Romano's haunting eyes met mine in the rearview.

He raised a subtle brow. "You're growing sloppier, Assassin. You are supposed to be invisible when you attempt to attack me."

I frowned. Why hadn't he called me Little Assassin?

I pulled out my revolver from my holster and didn't bother with my blade today. Aiming it at the back of his head, I eyed him in the mirror. "Am I now, Mr. Romano? Says the Don who left his car unlocked and unsecured."

His lip twitched. "Press the trigger," he challenged.

My finger tightened against it.

Surge Romano tilted his head as his intense eyes landed on me again. My cheeks warmed under his gaze. I didn't want him looking at me like that.

"Maybe I intentionally left my car unlocked."

I raised a brow before scoffing.

"Maybe I had seen your ninja-dressed ass from miles away."

Miles? I had only been a few feet away from him.

His eyes lit up like I was his friend now, and not an assassin who planned on murdering him... one day. Soon. Very soon, I promised. That day would come.

I had my muzzle pressed against the back of his head, and he still wanted to play coy with me? "Who are you calling a ninja ass? You sure love to talk so much when I'm the one with the gun, gripping your balls."

He shook his head slowly. "If you had any balls, you would shoot already."

My lips parted and I wanted to leave a dent in the back of his head. I wanted to squeeze the trigger and scream, *die already!*

He gave another knowing look in the mirror before training his gaze on my mouth. My breath caught in my throat, and he returned his attention to my face. His eyes searched mine.

I wasn't sure for what, exactly.

"Remove your hood," he commanded softly.

He didn't have to raise his voice for me to listen.

I squeezed my lower legs tightly, hoping to stop the trembling there. With hesitation, I reached up a free, trembling hand and pulled my hood down over my face. I avoided looking into his eyes as I focused on the gun pressed against him instead.

"You're wearing red today. Red lips."

His voice was oh-so-low as he spoke.

I swallowed the lump in my throat.

I couldn't see anything outside any longer. The snowflakes covered the windshield and windows from all angles. I tried to focus, but his words distracted me.

Red is a nice color on you.

I squeezed my eyes shut before slowly opening them again. I refused to look at him. When I was on an assignment, I never wore red lipstick. I wanted no more attention drawn to me until… now.

"If I had known you would've unknowingly listened to me, I would've asked you to wear a dress instead of those morbid black clothes," he continued.

Insulted, I flicked my gaze up at him and his eyes bored right into mine. I wished my fingers would listen to me once again as I pulled the trigger and ended this once and for all. But they had wrapped themselves around my hand like they were in control. They took my control right out of me.

Were my disobedient fingers punishing me because he'd sliced his own? Curious, I glanced at his white, bandaged fingers. My eyebrows furrowed, and a crease filled my forehead. I lifted my head as I caught his attention.

"You do that a lot, you know?"

His gaze observed me.

I gave a tight-lipped smile in reply.

"Stare at my injury," he finished. "Isn't your dead soul excited that I'm hurt?"

He's hurt.

I winced silently.

Stupid, stupid, stupid girl. Focus on killing him, my inner voice chided.

You kill him! I roared in my mind.

Pass me the damn gun then, sister, it replied.

I did no such thing.

"You don't want to run your mouth anymore?" he taunted under his breath.

My eyes flared, and I was about to cuss at him instead.

"Why don't you do us all a favor and drop dead already?"

He shrugged boyishly. "For me to drop dead, you'd have to press the trigger."

I was ready to scream my head off at him. "You are such an annoying and frustrating person to be around. Who in their right mind made you, their Don?"

He only looked at me through the mirror before shooting out, "Who made you an assassin who can't even press a trigger?"

My eyes flared.

"If you really want me to kill you, I will gladly do it."

He stared at me, seemingly unimpressed and bored.

"I have been waiting since day one."

Repulsed, I pressed the muzzle deeper into his hair and his head jerked forward. His lip curled up in a cruel sneer before he turned around and snatched the gun right out of my hand.

"If you don't know how to play with some toys, then don't pick them up," he chided under his tongue as he threw the gun at the seat next to him.

Surprised, I lunged for the gun, but his hand caught the back of my hood, drawing my face just inches away from his. I held in my breath as my gaze crashed with his. His bandaged hand came toward the other side of my face as his fingers dug my hair out from my hood until it fell in loose waves around my breasts. I yelped, startled, as I glanced up with my mouth open. "What in the world are you doing, you carrot head?"

The Don tilted his head as he gazed at me. His eyes narrowed before they regained their usual composure.

I swallowed thickily.

"There, you look more like a woman now."

I huffed under my breath. "How dare you — "

"Stop hiding who you're meant to be."

I paused.

His emeralds were brighter and watery, even now. Must have been the effect of the snow. His skin was no longer pink and flushed, but his freckles were still prominent. My fingers itched to glide across his skin. I'd never seen freckles like them up close. They dusted across his nose and decorated him like ornaments on a Christmas tree. I wondered if his entire body was covered in freckles as well.

A flush ran through my skin. My soon-to-be victim shouldn't look like him, and he shouldn't be looking at me like I was a fascinating science experiment.

His hands still dug into my black and golden locks until his uninjured hand snaked around the back of my neck and pulled my face closer to him. I gasped, and my breath hit his lips. I held in my breath as I stared up at him.

"You still haven't told me who you truly are," Surge said. "I feel I know you from somewhere, but I can't seem to recall where."

My body stiffened and turned rigid. I averted my eyes and pulled back, but his fingers never left my hair, and it only drew me back to my original position.

"And why are you trying to kill me?" he continued under his breath.

I didn't answer any of his questions.

He met my stare head-on.

"And why is it that one of your irises is larger and blacker than the other?"

My breath hitched and my eyes dropped low.

I didn't want to talk about that at all.

I had nothing left to say.

"What happened to you?"

His voice dropped dangerously low as it purred violently against my face.

His breath hit my face.

Morning coffee.

Mint.

Him.

I tried to turn my face away, but his fingers tightened against my scalp. It brought out a sweet sting, and I whimpered quietly.

"Tell me, my Little Assassin. Who hurt you?"

My. I hated how my soul came alive whenever he was near.

Would it die again when I finally killed him?

"Besides me, who's been hurting you?"

I almost cracked a smile. *Almost.*

Sighing under my breath, I threw him a malicious glare.

"Paws off, Surge," I jabbed, poking deliberately at his Family's symbol.

He blinked, not reacting like I wanted him to before he pulled back and his gaze fell to my gloved *paws* now. His grip on my hair loosened.

"How is your hand healing?" he slowly spoke. His eyes lifted to mine, and I sensed the curiosity and awareness filling his mind. "Let me see it."

I didn't react this time.

I trained my face to be as neutral as possible.

My hand was healing just fine, but I knew that wasn't what he truly wanted to see.

I hated that my words had filled that thought in his mind.

"First you injure my hand, and now you want to mollycoddle me?"

I tried to distract him.

It would only take a snatch of my glove from my hand to reveal my identity.

Every New York Family had a symbol on their hand, showing their ranks.

I didn't belong to the Italian Families.

I belonged to the Bratva Brotherhood, but they carried a similar tradition.

The followers had a cobweb, and the leader had a spider tattoo.

The Don's eyes narrowed in his cunning way, like he was assessing me all over again. His hand dropped low to my leather-gloved hand, and my gaze followed him. I didn't want to hide my hand from him. He would only get confirmation of his suspicions.

"It would be impossible. It *must* be impossible," he mumbled under his breath.

He spoke softly like he was speaking to himself and not with me, like he debated an inner turmoil with himself. His head flicked to face me as he eyed me curiously.

The more he leaned in closer to me, the more my back jerked toward the seat behind me. His looming figure deliberately rose from his seat slowly, like he wanted to spook me. I held his gaze, meeting his challenge. I refused to cave in.

Without warning, his hand grabbed mine.

The uninjured one.

I protested, "Hey!" before reaching out to punch him across the jaw with my injured hand. The Don grunted, but he didn't stop. I muttered cuss words under my breath as fresh pain burst through the injury. I hoped I hadn't ripped the stitches. "Didn't anyone teach you to keep your hands to yourself?" I called out.

Surge looked at me like I was an idiot.

"Did you forget what you do for a living?"

I took another swing at his face, but this time, he blocked it with his thick forearm.

Then, he ungloved my slim hand and stared down at the tattoo on it.

The same cobweb the *Vors* had, the mark of Russian soldiers.

"Impossible…" his stunned voice came out as his confused eyes met mine.

I swallowed thickly. A lump formed in my throat and refused to go down.

Bile singed the back of my throat.

Oh, no… I had let things get too far now.

How did I return to normal after this?

"My rivals don't have any female *molls* in them."

A moll was associated with the term *female gangster*.

His voice still came out puzzled, refusing to believe the truth.

I prayed he didn't.

He took my limp hand and wiped furiously on it like I was tricking him.

He scoffed under his breath, like it was all an illusion. I wished I had covered my hand with makeup. It was never supposed to happen like this.

"I don't know who you are, but you are definitely not Bratva. They used to sell women and use them as drug mules. There's no fucking way they would've a female be part of their mob besides being trophy wives. Not even the Italians have them as part of their organizations." He shook his head like he was still in disbelief.

I tried not to be insulted. After he was done vigorously wiping my permanent tattoo, he fell back into his seat and stared at me with a new perspective.

"They upgraded," I only replied as I slipped on my leather glove again.

There was no point in lying anymore.

The truth had been revealed.

This was a dangerous game I was playing.

Never in my past five years as an assassin had a target seen my face, much less figured out my identity.

Surge Romano was a dangerous man.

He threatened my entire existence.

My very being.

As long as he lived, he would always be a threat.

The Don fell silent as he assessed me again.

"Maybe you should take notes." I pointed a finger in his direction before shrugging carelessly. "I serve my *Pakhan*, Alexander, and maybe you forgot, but his equal and fellow leader is his wife, Ghislaine Khalil Nikolaeva. She rules with him."

His jaw clenched for a moment and loosened.

"Why does Alexander want me dead?"

Beats me. I shrugged again.

"No idea. I just get orders. Why don't you try asking *Pakhan*?"

Bad idea. Stop giving him ideas.

"You two aren't exactly on friendly terms, anyway. It's common knowledge that the Russians and Italians have been at war with each other for years."

He raised a refined brow as his uninjured finger grazed his lower full lip.

It caught my attention, and I stared at his pink mouth. It looked soft.

"And you are their assassin."

It wasn't a question but a statement.

"Their secret weapon."

I didn't want to ask if he would leak that information, nor did I want to give him any more ideas, so I kept my mouth shut this time. Not only would it place a target on my back, but the Brotherhood's strategy would also be exposed.

Today's visit had slapped me across the face.

"I should never have come here," I admitted in a low voice. "I should've killed you the day I laid eyes on you, and you should've killed me by now."

The vulnerability slipped out and I hated it.

I gave him yet another idea, although I was more concerned that he was planning on exposing me now. The Brotherhood was everything to me. They were my family. My family for the past seven years. They were all I knew and remembered since I was a child. I tried searching his eyes for any kind of mercy, but he was a hard shell, and he was impossible to read. Dons gave no mercy. It was a sign of weakness to them.

"I don't belong here with you," I muttered as I rubbed my forehead fiercely.

His alluring voice came a beat later. "You look fine right next to me."

I bit down on my lower lip. I probably ruined the lipstick on it. Avoiding his stare, I fiddled with my fingers instead. "I don't know why I'm even having a conversation with you and not slitting your throat instead," I exclaimed under my breath, ready to lose my shit any second now. "What am I even doing here with you?" I scoffed again.

Surge's voice purred this time. "What are *you* doing here with me?" The timbre in his voice grew, the bass of his voice deepened, and the huskiness of it returned.

Without meeting his gaze, I leaned forward and grabbed my revolver from his seat. I needed to leave right this instant. My mind turned into mush around him, and it caused me to think about things I didn't know I could. Things that were out of my reach. I was bound to my world, my cause, and my duty.

We were two different people from two separate sides of the world. People liked to believe there was only one world, but that wasn't true at all. There were smaller worlds within that larger world, and some couldn't leave their own world to be a part of the other.

Shrugging off my thoughts, I caught a whiff of his scent and my eyes turned hazy. I avoided looking at him as I returned to my seat. "This belongs to me," I reminded him. "You have stolen most of my daggers already."

I turned to leave and pushed the door handle.

A chuckle filled the air.

The Don was *laughing*.

The sound was pleasant.

It rumbled in the car as it wrapped around my soul and squeezed tightly.

I was surprised he hadn't put me down already.

Made men and their mind games were so confusing sometimes.

If he was a *vor,* he would've killed me.

Surge

7

It had been two weeks since my last encounter with that mysterious Russian woman.

She was part of the Russian mob.

She belonged to a different world.

It left a bad aftertaste in my mouth. It would've been a nice, twisted story to tell my children one day. Oh hey, I met your mother when she tried to assassinate me…

The image of the tattoo on her hand replayed in my mind constantly.

I still didn't know what her name was. I knew what organization she belonged to, though. I still found it hard to believe sometimes. It was uncommon.

She was uncommon.

Her kind didn't exist in our world.

I wondered why Alexander allowed it.

I'd never met her before or come across her. Typically, I avoided the Russians, and now, for some reason, they were out to get me. Maybe it was because of the Berlusconi alliance I still had and the business I still did with them. I knew it broke off when some of the members tried to assassinate the leader of the Nikolaev family.

Well, it wasn't me who'd been their target, so I still chose to keep them around. Most of the New York Families kept ties with each other except for the Vitalli and Moretti Families. They hated each other, and there was no point in wasting men and resources over the drama between them.

My Second in Command, Diego Bianchi, walked to my right and my Enforcer, Andrea Ricci, walked to my left as we entered the red and white hall.

Maybe I shouldn't have come here, but I had to. It was better to keep my enemies close and look them in the eye than have them try to assassinate me. I pulled my satin black suit's collar close to my neck as I fiddled with my tie.

I hated dressing up for the most part, and I missed my leather jackets already. My ears perked up at the chattering around me. Crowds gathered around the hall as people continued their conversations. I'd purposefully missed the wedding ceremony today, and I stopped by the reception to show my face at least, for the sake of appearances.

I murmured greetings under my breath and nodded my head toward people I knew. I was the only remaining family member of the Romanos' empire in New York. Annalisa was studying abroad and safe from the chaos of mob life. My step-grandmother, on the other hand, was in Paris with her. If her father had been alive, she would have been married off by now.

My stepfather had died in prison, and my mother had passed away shortly from leukemia. I had no other siblings. *Famiglia* was everything in my world, and I had no one left to call mine around.

My greens fell on the newly wedded couple. The bride wore a silky white gown that ended at her ankles. A one-year-old toddler clung to her leg. It was her hair that caught my eye. Such long, golden-brown hair… it almost reached her knees. It would be longer if it weren't for the braid flowing behind her. She might as well be a real-life princess. Light brown skin, petite, and bubbly. She was the opposite of her husband.

She laughed as her stoic man whispered something to her. I wondered what he must have said, since he didn't have any clue about how to make a joke. I stared at her giant husband. He was closer in size to me. As if he sensed someone staring at him, his blues narrowed in on me. Raising a hand, Dimitri Nikolaev wiggled two fingers at me in hello. I nodded and moved toward the *Pakhan's* brother.

It was their wedding. Like I said, keep your enemies close. They didn't know that I knew the truth. Granted, we were never close but casual acquaintances, so I hadn't expected them to order a hit on me. I wasn't disappointed nor did I feel betrayed, just merely surprised. I moved to the newly wedded couple and stopped right before them.

"Congratulations, Dima," I murmured slowly. "And to you too, Zara."

I caught the eyes of his wife. She smiled sweetly in my direction, and I wondered what she ever saw in Dimitri. He didn't even know how to smile. From what I'd heard, she was his assignment, one of the drug mules before they got hitched.

"Thank you," she replied chirpily before reaching down to grab her toddler from the floor who was demanding to be held.

"You could give me a break today, Ilya. It's your parents' wedding." The baby only sucked on his thumb as he blissfully sighed and buried his head in the crook of his mother's neck. The baby had hazel hues like his mother.

Dimitri had azure eyes.

They reminded me of the mysterious assassin I had met.

Was she related to the Nikolaevs?

Snapping out of my thoughts, I focused on Dimitri as his wife mingled with the guests. He stood out like an outcast in that black suit of his. Maybe he had been forced into wearing it.

"I'm surprised someone wanted to marry you."

Dimitri's cold and icy blue gaze landed on me. His features were sharp enough to cut through glass. "You sound jealous, since no one wants to marry you." His deep voice rumbled as he spoke low. He spoke similarly to me. I didn't raise my voice either.

My lip twitched.

All right, he was humorous sometimes without trying.

I was about to reply, but another voice beat me to it.

"Well, if it isn't Grandpa Surge." The deep voice flowed smoothly like honey.

I looked up as my gaze landed on the *Pakhan's* black eyes.

Alexander Nikolaev fiddled with the purple cuffs of his black blazer as he continued staring at me. I caught his inky skin filled with tentacles beneath his sleeves. I met the teasing eyes of the man who had ordered my death warrant.

Had he always been this savage? He was pale, haunting, and tall, like a morbid vampire. I didn't know he would turn out to be a bloodsucker as well.

"Daddy!" a high-pitched voice squealed from behind Alexander.

He turned around and I followed his gaze. A young child, no older than six, stood there in her white and golden dress. Her hair was pulled back in a loose ponytail and bangs framed her little face. She looked right at me and her warm, honey eyes beamed at me. She reminded me of sunshine.

Children were such innocent creatures among us predators.

"Hello, you." She hopped right over to me and said, "Whatth your name?"

I studied her mispronunciation before remembering she had a lisp when she spoke. "Surge," I replied slowly.

She nodded like it made perfect sense before grinning. "Thurge… I'm Noura." Then, she pointed out to the woman chatting with Zara now. "That's my mommy."

She pointed at a tall, golden-skinned woman in a pink, silky dress.

Ghislaine Nikolaeva.

I knew who she was. Everyone knew about her.

Former agent turned mafia queen.

She looked elegant and regal as she stood there, speaking with her sister-in-law. I studied Alexander's wife with long, flowy brown hair. The child would look just like her mother when she grew of age. Alexander caught me looking at his wife, and I wanted to look at her some more just to piss him off.

The child burst my bubble though, as she stood right underneath me. I could probably stomp on her with my feet. I don't know how well that would settle with her father, though. I was several feet taller than her, but it didn't intimidate the little girl. "Why did Daddy call you Grandpa? You don't look that old."

My lip twitched.

"I'm a young grandfather," I joked with the child.

Her smile widened as she tilted her head at me in curiosity.

"Go play with Ilya," Alexander shooed her from behind.

Noura only huffed. "Ilya itth only one year old!" Her lisp slipped through again. "He'th a baby. Jutht a baby," she protested.

"And what do you think you are?" her father teased, the affection for his adopted daughter clear as day. She was his wife's biological daughter from her first marriage.

"I'm not a baby!" she protested as she pointed to herself. "I'm six."

She waved her fingers in the air, trying to convince her father before glancing up at her uncle Dimitri who only shrugged.

Her father chuckled before gently pushing Noura in the direction of her mother. She huffed under her breath like a *baby* who was one second away from having a tantrum. She folded her arms across her chest as she scattered away to her mother. Alexander kept an eye on her before returning his attention to me. "You're the only Don left who hasn't been married," Alexander chimed as he returned to his original words, and we shook hands.

I couldn't resist but slip out, "Berlusconi is single, too."

The *Pakhan* lost his familiar smirk at the jab I'd just made.

"Speaking of him, Duran isn't here today?"

Alexander's eyes narrowed before replying calmly, "He's not here. Although, one of his people came here to pay their respects."

Before I could reply to him, a deep and edgy voice came from behind us.

"I didn't know you were coming today, Surge."

All heads turned to the new edgy voice.

The man had his hands tucked into his pockets as he staggered over to us. His inky-black hair was styled messily, and a few strands fell on his face. His tanned skin had grown darker from where he had been living these days. He wore a black suit like the rest of us, except he didn't bother with a tie. The first two buttons of his shirt were unbuttoned, revealing the edges of the sculpted wings engraved on him. A dimple filled his cheek as he finished with, "I haven't seen you in two years."

I blinked as my lip curved up in a smile.

"Vlad," I acknowledged as we shook hands.

And he was right. Vlad Vitalli was often missing for most of the year. Not many people knew where he truly lived besides abroad. "I met Ilya and Noura," I continued. "Where are your mini versions?"

His icy, wolf-like eyes looked across the hall at a woman seated with two children. I didn't focus on the twin children, since his pregnant wife was a sight to look at.

Dahlia Hadid.

Her long, midnight hair draped over her golden dress as she smiled at her daughter. Her fair skin stuck out in that dress like it was made just for her.

Her children were still young, yet she was already pregnant again. Well, if I had a wife like that, I wouldn't mind getting her big either. She sat with a redheaded woman as a man stood beside them. I did a double take when I saw Chief Miran Demir before glancing at Dahlia again.

I averted my eyes before Vlad could give me shit about staring at his wife a little too hard. Hey, I was single and not *dead*. I'd use that as an excuse.

I was the eldest Don amongst them and unmarried. Everyone around me seemed to have a happy family of their own. I knew Moretti had one, too. Salvi wasn't here today though, since Vlad was present. Those two might kill each other if they were in the same room ever again.

"It's good to see you again, Vlad," I replied with ease.

It was a wonder he was related to Alexander.

Vlad nodded with a tiny smile.

"Now that the introductions are over," Alexander butted in. "I am starving."

His eyes searched his surroundings before motioning a hand to one of his men. A tall man in a black suit walked up to him. I didn't know who he was. He was tall with similar black eyes like the *Pakhan*. I'd probably heard of his name. I just couldn't pinpoint who he was exactly.

Alexander caught me looking. "This is Kirill, my cousin from my mother's side."

Kirill Volkov.

I'd heard of him.

Now, that made sense as to why they both had black eyes.

Alexander's mother had the same eyes, too.

My gaze was too focused on Kirill, though.

Dread ran down my spine as I studied the man before me. I didn't like him already, and he hadn't even spoken to me yet. He opened his mouth to speak, to acknowledge me, but then his gaze focused behind me.

The scent of vanilla hit me first. I remembered this scent from somewhere. I remembered thinking about it.

High heels clanked behind me, and a feminine voice spoke.

"Kirill?"

I stilled.

My body turned rigid.

I clenched my fists in and out as my knuckles turned white.

It was *her*.

I just knew it was.

I hadn't expected her to speak another man's name in my presence when I met her again.

That pitch in her voice…

I could recognize it from a mile away.

Her voice was smooth, deep, and flowed silkily.

It matched the kind of woman she was.

I knew she might be here, but if she was their secret weapon, I didn't understand why they would openly flaunt her.

Kirill's lips curved.

He fucking *smiled* at her.

Wrath churned through me.

Why the fuck was he smiling at her?

I hated how his eyes lit up at the sight of her.

"Yes, Anastasia?"

Anastasia. That was her name.

I savored that name on my tongue.

She still didn't know it was me, since my back was to her.

Kirill moved right past me. His coat slowly brushed mine, and I wanted to burn the fucker alive for touching me. Bolts of electricity flared under my skin, and I could just imagine my skin flushing and my freckles darkening. I held in my breath and wrath as I slowly turned around to face them. I lifted my eyes to look at her, but Anastasia hadn't seen me yet. Her cheeks turned pink at something Kirill whispered in her ear.

Why the fuck was she blushing for him?

I had never cussed so much in my life before.

Kirill caught me looking. "Oh, apologies. Hello, Don Surge." He finally acknowledged me, and he didn't sound sorry at all. "This is my wife, Anastasia Volkova."

Wife.

Wife?

Why?

The female I'd been seeing lately turned out to be someone's wife.

I shouldn't be surprised at all.

Every woman I'd seen tonight had been someone else's wife.

Anastasia's eyes were glued to the floor so I couldn't see the recognition in her eyes. Slowly, after several seconds, her familiar blue but kohled eyes met mine.

They crashed into mine and burned them.

"It's a pleasure to meet you, Don Surge," she spoke softly through her treacherous, red mouth that I wanted to suck on.

I didn't speak at all as I swallowed thickly. I swallowed the lump that grew like the size of a tennis ball in my throat. She wore a little red and black dress that ended at her knees. It fitted her like a glove. My breath hitched and caught in my throat.

There were numerous women around me, but I couldn't force myself to look away from her, even if she was another man's wife. I'd looked away from the wives of Alexander and Vlad, but with this one, I didn't want to look away.

She wasn't supposed to be anyone's wife. She'd never told me she was married. Well, why would she tell me that, anyway? I didn't care that her husband was now looking at me and noticing me openly staring at her. I didn't care for him at all when she was all I saw. He could choke on his own dick and die. Better yet, I would feed it to him one day.

Her shoulders were scooped, and her full ample cleavage was on display. I wanted to reach out a hand and trace the swells of her lush softness. I'd felt her against me every single time I had met her.

Which married woman did that?

Maybe she'd played me like a fool.

Her face was adorned with subtle makeup, her high cheekbones still pink and dewy. Her face was carved out like a goddess. Her eyes looked much too large for her small face. Taking in her raven with golden streaks hair, I realized it hung loosely around her in curls, as she played the perfect role of a stunning trophy wife. She looked tall, thin, elegant, and *beautiful* as hell as she stood there innocently like a gazelle like she didn't recognize me at all. She kept on with her charade, like she was completely innocent and unaware of who I was.

My lip curled down in displeasure as I stared harshly at her.

If I had known you would've unknowingly listened to me, I would've asked you to wear a dress instead of those morbid black clothes.

I hadn't expected to see her in a dress, glued to the arms of another man.

A man who was my rival, no less.

I glanced down at her hands clasped before her. The injured hand I had stabbed was no longer damaged. I searched for the scars on her hand, but they were no longer there.

Impossible.

It would have led to some form of scarring.

I swallowed again as I searched her other hand.

Only clean and unblemished skin greeted me.

No cobweb tattoo in sight.

Puzzled, I lifted my eyes and stared directly into hers.

There was still no recognition in her eyes.

Her leader had played dumb, like he hadn't planned on assassinating me.

And here was his follower, still playing a charade.

I inhaled slowly and released it when I spoke at last.

"It's an honor to meet you, Anastasia."

I didn't bother to say her husband's poisonous surname. She was not Volkova in my mind. She was just … just … the assassin I had pictured her to be.

Her throat bobbed as she swallowed.

Sweat clung to the slopes of her soft tits.

She *knew*.

She knew exactly who I was.

And damn her and her fucking husband.

I reached out a hand and she reached up hers to shake my offered hand. She thought I wanted to simply shake her hand?

How dead wrong she was.

My rough and calloused fingers engulfed her soft fingers before I pulled her closer toward me, away from her husband. I didn't like her next to him at all.

I wanted her to belong by my side as she should. She was a queen, and she shouldn't be married to a lowly peasant.

A tiny gasp left her sweet, pouty mouth.

Her small, upturned nose wrinkled, like she didn't know what to expect from me.

I knew everyone's eyes were on me, all of the leaders and their seconds in command staring at me as I snatched another man's wife right from him and toward me instead.

So, don't mind if I enjoyed this power play.

I stepped closer to her as my lips brushed against her left cheek, leaving a kiss behind before it brushed against her right cheek, leaving another mark of me behind.

"Little Assassin," I whispered as if only for her ears.

Her skin was so soft unlike the hard exterior she hid underneath. She was a woman underneath it all, and I couldn't wait to discover those parts of her. I inhaled her scent deeply. *Vanilla.* I memorized it in the back of my mind.

Her cheeks burned pink as she avoided staring at me.

It was common for Italian males to exchange kisses with each other and females to exchange with each other, but in our made world, kissing another man's wife was considered an act of war. Especially when an Italian mobster kissed a Russian mobster's wife.

Pleased, I met Kirill's narrowed and darkened gaze, but he did not say anything at all. Cricket silence came from him.

I was the Don, and he was not.

I ruled, and he only obeyed.

I held his gaze the entire time, daring him to challenge me and slit my throat, but he did no such thing. He did glance behind me though, at his leader, his *Pakhan*, who was also quiet.

I'd probably stunned them all.

Alexander would never openly declare war against me, though. I'd probably get a higher spot on his hit list.

Kirill's jaw ticked and clenched before looking away. Satisfied, I glanced at Anastasia in my arms, who looked dumbfounded like her husband. With hesitation, she glanced at him before looking up at him.

Her charming husband took the moment to entwine his fingers through Anastasia's. Automatically, my eyes narrowed in on that sight. His larger hand covered her pale and slim one. As if surprised by the gesture, she looked up at him with her eyebrows raised, and a shy smile formed on her lips. My fists clenched at the sight of that expression. She seemed to be playing the part of the trophy wife a little *too* well.

She glanced at their entwined fingers like it was the first time her husband had held her hand publicly. I wanted to grab her by the throat, slam her against a table, and pound into her senselessly. That would show Kirill who I was exactly. I glanced at him for a moment, and he seemed to be looking right at me with a sly smirk before turning toward her.

"Yes, Tasha, you were saying something?"

Anastasia's cheeks were still pink as she spoke.

"Yes, one of the men was looking for you up front."

Her voice sounded more breathy than usual.

Why did she sound breathless?

He gave a curt nod before saying, "Excuse me," to us before leaving. But not before he practically took Anastasia's arm and dragged her behind him. I still stared at their lingering backs and willed her to glance behind her to look at me.

Just once.

She didn't.

She gave me her back the entire time.

Her naked back. The same one with no ink stretched across her skin. It only showed smooth and unblemished porcelain skin. I curled my fingers in and out just so I wouldn't reach out to trace her soft skin. I continued staring as they disappeared around the corner. A figure in black and purple stepped right next to me and spoke.

"That's not a look you give to someone else's wife."

I glanced through the corner of my eye at Alexander.

His lips played a coy smile, and he raised a subtle brow.

I blinked slowly. "She reminds me of someone I knew."

Alexander looked at me in disbelief.

"Your stepsister? They're the same age."

I gave a slow nod. Well, Annalisa was no longer my stepsister, since our parents were dead, but that didn't take away from the fact that she was family.

A server slipped past us, and Alexander grabbed two martinis, offering one to me. I gave a slow nod before grasping it from him. Taking a slow sip, I muttered, "I'll see you around, Alexander."

His black eyes assessed me.

"Oh, you're not staying for dinner?"

No. You just might poison me.

I searched his eyes for anything that might give his intention away, but he was like a magician, so good at masking his feelings. I shook my head and made a show of glancing at my gold watch. "Afraid not. I must be going. Congratulations again to Dima and Zara."

Alexander shrugged. "All right. If you must."

I opened my suit jacket to pull out an envelope. "This is for Ilya instead. I'm not sure what to give a couple that already has everything," I admitted.

Alexander chuckled before taking it from me. "What's in it? A check?" he joked.

"Actually, it's an unlimited subscription for my amusement parks—only for Ilya."

His lip twitched. "Good seeing you, Surge."

He placed his treacherous hand on my shoulder as he turned around like we were still good acquaintances, and he hadn't ordered my kill. It was a pity, since Alexander wasn't that bad. We got along for the most part. Still holding my drink, I wandered toward the exit. The strong flavor of gin and vermouth melted on my tongue.

I could also taste the juniper berries as I savored the drink. I had a few sips left as my eyes swayed to the darkened hallway to my right. A figure in burgundy and black flashed before me, and my footsteps changed direction and headed toward it.

My lips against my glass halted as I came across a woman in red and a man in a suit at the end of the hallway. My ears perked up at their conversation as they spoke in hushed yet loud tones. Well, it was mainly him. She just stared at him with her mouth open. I could have recognized her beauty from a mile away in that little dress. It hugged her curves and edges like she was born to wear it. I swallowed at the sight of her again.

Her beauty was incredible. Simply stunning.

I hated how fucking beautiful she was. Who gave her the right to look like that? She'd caught my attention since day one, and she was married to another fucker.

Her glossy hair flowed behind her in loose curls and her skin was flushed. It brought a natural glow to her face, a natural sheen from her sweat. She couldn't see me as her husband blocked her view.

"Why did Don Surge kiss you?" Kirill's voice grew louder.

I smirked. So, I must have hit a nerve.

Anastasia crossed her arms over her chest. "I don't know. I didn't ask him to."

My smirk widened as I casually leaned against the wall and stared at them in fascination. They say there was no place for a third person in a relationship, and here I was, changing the rules.

My body was half cast in the shadows of the night. There was no one around in this empty hallway. Voices diminished at this end of the place. I couldn't see Kirill's fuming face, but I could imagine he was pissed.

"Don't be smart with me, Tasha. I've seen the way he looks at you."

Good. I took another sip.

Message sent clearly, then.

"Why didn't you stop him as he touched you?" Kirill continued shooting questions.

Anastasia's eyes flared as she threw up her hands in the air.

"He's the Don, and it's common in Italian culture to kiss on the cheek."

Kirill stepped closer to her and jabbed a finger in her face.

"We are fucking Russian."

She raised an eyebrow and huffed out, "It's also common in our Slavic culture to kiss on the cheek, at least three times. I even saw a man kissing another man on the lips. You're lucky Don Surge didn't try that with you."

I held in a laugh at her sassiness.

Yes. That's my girl.

"We don't do that with strangers! And he was meeting you for the first time," Kirill protested. His voice had a deeper edge to it now.

Was he admitting to kissing men on the lips now?

"And he didn't try to kiss me! I'm sure this tradition works both ways."

Laughter bubbled in my chest, and I had to bite down on my lip to stop the laughter from bursting out.

Did he want me to kiss him now?

Anastasia let out a long sigh, like she was frustrated.

"Why are you upset with me, Kirill? I didn't even do anything. If it bothered you so much, you should've confronted him about it. Why argue with me now?" She shook her small head before turning away to move past him.

He turned around and his fuming face screamed, "Don't you fucking walk away from me! We're not done with this conversation until I say I am. Learn your place as my wife and listen to your husband."

I lost my laughter and my smiles.

My lips halted at my drink.

My jaw clenched and my fingers tightened on the glass.

"I don't wish to speak about this, Kirill. Can we talk about this later at home? We have guests to take care of right now," Anastasia protested as her footsteps quickened like she was in a rush to escape him.

"I said, I'm not done!"

The edge in his voice had grown thicker and harsher. His tone grew louder. I'd never spoken to her in such a way. I didn't like raising my voice.

Kirill's face distorted into an ugly snarl as he lunged forward and grabbed the back of her scalp and tugged her back.

Anastasia's feet halted and she hissed under her breath. Her hands automatically rose to her hair as her head was pulled back.

"What are you doing, Kirill?" she protested in a low, hurt voice.

Her voice ached.

It fucking *ached.*

My jaw tightened and I ground my teeth against each other.

Blood whooshed past my ears as my pulse spiked.

Straightening my back, my eyes narrowed, and I was ready to slam my drink to the floor. I didn't care if I didn't have a say in their marriage. He couldn't harm her in my presence.

I turned my body and headed in their direction. My hand was already curled in a fist, ready to hit his damn sneering face. I was only a few feet away from them.

Anastasia glanced to her side before reaching out to jab her elbow in his face.

He grunted and loosened his hold on her hair.

My feet halted.

A few pieces of her broken hair strands were in his fist.

Kirill snarled as he glared at her.

"You hit me!" he accused.

I tried not to roll my eyes at the irony as I watched them.

He quickly reached out for her again, but she turned and captured his hand between her hands like lightning, ready to strike down a tree. She pushed two of her fingers on his middle finger, adding pressure and pushing it in the opposite direction.

Kirill grunted, and his face contorted into a grimace. Anastasia's face was void of emotion as she continued staring at him, adding more pressure to his middle finger like she wanted to crack it. Any more provocation from Kirill and she just might.

A flicker of determination shone through her narrowed gaze and filled her face a moment later. She had no mercy for him right now.

I wasn't looking at Anastasia. It was the assassin taking over.

I blinked slowly as I hid in the shadows again.

She didn't need my help after all.

"Tasha, what are you doing? I'm your husband!"

His voice held a plea. It sounded like emotional manipulation at its finest, an attempt to guilt trip her when he had been the first to yank her hair.

A pathetic husband.

Anastasia immediately dropped her hold on him as she stared up in surprise. Kirill's eyes widened as he stared down at his hand. So many emotions overcame his face, like he couldn't believe his wife had defended herself against him.

Anastasia's trembling hands went toward her hair as she pulled it down. "It was just a defense reflex from my training, Kirill." Her voice trembled in puzzlement. "I didn't want to harm you. You were... and I just..." Her voice trailed off as she looked away.

I wanted to snarl, *Never apologize.*

But she beat me to it.

"I'm sorry."

Before Kirill could reply, Anastasia took off running in the opposite direction from where he stood. Puzzled by the sudden gesture, his head flew in the same direction she took off as he watched her scampering away like a ghost was chasing her. Instead of following her, he moved in my direction as he muttered cuss words under his breath.

I slipped further into the shadows, hiding completely from him. When he swept past me, I wanted to trip him on his feet. It took all my willpower not to beat the shit out of him and possibly leave him fingerless and blind.

Once his shitty ass disappeared from my sight, I turned my head to where Anastasia had run off to.

Without second-guessing myself, my feet turned, and I followed her. As I walked through the hall, I noticed that her scent still lingered in the hallway.

I wouldn't leave without meeting my Little Assassin again.

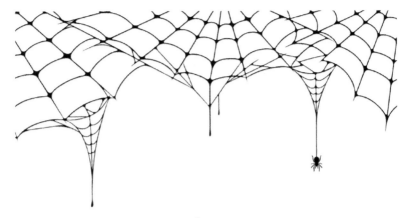

Ana

8

I ran until I found an empty restroom I could slip into. After slamming the door behind me, I leaned against it. Rough pants left my mouth as I tried to control my breathing. It was no use though, because my entire being shook uncontrollably. My breasts heaved and I crossed my arms over them to stop myself from trembling.

What the hell was that?

Kirill had never yanked my hair like that in the middle of an argument. I hoped he wouldn't do it again.

It just happened once. I tried to repeat this to myself, but my inner voice decided to come at the wrong time.

It only takes one incident for it to happen again.

I shook my head in disbelief.

No, Kirill would never try to harm me.

I sighed restlessly as I moved away from the door and stared at my dreary reflection in the mirror. A girl with red-rimmed eyes stared back at me.

I didn't recognize myself in the mirror.

I'd been excited to attend Zara and Dimitri's wedding. I'd even dressed nicer than usual, too. Raising my heavy eyelids, I focused below my waterline where the mascara and kohl had smeared slightly.

I reached up and rubbed the back of my head. The lingering sting was still there as I recalled seeing the broken pieces of my hair in his hand. I turned the faucet's knob and dampened the spare charcoal-colored face towel in the bathroom to clean my eyes with trembling fingers. The makeup must have smeared when I squeezed my eyes shut the moment Kirill pulled on my hair. I'd spent hours applying my makeup carefully. I didn't usually wear much, but I liked the look of it. I felt pretty and feminine. Different from my usual bare face.

Stop hiding who you're meant to be.

A rich voice echoed in my mind.

Swallowing thickly, I closed my eyes and wished I could stop thinking about it. The makeup was a pleasant change. I wished men would stop ruining my hard work in the process. My mascara cost me about fifty dollars. Yes, I was married to a wealthy person, but that money was all Kirill's, and I wasn't allowed to touch it. The money I was paid by *Pakhan,* Kirill always collected. I never saw it. I didn't question Kirill's intentions for taking it away from me. He was my husband. What was mine was his.

The face towel didn't help much, though, as it just made my eye makeup smudge even more. I resembled a raccoon with two black eyes now. Stupid shaky fingers.

I sighed before throwing the towel in the sink. Clenching the edges of the vanity table, my knuckles turned white, and I stared down at the running water. A distraction seemed nice right now. My ears perked up as the doorknob behind me twisted.

Had Kirill followed me?

I wasn't in the mood to deal with him right now.

With my dimmed soul, I straightened my spaghetti-like back before flopping it back. It took too much energy to be strong. I wanted to be exhausted for once, sleep for days, and eat ice cream so I could feel better. However, I wasn't allowed that luxury.

Every day, I was supposed to be working. If I wasn't working, I was planning. There were other assassins in the Brotherhood too, but I was the only one who received the deadliest jobs. They sent me in when there was a risk. Even if I got caught, no one would believe a female was part of the Bratva. At least, it was supposed to be that way.

My ears perked up again as the footsteps of my husband invaded the bathroom before closing the door behind him. I wished I'd had a few moments of privacy before he came.

Was he here to apologize?

My stomach churned and twisted at the thought of an apology. I didn't know why I was trying to make myself feel better. Kirill never apologized because he was never wrong in his eyes.

I inhaled tightly. Then, I released it.

Lifting my hopeful eyes, I prepared myself to meet his black ones.

A pair of emeralds greeted me instead.

I blinked a few times and thought I had imagined it.

Clear wet mosses stared right back at me. I swallowed, and then wondered what he was doing here. I didn't speak at all for a few seconds. He'd sucked all the words right out of me. My breath came out sharp and shallow as my hallowed eyes met his.

His suit was snugly fitted around him, molding against him like a second skin. Gone was his leather jacket, and his face was clean-shaven. No stubble in sight. He smelled of a clean shower and aftershave, and I tried not to inhale him further.

His chiseled jaw tensed as he stared directly at me. His thick, reddish-brown hair was combed neatly over his head and tucked behind his ears.

I stood up straighter, fixing my spine as I forced myself to smile through my trembling lips. I hoped it reached my eyes. I lifted my chin as I turned around slowly to meet his haunting stare head-on.

"Hello, Don Romano." I gave a curt nod as I spoke softly. "This restroom is currently occupied, but I can leave right now if you prefer." Without waiting for his answer, I turned to leave, past him. I was just about to turn the doorknob when he spoke.

"Anastasia."

My hand halted on the doorknob.

I closed my eyes at the way he said my name.

Anything that came out of that mouth of his was poetic.

He sounded calm, and I could hear the admiration in his voice.

"Ana. It has a nice ring to it," he continued. "It sounds better than simply calling you *assassin*."

My shoulders tensed and I turned around slowly. "I'm not sure what you're talking about, Don Romano." I shrugged innocently as I averted my gaze from him.

"It's Don Romano now?" he asked quietly. "Just weeks ago, you were already on a first-name basis with me."

Swallowing thickly, I lifted my dimmed eyes to meet his. "I don't know what you're talking about. You must have me mixed up with someone else."

His lip curled in a knowing smirk. Crossing his arms over his chest calmly, he continued, "You never told me you were married." His voice was laced with disappointment.

I raised a subtle brow before politely changing the topic.

"I am leaving now. You may have the room to yourself."

I avoided looking at him as I tried to slip past him again, but he moved to block the doorway. My tired eyes lifted, and I wondered what he wanted.

"What does Anastasia mean?" Don Surge's deep voice came.

Although I kind of liked listening to his low, rich, and rumbling voice, I would never admit that to him. It was nice to the ears, and it haunted my very core. Those eyes of his haunted me. Not only that, he *hunted* me like a spider casting a spell on its prey and drawing it to its web.

He was like the very web I'd call home.

My heart stuttered at the startling thought.

I didn't know why he felt familiar when we were two strangers who were trying to kill each other. I didn't even know why we couldn't bring ourselves to slaughter each other already.

What was holding us back?

Holding in a sigh at the endless questions brewing in my mind without any answers for them, I turned around and faced the mirror again. My backless dress was to him, and I stared at his reflection in the mirror as his gaze swept over my bare skin. I didn't have any other tattoos on my back, just one in particular. Kirill didn't like tattoos on me.

"I don't know, Don Surge," I lied at the tip of my tongue. "I would ask my parents if I could." My body stilled at what slipped out. He wasn't supposed to know that.

His jade-colored eyes clashed with mine in the mirror.

Beautiful.

His eyes were beautiful.

Green was the rarest eye color in the world, and he had two of them.

Out of everyone in the entire world, how did he find himself lucky to be part of only two percent of the world population who had eyes like that?

They were different every time he looked at me. They'd turn soft and glassy like a forest after a rainy downpour whenever he teased me. When he wanted to behead me, they morphed into an olive-green color like poison oak. Bold and beautiful.

I wanted to vomit at my treacherous thoughts. After I finished scolding myself, I studied him some more. He looked different today. Dapper and polished, unlike the rugged look he had whenever he wore a leather jacket. My eyes swept down to his thick biceps hidden underneath the layers of satin he was wearing. Lifting my gaze, I avoided looking into his eyes and began counting the freckles on his face instead.

1. 2. 3. 4. 5. 6. 7. 8...

"Where are your parents?" His lyrical voice came a beat later.

Shit. I closed my eyes before slowly opening them. I hoped no one would find us alone in the bathroom. It wouldn't end well for either of us.

I was a married Russian woman, and he was an Italian Don.

The Don who also happened to be my rival.

My *husband's* rival.

The thought of my husband brought my hand back up to where Kirill had pulled off some strands of my hair. I rubbed the sore spot and wondered if there was a tiny bald spot there. I kind of liked my long hair a bit too much to go bald now.

Surge's hollow gaze went toward my scalp, and I froze. His eyes returned fiery, like a midsummer forest under the blaring sun. His jaw ticked, and I wondered if he'd seen what had happened between Kirill and I.

"I don't remember my parents," I admitted after a moment in a low voice. I didn't know if I could get away without telling the truth. I could attack him, but I didn't want to expose myself publicly. I was supposed to play the part of a respectable wife and a meek, timid woman right now.

Surge's eyes hardened before a crease filled his eyes.

"You don't remember, or you can't?"

Wasn't it the same thing? I shook my head slowly.

"Can't," I confirmed. "Amnesia," I mumbled.

Surge tilted his head at me, and my breath hitched at the movement.

He really needed to stop looking at me like that.

I was married. I was... married. I ...

He bit his full bottom lip as if thinking hard, and my treacherous eyes dropped to them. They were pink. Extremely pink for a man. I thought it was because he looked like a carrot, but now I was unsure. Good, strong genes, though.

That suit did look flattering on him. I flicked my gaze to his eyes and realized his eyebrows were still furrowed. Deep lines filled his forehead. Despite our age difference being sorely apparent, he was attractive. My cheeks warmed. I wished I didn't think he was. I tried to count his little brown freckles again.

10. 11. 12. 13. 14...

"No one's ever looked for them for you?"

His voice interrupted my count again, and my face burned at how he was digging his nose into my business. He still blocked the doorway with his back and stood there, casually leaning against it as he met my gaze in the reflection of the gilded mirror.

Maybe I should take this opportunity to stab him right now. I had my blades clipped to my thighs. Simple enough. If he were to end up dead out of nowhere, it wouldn't be connected to our organization. No trail that would lead the authorities to us. Fewer enemies. No war.

However, I couldn't annihilate him at a Bratva *wedding.*

I wondered if I should scream for help instead. Maybe then, the Bratva would have a reason to kill him or declare war against him. My heart sank as dread filled it. I didn't want to falsely accuse him when all he did was stand there, trying to get to know me like I was some fascinating alien species. Even though he had no right to get to know me, a treacherous part of me wanted to fess up my truths.

No one had ever asked me that question before.

I sighed silently. "My people did," I replied. "I was told my parents died."

Surge's eyes turned to slits. "Did they take you to see their graves?"

I stilled for a second before glancing over my shoulder at him.

What a strange thing to say...

I frowned. "No. I was fourteen when they told me about their deaths. They didn't allow children to go to their graves. They said it would spook me."

Surge crossed his bulging arms over his chest as he stared down at me and made himself comfortable against the door. He was a good seven inches taller than me. I was not short by any means, but he was one of the tallest men I had ever seen.

A giant underneath the suit.

"Who is this 'they' you speak of?"

I didn't want to mention Kirill's name without remembering the earlier incident. I returned my gaze to our reflection again, and his eyes held mine one more time.

My feet stayed rigid, holding me in a chokehold like I had no control over my body but to stay with him and answer his questions. I glanced down at my wrist and played with the golden bracelets wrapped around it.

I spoke calmly. "While it was nice speaking with you, Don Surge, I must leave now. Everyone must be wondering where I am." I didn't know why I was lying. No one probably gave a fuck either way.

"So, after they found you, they turned you into one of their assassins?" Don Surge completely ignored my request as he interrogated me yet again.

My eyes narrowed and I held a groan in. Careful not to reveal anything, I widened my eyes dramatically to play the role of a ditzy, trophy wife. "Assassin?" I brought my hand to my chest. "Dear Lord, what are you speaking about, sir? I wouldn't even hurt a fly." That was true.

I didn't kill insects. Just humans.

His jaw clenched.

If I stared closely, I could count every tic on his prominent and angular face.

My eyes brightened.

Score. I blinked innocently and rapidly, like I had the wings of a butterfly attached to my eyelids.

He didn't seem to like that I was toying with him. His spine straightened as he stalked toward me. I held in my breath as he filled the distance between us.

Now, he was directly behind me.

Too close behind me. He invaded my personal space on purpose. I could feel every inch of him pressed against me— against my back, my ass, and my legs.

My ass brushed against his groin. His *hard* groin. I could feel the erection through his pants. My cheeks warmed and I stared at the mirror again. My cheeks were flushed, my loose curls now tangled, and my kohled eyes watery. He hadn't even touched me yet and I was already sporting the afterglow many women bore after tumbling in the sheets. My cheeks turned pink. No sheets around, just hard surfaces.

Tables. Walls. Shower… I swallowed.

Every inch of me heated as the tension thickened.

My pulse drummed against my ears as my heart raced.

A moment later, Don Surge's arms reached out and his hands landed on the edges of the white marble table in front of me. His leather scent, combined with the cologne that he wore, fluttered under my nose. I hated how I could still remember his scent. It was as if it were embedded deep into my skin, following me around wherever I went. What's even worse was that I couldn't get enough of it. Every time I got a whiff of it, I got into this natural high a junkie always seeks. I forgot what I smelled like whenever I was covered by the overwhelming scent of *him*.

I didn't know where I began and where he ended. My body tingled, pinned against him. Unfamiliar sensations crawled over me, and I wanted to cross my legs together to stop the ache forming between them. His presence consumed mine until I dissolved into mist. I held my breath just so I could stop sniffing him, but then I stopped when I couldn't breathe.

I was tempted to cover his hands with mine, but I stayed still. His suit was soft as it brushed against my naked back. A terrible thought crossed my mind at the thought of leaning against him like he was my personal comfort pillow.

A shiver ran up my spine as I felt his burning stare on every part of my body. Everywhere his fiery eyes landed, they left a destructive fire in their wake. I might as well be nude from the way his burning gaze bored into me invasively.

Now, I didn't react and stayed still as I waited for him to speak. His eyes dropped down at my hand before flicking back up to meet mine. That gaze of his spread through me like wildfire, burned into me like coals and left nothing but ash in its wake.

"Who else knows you're an assassin?"

My throat ran dry, and my heart almost fell out of my chest at the sudden question.

His lip twitched. "I'm assuming the rest of the Families are unaware?"

I exhaled. He leaned in closer until my thighs bumped into the vanity table. Lightning bolts exploded in my soul at his nearness. Wild tremors ran throughout my tormented body as the hair on my nape stood up.

He was like the moon's pull on the ocean's tide, leaving my body swaying from his intensity, but I willed my mind to remain strong. Surge's firm grip on the edge of the vanity tightened until his knuckles turned white.

"Mr. Romano, I don't know what you're — "

Surge lifted a hand and turned on the faucet. Puzzled, I stared at the clear water pouring out of it. Bewildered, I continued to stare as he pressed his hand under a dispenser until soap emerged. Now, his hand went toward mine, which was clasped.

My eyes widened when I realized his intention. I leaned back to pull away, but my lower back bumped into his hardness again, and he grunted softly. He snatched my hand and held it right under the faucet. Water poured down on it like a broken dam. I pulled back again, but his grip remained firm.

"What are you doing?" I gritted out, losing my façade of niceness.

I tugged my hand again, but he continued to lather it with soap. I stared as the mixture of warm water and soap. My breaths came out rougher as he began to wash my uninjured hand clean. Little water droplets smothered my soft skin before they fell off it, leaving my skin glistening. Slowly, the black ink marking my skin began to show.

Setting my jaw, I hissed, "You already overstepped your boundaries when you kissed me in front of my husband. Has no one taught you to keep your hands to yourself?" I spat out.

I was a hypocrite for throwing that last line at him, but I didn't care right now.

Too late. Now, my hand was completely clean, and a shiny black tattoo glared at us.

Surge stopped washing my hand and we stared at it in silence.

I wished he hadn't come here. Not just in the bathroom with me, but at this entire event. I should've feigned illness and skipped out on it. If I had, I could've avoided this confrontation. He figured I belonged to the Brotherhood, but he didn't know my name or my exact status. It was game over when our eyes met the moment Kirill introduced us.

Now, the theatrics were officially over.

My hopeless shoulders sagged as I stared with dimmed eyes at my hand.

The cobweb tattoo taunted me as I stared at it in defeat.

The funnel-shaped design spread out like a leaf. *Pakhan,* his father, and the leaders that came before him all had the same tattoo of a red and black spider. I heard it's one of the deadliest ones out there. *Pakhan's* followers, on the other hand, had cobwebs to signify their allegiance to *Pakhan* and his family. Just like me. I lifted my head and glared at Surge Romano.

Snatching my hand from him, I shot out, "Are you fucking satisfied now? Are we finally done here?"

The Don's eyes assessed me. "It's an honor to meet you, Little Assassin."

He'd said something similar back at the wedding as well.

My lips parted as his crinkling eyes teased me.

I wanted to throttle him already.

His gaze set me on fire.

It compelled yet disturbed me.

It was alluring and magnetic.

My breathing was shallow as my heart skipped a beat.

My heart was better off dead.

Why did dead things need to beat again?

His smirk deepened like he knew the effect he had on me.

"I wish I could say the same, *Don*." I spat out his title like it was poisonous.

His eyes softened for a second as he eyed my face. He frowned, and I wondered what he was looking at. He reached up with his clean, non-soapy hand, and with his pinky, he wiped the corner of my eye.

I gasped when watery kohl emerged, coating his finger. My husband's doing. I'd never had someone wipe my eyes before. My chest heaved and I wanted to look at anything but him. As if I had no willpower left, I stared with my mouth open as he took that same pinky, put it in his mouth, and sucked it clean.

I couldn't believe he'd just licked my tears!

The Don was insane.

Malicious and monstrous.

Frowning, I threw invisible daggers at him through my eyes.

I hated how he'd revealed my tattoo like it was so obvious that it was there, and now he was licking my tears. I always covered up the tattoo at parties. Nobody was allowed to know that I was initiated.

I blew out a rough breath and stared at him in annoyance. "If you don't move away from me, I won't be responsible if my elbow ends up in the back of your throat, Surge. This is my people's wedding, and you're a guest. You don't get to come in here and wreck my world — "

His eyes flared and darkened. "Wreck *your* world? You're the one who came into my life out of nowhere when I was just trying to drink in peace. You started it."

The bass in his voice deepened.

He so rudely interrupted me again. I wanted to plaster his big mouth with tape.

"You sound like a five-year-old instead of the mature forty-year-old man you're supposed to be," I huffed.

When he didn't bother to move, I jabbed both of my elbows into his stomach. He lost his expression, and, taking the opportunity, I clutched the edges of the table in front of me and shoved my back against him.

He fell back a few feet behind me. Not as far as I'd like, though, since this bathroom was massive enough to fit ten people.

"This isn't over, Don. I will bring your head as a souvenir to my people."

I turned away and stomped over to the door. I flung it open and managed to take two steps out of the door but stopped in my tracks. I looked around frantically with flushed cheeks. No one was around.

Sighing in relief, I took another few steps. Rummaging through my golden clutch draped around my shoulder, I pulled my travel-size perfume bottle out and sprayed it over me. I couldn't smell like him when I returned to my husband.

A man could tell another man's scent.

I moved another step but paused when I heard his alluring voice again.

"Not if I steal your soul first and keep it as a souvenir, Anastasia."

Anastasia...

I liked how his voice rumbled as he spoke my name.

It sounded even better than Little Assassin.

My heart drummed with each passing second.

"Dead people don't have souls, Surge," I said, glancing over my shoulder as I continued to walk away from him

He made no move to follow me.

The Don leaned his arm against the doorframe as his haunting gaze remained glued on me. The hue of them reminded me of the spring's promise of a new beginning. He couldn't be anyone's beginning, though. Just everyone's end. The destroyer of all sunshine and all things floral.

My legs almost turned to jelly.

I braced myself against the wall before I could slip.

"Those who were resurrected do. Isn't that what Anastasia means?"

His voice echoed in the empty hallway.

It was so deep that I could feel it in the pit of my stomach.

The corners of his lips lifted, and my heart skittered to a stop at the small action.

My lips parted and I almost halted in my tracks.

He knew what my name meant all along.

Bolts of electricity ran through me at what sizzled between us.

"You, Anastasia, are the epitome of the word resurrection. You're dead to the world but alive to others... to *me*."

His voice dropped low as he took one last look at me. I took one last look at him too, because the next time I met him, it wouldn't be as Anastasia.

It would be as the Assassin.

Surge

I shouldn't have done this, but fuck it, it was too late for regrets now.

A pair of men were guarding every entrance, hallway, rooftop, and exit.

Anastasia wasn't allowed to be in here today. It wasn't like she asked for permission, anyway, but still. There was no way she could sneak in. Not with my security camera doing surveillance on the warehouse. I didn't tell my men about her, though. They didn't see her face when she broke into my home, only knew that she was a female.

Today, my doors were closed to her. It wasn't that I was beginning to grow afraid of her. I had a different agenda planned for today. Something she couldn't see because she just might never forgive me for it. She already hated my guts, that much was obvious. That hatred wasn't because of me, but because of the bad blood between our worlds and communities.

I shoved my hands into my black leather jacket as I paced the charcoal-colored granite floor. I'd returned to wearing it again. My footsteps were deliberately slow as I paced. Pulling out a joint from my jacket, I lit it up slowly. The flame lit up the dark warehouse.

I blew out a breath and it came out as white puffs in the chilly atmosphere. There was no heating system here in this warehouse. It was one of the oldest in the city, built a very long time ago.

I glanced around my isolated property. Not only did I do most of my trade and business matters here, but this was also a special place for those I didn't like. The walls were painted a charcoal gray with a dark brown color splashed across them.

It used to be burgundy. The color of metallic blood as it oozed out of the bodies of traitors, enemies, and rivals, and splattered the walls like a streaming river. I blew out the smoke in my mouth. Not many people knew I smoked joints. They couldn't detect it on me.

I continued pacing as the smoke curled and uncurled around me.

Any second now...

"Let me go! Who the fuck are you?"

There he is.

Ignoring the deep and masculine voice, I took another drag from my joint. A man in a black hood was brought out in front of me at gunpoint before he was tied to the wooden chair with a rope. His chest, arms, and legs were trapped. He had nowhere to escape. Blood surged through me as I studied him. His hands were also tied to the chair.

As I lifted my head, I nodded at the two men who'd taken a step back.

The hood stayed over the man's head as I had instructed them to do earlier.

Adrenaline rushed through my very flighty veins. The man still screamed and protested as I headed toward him. I stalked toward him until I was standing right behind him. He stopped screaming, and my lip twitched. It was as if he knew someone was close to him. My men had picked him up when he'd left the wedding hall's premises and headed straight home. His wife wasn't with him.

I sensed a quarrel between them. Perhaps, she'd left without him. My fingers tingled in anticipation of the chaos to come. His people would search for him, but no one would find him until I wanted him found.

Leaving the joint still lit in my mouth, I stared down at it for a moment as the ash built on the tip of it. The joint helped camouflage mine as well as the warehouse's scent.

The bound man was wealthy enough. If he was intelligent enough, he could sniff out the cologne I wore and assume it was an expensive one. Then, he would associate that with wealth… and he could probably deduce who among his long list of enemies was the culprit from there. For now, it was better if he thought of me as a street thug and not the Don I was.

I didn't speak at all, since he might recognize my voice.

The atmosphere thickened with tension. No sound came from my men, either—only the sounds of erratic heartbeats and shallow breathing. I reached below and jerked the hood from his face. For what I was about to do, I needed access to his head.

He cussed before yelling, "Let me go! You don't know who you're fucking with. You're all dead!"

I did know who he was. He just didn't know who *I* was.

He didn't know just how powerful I was.

I was the eldest Don from the Fourth Family of New York.

Without any blood relation or any mafia prince status, I'd been ruling the Romano family for the past seventeen years. From a street thug trying to get by on the streets to a mob boss.

No one could hold a candle to me.

I'd seen more than the other Dons. I'd consumed more lives than them. I'd buried more people than anyone. I'd lost everything yet gained so much more.

My childhood innocence was all gone.

My feet remained glued to the ground as one of the men who stood near me blindfolded the man. Now that his vision was taken away from him, he was protesting again. I didn't muffle his voice, though, because my ears craved to hear his screams.

I grabbed the joint from my mouth and brought it near his scalp.

Then, I jammed it right onto it.

He hissed like a bitch before grunting, "What the fuck?"

I pulled it back after a couple of seconds and admired the circle-shaped burn mark it left behind. He tried to glance behind him, but I jammed the lit joint onto his head again.

Again and again.

I found another spot on his scalp and pressed the joint against it as well.

His body shivered uncontrollably in his seat, and he tried to move his head forward to avoid my murderous hands. I only pressed the joint against his scalp harder.

The butt of the joint met his scalp one last time before I dropped it on the ground. His yelling and cussing continued for a good minute or two as my eyes assessed my handiwork of the five burn marks I'd left on his scalp. Now, he wouldn't be able to sleep for days without grunting in pain the second his head touched his pillow.

Days weren't enough, though. I needed his pain to last weeks. Months even.

I still remembered those four silky tendrils in his hand.

The ones that didn't belong there.

The ones he'd forcefully snatched away.

I didn't speak. There was nothing to say anymore. I didn't believe in second chances. Stepping away for a moment, I moved over to the table behind me before grabbing a can of liquid. As I uncorked it, I stared dimly as the bound man continued protesting and screaming. His nape had a flush running across his body. Stepping toward him again, I stared down at him as he panted and breathed shallow breaths.

"Stop. Stop it!" he protested.

I didn't listen.

Reaching forward, I reached out a gloved hand and yanked his thick, black hair with all my might. Noises of agony filled the atmosphere. I swore my pupils dilated. My pulse spiked and blood whooshed past my eardrums.

I needed more. More screams. More pain.

I wanted to feed on his deprivation and make him suffer. I wanted to punish and torment him. I wanted to do those things that normal people thought twice about doing. I wanted to give in to the thoughts that entered their minds, but they chose not to act on them. Maybe it's because they were afraid of jail, or they had a moral conscience and couldn't stand the guilt that came from hurting others. I wasn't afraid of these things.

A made man didn't live his life in fear.

They were prepared to die from the day they were initiated.

I poked at the fresh burn marks I'd embedded into his skin and dug my fingers deep into his flesh. He twisted and grunted in his seat before cussing again. I yanked again until his seat almost tilted backward, but I caught it with the back of my other hand. His face faced the ceiling now as his neck bared out to me. I could easily reach out for my blade and slice across his neck. Bright red would pour out of it and a pool would form underneath him.

Focusing again, I pulled my hand away and my fingers returned bloody. I'd broken into the skin of the burn marks. I hid a smile as satisfaction settled into my soul.

I stared at the broken locks of hair before dropping them on the floor.

That looked familiar.

His head was still tilted back as he breathed like it was his last. Then, I lifted the can and poured gasoline on the back of his head, just at the tips of his locks.

It only needed a spark to spread.

A spark for combustion.

He hissed before sitting upright and glancing around, even though he couldn't see.

"No! You want money? I'll give you any amount you want. I'll spare you if you stop now."

A dry chuckle left my lips.

I gave the gas can to one of my men and pulled out my lighter.

The tied man no longer shook anymore. He couldn't tell what I was doing. Perspiration trickled down the back of his neck and his shirt grew damp with it. I wondered if he'd already pissed on himself. I wouldn't be surprised if he had.

"My people won't spare you!" he warned, like he commanded this warehouse and not me.

My lip twitched as I stared at his glistening, oily locks. Bloody droplets still oozed out of his wound. It was cute how he thought he could threaten me when he looked like shit.

My Family's ties went to the late eighteen hundreds. I wasn't just older in age compared to the other Dons' families. The Romano Family was also the eldest. The people that came before me had the mafioso in their roots for hundreds and hundreds of years. His people, the Solntsevskaya Bratva, only came in the late nineteen hundreds.

If his family knew I'd taken him captive, they wouldn't stop coming for me, though. The *Pakhan* wasn't just his leader, he was also his cousin. They had a blood relation.

Anyone would do anything for their family, just like I was willing to do anything for mine. I'd gone off the rails now after he'd tempted me last night.

I couldn't attack him then. Through my hollow stare, I ignited the flame and held it right above the edge of his hair. I filled the distance between the flame and the tendril, and the lock immediately caught on fire.

"What are you doing?" he screamed hoarsely.

What are you doing? You're hurting me.

Familiar words echoed in my mind of the night before.

I stared in fascination as the inferno consumed many, many hairs along the way. He jumped in his seat as he shook his head vigorously. Tormented screams filled the air as the fire ate away at his hair. He would have none left when this ended.

It was no use shifting around, though. He was bound. He jumped in his seat and his wrists had turned red from trying to escape the flames. The flames were a part of his hair now.

"Shit, my scalp burns! Who the fuck are you?"

My scalp burns.

At least the fire warmed this place up a little. I ungloved my hands and reached out over his flaming head like I was warming myself by the fireplace. It calmed the icy skin on my fingertips. The winter this time of the year had been merciless. It was nice and toasty as I rubbed my hands together to generate warmth.

Another chuckle left my lips.

I'd used his head like it was my private chimney.

"You will regret this! Let go!"

Let go.

She had said those words, too.

The fire burned through his hair, and some of it fell away to the ground. He resembled a man from Hell, like Judgment Day had come too soon for him. The scent of burning flesh and scorched locks filled the air. I had a feeling the dirty, sulfuric scent would linger in my clothes for days.

He continued screaming and my ears continued relishing the noises he made. Music to my fucking ears. The sounds were simply melodic. I took my cell phone out and recorded his screams. I would listen to them later.

I didn't care about this man when all I saw was her.

I wondered if he felt the same way she had when she asked him to stop pulling at her hair.

His screams stopped after a few moments.

My fingers halted, and I flicked my gaze up.

His body seized, and he looked like he was going into shock.

I nodded at my men as I turned around and swiftly headed toward the exit. Immediately, they ran toward him to put out the fire with a large blanket. They were prepared. Everything was planned. They wrapped his head with it before throwing a bucket of ice-cold water on him. It extinguished the inferno within minutes.

Later, they would throw him outside of his premises.

A welcome gift for his wife.

His pride would be crushed, and his ego would be challenged.

He should be glad I left him alive.

I still wanted to kill him, and I'd never left a kill unfinished. It took every inch of my willpower to walk away.

My hands curled and uncurled in fists. I was half tempted to return and finish the task. He was mine to harm, but not to slaughter.

Anastasia held the right to that.

Kirill Volkov would be punished again.

Only next time, it would be by her hands.

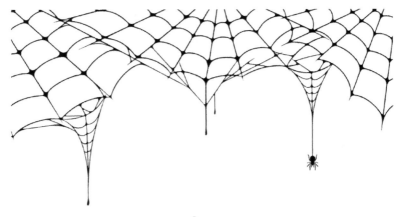

Ana

9

PAST
SIXTEEN YEARS OLD

I had gotten used to my new life with the Bratva.

I didn't live with Kirill, but his home was nearby. I saw him almost every day since he trained me to fight and use weapons. I stayed in an apartment with one of the housemaids named Maria. I still didn't remember anything about my past. The questions I had to find out where I came from were long forgotten. During the day, I attended the local high school, and during the night, I often sparred with him.

This became my life now ever since I became initiated three months ago. It didn't matter to me who Kirill Volkov was and where he came from.

He'd sheltered me and provided food for me to eat. I didn't know anyone else out there. I was told I had no other living relatives. It was strange, though. Just today afternoon, I headed toward the chauffeur who always picked me up after school when someone had called out to me, "Ana!"

I paused and glanced behind me, but I didn't recognize the person. The person had raven-black hair and brown eyes. Puzzled, I stood there silently for a few seconds as I debated whether or not I should talk to the stranger.

I tapped my foot on the ground as I waited for the stranger to say something. When the stranger didn't say anything, I shook my head and slowly turned around to head toward the black SUV that was waiting for me.

"Princess!"

I stopped in my tracks.

Dumbfounded, I wondered if they thought I was their princess. A giggle slipped out of me a second later.

A princess?

Yeah, right.

I swung my bookbag over my shoulder as I glanced back again. The wide-eyed young woman still stood there, staring at me directly. She rushed in her footsteps before her wild eyes met mine. I only stared at her with raised brows. She pushed past the incoming crowd of students before moving toward me. My feet were glued to the spot as I continued to stare at her silently.

A figure in a black suit stepped next to me.

Snapping out of the trance, I glanced up at the driver named Matteo.

"Shall we go, Miss Anastasia? Sir Kirill is awaiting your return."

I nodded slowly, biting my lip as I glanced at the lady still running toward me. She was only a few feet away and my curious heart wanted to hear what she wanted to say. A moment later, Matteo's hand tugged gently on my arm as he moved toward the car.

"School is over, Miss. We must return home."

"All right," I mumbled.

Matteo glanced over his shoulder at the woman who kept shouting, "*Princess! Princess!*" I tried looking at his eyes to see his expression, but damn him for wearing black sunglasses.

Did he know her?

Did *I* know her?

My pulse spiked as I continued to glance behind me to gawk at her. I wasn't sure if I knew her. Did she know who I was?

A ray of hope stirred in my heart, and I opened my mouth to speak but then clamped it shut.

Once I was in the backseat, Matteo quickly started the engine. The roar from it sent tremors throughout my body, and I was left staring out the rearview window at the woman whose muffled shouts still echoed in my ears.

My pulse spiked and my breathing quickened. From the distance, she grew tinier and tinier until the vision of her faded away. Turning around, I chewed inside my cheek as I tried to understand what just happened. I crossed my arms over my chest as I tried to catch Matteo's eyes, but he only stared straight ahead as he drove.

Why hadn't he spoken to her, though?

And why did she keep calling me a princess?

I wasn't a princess.

… Was I?

❖

Kirill didn't seem too pleased about my encounter with the stranger, because I stopped going to my high school a week later.

He offered to homeschool me instead. I shrugged off the sudden decision because I hated waking up in the mornings, anyway.

One night, I fell asleep earlier than usual when something sharp like a knife's edge poked the side of my neck. My heavy-lidded eyes burst open, and through my groggy eyes, I stared into the secluded shadows. I couldn't see anything at all.

What the...

Sweat clung to my nape and my loose limbs moved under the bed's covers as my eyes closed shut.

The next time I woke up, I couldn't move.

My vision became clearer as I stared into the shadows of the room. I hissed under my breath when I glanced down and found myself bound to a chair with a rope. Unease crept up my skin. I still wore the same blue pajamas that I'd worn the night before. My chest expanded as shallow breaths escaped my lips. My pulse throbbed and I winced when I tried to move.

The ropes were tied so tightly around me that I could feel them cutting into my skin. I groaned when something red trailed down to the chair's armrest. Lifting my heavy head, I glanced around for anyone in sight. Not a single person was around.

This seemed like something out of a horror movie, and I didn't know why I was tied up. Icy shivers ran up my spine and the blood in my veins jittered. My mind ran in different directions as it filled with thousands of questions, I had no answers to. Unsatisfied, I swallowed the scream that wanted to erupt out of my mouth.

"H-Hello?" I croaked.

No answer came.

My heart hammered in my chest.

My tired and fleeting eyes searched through the vacant room. It looked like a room of a house or an apartment, but it had no bed or windows. I didn't even know if it was dawn or dusk outside. It was simply dark everywhere I looked. The fluttering in my veins increased as I scanned the room. My breathing deepened and my chest expanded as I tried to calm my nerves.

The only artificial light that came was from the ceiling above my head. The walls were painted with gruesome charcoal colors that only reminded me of the utter desolation I was in. It cloaked me with its unfriendly blackness. The empty room was deafeningly quiet, and the only sounds that existed were my rapid breathing and erratic heartbeat.

My feet were sockless and the cold, wooden floor left peppered kisses on my skin. Time slipped by slowly as I continued to move and struggle to break out of the rope. No one had taught me how to break out of ropes. Although I was taking advanced training with Kirill, I didn't think it was possible to be taken away from my home again. I wondered if I could chew through the ropes.

They were thick and heavy, and the more I moved, the more they cut into my skin. Trying to breathe through my clogged nose, I bent down so my teeth could catch the rope binding my wrists. My chest wasn't bound. I began biting on it, but after a few minutes of slowly sawing away with my teeth, I hadn't made much progress. The binds were too strong, and I was afraid my teeth might just crack.

Sweat trickled down the back of my neck as I continued to hack at the rope. My nightshirt clung to my sweaty back. My hair was also drenched and matted against my face. My teeth grew sore from gnawing, and, after a few seconds, I stopped.

I stared with dimmed eyes at the binds again.

They were constricted enough to cut into my skin.

I needed to get out of here. *Now.*

My ears perked up when the doorknob turned and artificial light from the hallway poured into the room. My eyes narrowed at the three hooded people in black outfits, covered from head to toe. I couldn't even make out their eyes. The area around their eyes was thinner than the rest of the hood, like a thin veil.

I held in my breath as they came up to me.

Three figures. All large.

I was still young compared to them, but I grew taller every day. I swallowed the lump forming in my throat.

"W-Who are you?" I croaked out again.

I licked my dry and chapped lips, wishing I had some water to quench my thirst.

Their mouths remained shut.

I eyed every one of them. They all had weapons attached to their hips. Maybe if I was untied, I could snatch one away from them. I moved my arms again, but the ropes only cut deep into my skin again and left my wrists raw. They weren't going to look pretty afterward. Sighing restlessly in my mind, I sniffled and glanced up again.

Were these the enemies of Kirill and the Bratva?

"No one could ever find out who she is," one of them whispered to the other. They were speaking with each other like I wasn't even there. Their voices were low, hushed, and they came out muffled. I couldn't recognize them.

"Her people are still looking for her," the other deep and masculine voice replied.

My heart skipped a beat.

Their words chilled me to the bone.

What? My people?

I thought my family was dead?

It was strange how I'd never seen a picture of myself on television. It was as if no one was looking for a missing child …

It was like I was a ghost now.

Anastasia.

I didn't know anything about who I was.

It was strange that the Solntsevskaya Bratva's oath became my life.

I have no body, no soul, no name. I am Bratva.

My life had been long forgotten.

My true identity was completely wiped from history.

Kirill mentioned my parents' names were George Popov and Olga Popova. According to Kirill, they were from the smaller side of town. Sometimes, I wondered if they even existed, because I couldn't remember them at all.

Not even the slightest of memories came into my mind whenever I thought of them. They had no relatives that I could trace my roots, and I had no siblings to share the burden of being an orphan with.

I had assumed I'd been traveling with them before I was separated from them. The unfamiliar names still echoed in my mind sometimes, but I felt no connection with them. The only person I had a connection with was Kirill.

Bewildered, I flicked my gaze between each hooded person. An ache throbbed in the back of my head. I didn't understand what they were talking about. I tried to open my mouth to speak but closed it shut again. I couldn't bargain with them, and no one took someone intending to return them.

I gazed around my surroundings to map them to my mind, but it felt like a lost cause. I wished I had my blade. I always slept with it under my pillow, but I didn't think it would have been helpful if I had it under my clothes as well.

Shoot. Maybe I should've slept with it on—but then again, they would've searched my body for weapons. The chances of coming out of here were less than zero.

Footsteps came up from behind me and I glanced over my shoulder. Before I could lift my head to look at him, he grabbed a hold of my loose, sticky mane and tugged at it. I bit down on my tongue to stop from shouting cusses at him.

Never let them see you in pain.

Kirill's words echoed in my mind.

Where was he?

Did he know I was here?

Panic wanted to settle in my soul, so I closed my eyes instead. Sometimes, it was better to ignore reality than to face it. Life around me disappeared as nothingness greeted me. The pure blackness of the chaos swarming in my heart filled my mind. A sharp sting greeted my hair again and I bit down on my lip harder until I tasted something sticky and metallic like blood. I opened my eyes as I licked my liquid-covered lips. I had bruised myself.

My eyes widened when a looming machine with a silver end pointed right near my eye. I jerked my head back from it and shouted, "What are you doing, you sick freak? Why have you taken me?" They continued to ignore me as a sharp sound emerged from the machine. I didn't dare look at the heinous device.

Thump. Thump. Thump.

My heart beat wildly.

I had no idea who these sadistic creatures were.

I closed my eyes again and angled my face from it. The sounds coming from it made my skin crawl. I couldn't move any further than the seat until a sense of hopelessness settled over me. There was no escape. A choked and broken noise left my lips when my hair was yanked again, and fingers pried my eyes open. Unwanted water trickled from the corners of my eyes as I screamed, "No!"

Never let them see you in pain.

The command still echoed in my mind, and it was kind of hard not to break down when they threatened me with a deadly weapon. I still shook my head fiercely as one hand grabbed my jawline roughly until my teeth bit into my inner cheeks. More blood erupted inside my mouth. The other hand continued to pull on my hair as it lifted my head and granted them direct power over my eyes.

The hooded figure holding the device pried open my right eye before it made contact with it. I hurled a scream as he pierced right into my iris.

Pain.

God…

The pain of it was nothing like I had ever imagined.

I had nothing to compare it to.

I'd never felt such a burning sensation igniting my skin.

A rush of heat swarmed over my mind even though my body continued to remain cold. I didn't know how it was possible to be hot and cold at the same time.

It was like being sliced right open as they used the foreign object to invade my eye. It jammed itself right into one of my main senses. It hurt incredibly much, more than being in battle and being nicked by a blade.

I didn't know why they wanted to torture me instead of killing me.

I knew torture existed in our world, but they hadn't even begun to ask me questions about the Bratva, and they were already harming me. It didn't make sense at all.

They just needed to hurt me, to drag me into darkness until I didn't recognize myself anymore. This flicker of madness suffocated my very existence.

I'd been wiped from history before.

History was repeating itself now.

A piece of myself slowly slipped into the darkness.

Another piece of my identity I would never retrieve.

Specks of blood landed on my cheek. My chest heaved as despair took over my soul. I didn't know what I had done to deserve this. Had I killed one of their people? Maybe. I couldn't even move my head anymore, or my eyes. The power from my hands had left mine and gone into theirs.

One of the tall figures behind me spoke.

"Boss said not to leave her blind. He specifically ordered us to only damage one eye."

Boss? Who was this *boss* and why did he want to hurt *one eye* only?

Maybe they wanted to turn me into Medusa.

The hysterical thought made no sense at all.

I fisted my clammy and cold hands together as I struggled to not feel the pain in my eye.

My body shivered uncontrollably as shocks ran through me.

My breath hitched, and my tongue wandered loosely in my mouth.

My mind faded as I sat there, unresisting and unable to fight anymore.

I was afraid if I struggled some more, they would miss their aim and end up destroying the rest of my face.

My body made the wisest decision it had so far, granting me mercy.

The darkness around the edges of my injured eye took over.

My mind drifted off and my head lolled backward. A tiny part of me was grateful I had leaned backward, otherwise, that device's pointy tip would be sticking out of the back of my head.

Time froze and I stared vacantly as the device moved through a thick fog in slow motion. My surroundings became distant, like this had happened to someone else other than me. I couldn't protest and scream, even though I wanted to.

Thump. Thump. Thump.

My rapid heartbeat increased.

I just might die from shock today.

Before I lost consciousness, someone spoke again.

"The princess has a pair of distinct and healthy eyes. No one can recognize them now."

Princess.

That word again.

No one would be looking for a princess with damaged eyes…

Who am I?

Before I could ponder on those words some more, my world turned black.

I didn't have to face this cruel world any longer.

I didn't know how much time had passed when I woke up.

Alive. I was *alive*.

One of my eyes was closed shut, and I laid in an unfamiliar bed. A blurry figure in black sat on the floor beside me. I blinked and reached up a trembling hand to my throbbing, bandaged eye. My limbs weighed like concrete, and I had no energy left in me. After a fleeting breath, I whimpered in pain, and my hand collapsed back onto the soft, satin sheets. I wanted to sleep and wake up with a clean slate. However, vivid memories of what occurred recently flooded my mind, and I closed my eyes again.

"You're safe now, Tasha," a familiar voice cooed.

My eyebrows furrowed, but I didn't want to open my eyes.

"I found you before they could cause more damage."

Silence fell over us.

Both of my eyes throbbed now.

A pang of anger filled my heart that something had been taken away from me.

A part of me had been damaged.

"Too late," I whispered.

"*Malyshka*." His words softened.

Kirill.

It would be easy to curl up like a baby against him, but I didn't move at all as his hands smoothed my hair. His touch comforted me, but it wasn't enough. It never could be. I felt like I was in the wrong world sometimes, and my real world was something else entirely.

I exhaled. "They hurt me, Kirill."

He sucked in a sharp breath. "I'm aware."

I sniffled as numbness settled in my heart.

"They kept on saying I'm a princess," I said in a small voice.

I didn't recognize my voice. I curled up into a ball and draped my heavy arms around myself. A moment later, the comforter lifted and wrapped around me. *Kirill*. I snuggled into it like it was my new home.

"You are the Bratva's princess, aren't you?" I could feel the smile in his voice. "You might not be born into the lineage, but you're far worthier."

I almost smiled. *Almost.*

Oh. Was that why they called me that?

I had assumed otherwise.

What about the person I had seen at school?

Kirill sounded like he wouldn't lie to me, though.

His hand rubbed against my hair again and I leaned my head into it, against his comfort. I liked the praise that came from him. He seemed proud of me.

My eyes continued to remain closed, and only darkness filled my vision.

"You are very special to me, Tasha," he murmured.

I would smile if I could.

"You are the only female to be initiated in our organization," he continued. "Many people will not stand for that, not even my own, and there will be those who want to harm you to get to us... to *me*. Word had leaked out to the rival family members about you. They broke into the security system when they came for you. The housemaid and guards were dead when I arrived here." My pulse spiked. "You're our chosen one. Our secret weapon. *My* secret weapon. No one can ever know who you are. The same thing that others consider a weakness. Your femininity will be your strength."

My beating heart pounded in my chest.

"You're in my home with me. You're not safe in that apartment anymore."

I inhaled before releasing a breath. "Are they alive?"

"No," he replied after a beat. "Their eyes are gone now."

My soul jerked awake.

I cracked open one eye and met his dark ones.

Two pools of abysses greeted me. They were hollower than usual, like he was both tired and relieved to see I was alive. He looked like he hadn't shaved in two days, and a strange urge fell over me to reach out and touch his dark jawline. My cheeks warmed, and I brushed that thought away.

Kirill had always been Kirill to me...

I wondered how long I'd been gone.

His jaw ticked as he glanced at my bandaged eye. I still didn't know if I could see from it. Maybe my vision would be blurry in one eye. Not wanting to think about it right now, I flicked my gaze down.

"I recorded it for you," he spoke again. "Do you want to see it?"

My heart thumped once again.

My good eye prickled with water as I glanced up.

A sick part of me wanted to relish their deaths for what they did to me, and the sicker part of me wanted to see it on repeat.

Rage settled over my heavy soul.

I'd never felt this feeling before.

It was foreign.

Strange.

Unknown.

The need to hate, hunt, and harm ached in my fingertips.

I had killed other people before because of a higher order, but this time I wanted to kill someone of my own accord.

I wanted to end people's existence like they'd tried to end mine.

To see the same wounds, they had inflicted on me.

To see them suffer the same way I had.

They didn't show me any mercy as they cut into me.

I would show no mercy to anyone.

Every assignment I would now have was guaranteed to end with someone's death. I was already a killer, already initiated, but now, I would bloom into the assassin my world desired me to be. The bloodshed of my enemies would cover me like armor.

They would never see me coming.

I wouldn't be capable of mercy.

I hardened my heart as I met Kirill's gaze.

I could never come back from this now.

As the remaining shreds of my humanity fell, I replied in a clear voice, *"Yes."*

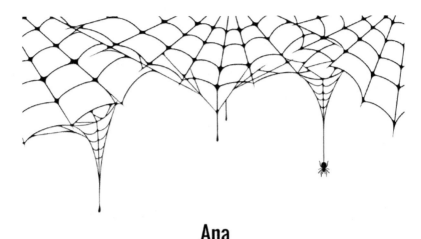

Ana

10

PRESENT

Nobody wanted to return home to a burned husband.

I stared in alarm as Kirill rested his head on the bed and I wondered who wanted to cross him. Still bewildered by the horrific sight, I could only gape as I took in the deep brown scars etched across his pale scalp. I wanted to hurl my breakfast at my feet but thought it would offend my husband, so I gagged silently.

Jagged scars were embedded into parts of his skin like mismatched socks. Some of the colors were bordering scarlet color while others were slightly pinker. Every inch of his scalp was filled with raw markings, strategically etched across his skin like someone had a personal vendetta against him. He was left in a terrible state, and by the looks of it, it would take months for him to recover. Those scars would stay on his skin forever. His hair would grow out eventually, but I doubted the marks would vanish.

Two bodyguards surrounded us in our room. I wanted to order them to leave, but maybe it was better they were here. I couldn't be with him always, just like yesterday.

A pang of guilt settled over my heart that I'd let him storm out of the wedding without me. He wasn't answering my phone calls, and I didn't know what I did to deserve his malicious behavior. He was the one who tugged *my* hair. As he laid there sleeping with a burned head, I wondered if karma got him for what he'd done to me.

I scolded myself for even considering such unsolicited thoughts. Studying him again, I realized that there were no gauzes or bandages wrapped around his bald head. The skin was still sensitive and raw.

Whoever did that to him intended to leave an obvious scar on his skin. Not only did the perpetrator make sure to scorch his flesh until it was black, but he also made sure it hadn't penetrated deep into the brain tissue.

He should've known better.

I remembered the time when those rivals had yanked on my hair to poke my eye. Don't get me wrong. A yank was painful no matter what. But there was a good yank and there was a bad one. A good yank caused a sweet sting and turned me on, but this bad kind of yank where water coated my eyes wasn't good at all.

I sighed silently. Kirill's karma seemed more humankind-inflicted than a god-inflicted one. *Pakhan* was already searching for whoever had harmed his cousin, but so far, there was no one to pay for what they'd done to him.

Kirill mentioned that he had been blindfolded when he was abducted, and he couldn't remember hearing any voices. It's as if no one had spoken in the warehouse intentionally. I tilted my head as I pondered over what he'd said. Voices were hard to distinguish either way, but it made me wonder if Kirill had known those men and that was the reason why they hadn't spoken.

I sat in the lounge chair across the bed. Kirill had been unconscious for the past two days now, only stirring in his sleep every once in a while, letting me know that he was still alive and breathing. He'd been hooked on IV medications, and the needle sticking to his vein was how they were feeding him.

I gritted my teeth as I sighed again. Slowly, I rose from my seat and caught the attention of the soldiers. They only nodded at me as they returned to guarding their superior. I had an assignment to complete. A pending assignment I had waited way too long to finish. Kirill had told me two weeks, but I'd crossed my third this week. I'd waited for him to scold me for disappointing him, but now this had happened.

I gathered my belongings as I exited the room. I carried with me a black, leather bag that held my outfit and my weapons. Currently, I wore a white dress that ended at my calves. Slipping on my black boots and a trench coat, I stepped outside before anyone could stop me. The soldiers didn't know what I did in my spare time.

Pakhan had ordered them not to stop me if I tried to leave the house. He knew I could handle my own. Gusts of wind fluttered against my cheek as I walked. My eyes turned misty as I stared into the horizon. I tried to focus on my blurry eye, but it was no use. I couldn't make my vision any clearer.

Dimness settled over me. It would be permanently scarred. Even if I had surgery, I don't think it would replace the enlarged black iris. Someone had purposefully made it that way. I moved along the pathway. The snow had stopped falling, but the frosty wind continued. It was January now.

I locked the door behind me, jingling my keys before pocketing them. More guards in black suits stayed outside like they were ready to go to war for their captain. They eyed me curiously, like they wondered where I was going. They only glanced at each other as I walked by, knowing it would be better not to question me.

I should have felt more upset about Kirill being harmed, but the feeling in me was now missing. Sure, I obeyed him. I would die for him, but not for the obvious reason that he was my husband. I'd die for him because he was my *leader*. I paused at my treacherous thoughts and shook them off.

I should still be playing the role of a dutiful wife, but I couldn't convince my mind to do so. I didn't know how to care for a cheating husband.

A husband who yanked my hair even though I had told him I didn't like it after what those rivals did in the past.

A husband who was immune to me.

A husband who didn't touch me.

Was there something wrong with me?

There is.

My soul sank deeper into my chest.

Did my scarred eye bother him?

Perhaps he considered me physically unattractive because of it. I was tempted to return inside just to stare at my reflection in the mirror. I'd always considered myself as someone who'd make anyone look twice, so why couldn't he?

My soul had detached itself from the pain that neither of us could fix.

I couldn't fix *myself*.

I'd always been a killing machine for my people's cause.

I hadn't felt something real in a while.

Emerald eyes flashed in my mind.

I almost toppled over my steps but caught myself. I blew out a shallow breath and stared as it turned into mist in the frigid evening air. Reaching up with a gloved hand, I tucked my loose hair behind my ears. I opened the back door of my car and dropped my bag onto the seat. A moment later, I slipped into my driver seat as I began the engine, turned on the heat, and waited for it to warm up. Cold air immediately filtered into the car, and it would take some time to warm up.

I rubbed my numb hands together. Even with the gloves on, they had turned as cold as a popsicle. I rested my arms on the steering wheel as I pondered about running away from all of this chaos and returning to killing instead.

I wanted to butcher Surge Romano, but his teasing eyes filled my mind again. My heart sped up, but not in the way I wanted it to when I thought about killing someone. I groaned and scolded myself for thinking about another man.

Why not? Kirill sleeps with other women, my inner voice countered.

My eyes misted as I blew out a breath.

Shut up, I warned.

Maybe if you fuck another man, he will notice.

My body stilled at the thought.

I flinched, disgusted by the absurd thought.

Think about yourself. I shook my head fiercely. *He doesn't care about you.*

He's my husband, I wanted to scream.

That doesn't mean he gives a shit about you.

I should be more sympathetic toward him since he'd been hurt and left for dead. One of our bodyguards standing guard outside of the house had found him unconscious in our yard. Apparently, someone had kicked him out of a moving van before driving off.

Unease ran over me.

He didn't deserve that.

Yes, he did. He pulled your hair, remember?

That punishment was too severe for the one he paid.

An eye for an eye.

I glanced at my damaged, cerulean-colored eye in the rearview mirror before looking away.

Whoever had hurt him must have planned on leaving him traumatized.

And what about the trauma he's given you over the years?

It wasn't the same thing.

The man doesn't even bother to take a shower before coming to see you after tumbling in the sheets with someone else.

I remained quiet now.

You can smell the other woman's fucking perfume.

I still didn't reply.

My inner voice sighed, most likely thinking it was pointless to talk sense into me before it gave up on me.

But not before it retorted one more time.

How have you not killed the whores he's fucking?

I shook my head slowly.

They weren't whores. The biggest whore was my husband.

I should kill him instead.

I hissed at my response before reaching up to pinch the bridge of my nose. Tormented by my own thoughts and my inner voice doing happy little jumping jacks in my mind, I willed it to shut up before it could cause any more damage.

My battle wasn't with the other women in his life.

It was with the man who laid in my bed.

I clenched and unclenched my jaw.

"Why did you marry me, Kirill?" I murmured.

Then, I froze.

My eyes widened at what slipped out, and I glanced around the Jeep.

I hesitated as I flicked my gaze up at the ceiling.

I wouldn't be surprised if Kirill had cameras in the car he'd given me.

I shouldn't have spoken out loud.

Too late for regrets now.

I shut off my wandering mind as I drove before I did something insane like reverse the car and shoot my now-bald husband in the throat. I winced again at the terrible thought. I wished it could remove itself permanently from my mind, but it seemed like it was here to stay. Picking up speed, I drove through the dark night. Even with my windows rolled up, I could feel the gust of heavy winds pushing against them. My mind was now vacant, but my hands still knew what to do.

I parked two blocks away from the warehouse I'd expected Romano to be in before planning my entry. Unlocking the car, I grabbed my leather bag from the back and rummaged through my belongings before picking out my outfit. I had already removed my trench coat and wool dress by this point. Goosebumps erupted on my warm skin as the car's heat ran over it. I rubbed my hands together as I prepared to dress.

I paused when footsteps emerged from the side of my car's door. My chest heaved as I grabbed my revolver from the bag. I turned around and my hair flew with me as I faced the backseat and the emerging footsteps. It must be one of the made men scouting the area. Maybe they had prepared for my arrival? Unease filled my spine as I straightened my back. My body stilled as I waited for the door to burst open. I didn't bother locking it. The need to kill filled me as I held in a twisted smile.

I glanced out the window, but the dusky evening had darkened, and no streetlights were on around this isolated area.

My breath whooshed past my ears as the door handle flung open. I kept my hand steady, my mind clear, and my breaths light as I focused. My fingers tightened on the trigger, ready to pull it any second.

What I didn't expect to see was a ginger in the middle of the night.

The first thing that entered my car was his scent.

I hated that I recognized his leather aroma. He smelled like the way he looked. The way he dressed. His scent was like that of a clean car. The ones people were addicted to smelling and they craved it like a junkie craving a high a drug gave.

I stopped breathing, and Don Romano gave me a look like he knew what I was doing. His relentlessly intense eyes were already scolding me, and I wanted to huff at him.

I kept my face stoic as he entered my vehicle, closed the door behind him, and made himself comfortable in my car. He pulled the halves of his leather jacket closer to his body as his gaze lifted, and his jade eyes met mine. I frowned as I glared at him through my eyes.

His hair was still damp and tucked neatly behind his ears like he'd taken a fresh shower. His cheeks had a light, day-old stubble on them, and my fingers itched to run across his face. He only shrugged boyishly, like I wasn't holding a gun to his face, before his eyes wandered lower to my body.

I only had my bra, underwear, and knee-high combat boots on.

Shit. Damn him for finding me at the wrong time.

Couldn't he have come a minute later, after I had changed?

My fingers quivered on the trigger, and I used my free hand to steady myself.

I still aimed my gun-holding hand right at his face.

Don Romano leaned back into the leather seat of my car like it was his new home as his eyes remained glued on my body. I swallowed, wondering what he thought about me. I glanced down at my body, trying to look at it from his perspective. My loose chest-length hair framed my body. I had full breasts, dainty collarbones, a soft stomach, and long legs. I didn't have freckles like him, and now I kind of wished I did. They made him look even more appealing.

Attractive.

I wrinkled my nose at that thought. I didn't give a shit about his opinion. Still, I returned his curious stare. My cheeks warmed when he bit down on his lower lip. His teeth sank into the fullness of it, and I wanted to touch it to see if it was as soft as it looked. His thumb reached up to graze across his lower lip.

The Don's eyes glided smoothly across every inch of my skin, and everywhere he glanced, a flush of pink followed. I wanted to squeeze my legs together, but it was impossible to do so with the way I sat. My core pulsated and I wanted to scream at it. I hated how he openly stared at me when I had the damn gun aimed at his face. I felt like my control was slipping out of my fingers and into his hands.

Finally, after what seemed like forever, his head lifted to look at me.

I opened my mouth to cuss at him, but my voice was sucked right out of me when I caught the dilation in his eyes. They were darker, looking like an ominous and foggy forest.

Only sheer *hunger* shone through them.

My fingers shook again.

I hated the damn things for trembling.

My cheeks grew hotter, like a scarlet woman who'd been caught committing adultery. I'd never had a man look at my half-nude body before. I hadn't planned on anyone seeing me naked this way… or at all.

His lip twitched as he spoke in his rich voice. "I didn't peg you as a person who wore pink. You always dress like it's someone's funeral. Lately, I suppose, it's mine."

My eyes widened at his comment, and I glanced down at my pink undergarments.

Out of all the colors I could wear, why didn't I choose black today of all days?

"You look feminine," he murmured.

My heartrate accelerated as I met his heated eyes again.

"Womanly."

It was better when he thought of me as a man.

I'd been so used to pretending to be a male assassin this whole time that I'd forgotten what it was like being a woman.

The area between my legs felt damp again and my nipples tightened. They itched and throbbed under his leery gaze. His eyes zeroed in on them as if he noticed they were undeniably erect and wanted to break out of my thin bra. I wanted to hide from his stare. "Stop looking at me," I shot out under my breath.

He raised a light brown eyebrow. "You look soft," he continued, his voice becoming more teasing and taunting by the second. I was ready to jam the barrel of my gun over his head. "But still a damn badass, holding that gun." He sounded almost proud, and my treacherous soul craved more of his praise. "Although, I do wonder sometimes, do you know how to use it?" His smirk deepened.

I clenched my jaw. "Why don't we test that theory out?"

The asshole already knew I could. I'd killed his soldiers in front of him before, yet he still wanted to be a pompous ass.

My finger loomed over the trigger button, but he reached out like lightning as he pulled me from my driver's seat and onto his seat.

My reflexes kicked in and I grabbed my blade from my still-open bag. I might not have been able to shoot him yet, but I sure as hell could stab him. I landed right on his lap with my gun pressed to his forehead and my blade pressed against the side of his neck. My soul gleamed and my heart did flipflops at the thought of killing him then and there. His body stilled at my threat, but his eyes remained unaffected.

"Don't you dare move," I warned. "You pull out your gun on me, and I swear, I will stab you." My voice came out too low and too breathless for my liking.

He didn't dare move, but his deceitful eyes dragged down to my breasts that were smashed against his rock-hard chest. From my angle, my chest looked rounder than usual. "You can't move your eyes, either," I hissed, shivering at the coldness of his leather jacket against my softness.

His carnivorous gaze flicked up to meet my eyes, and his hands glided up the sides of my waist. I swallowed and my breath was caught in my chest as his large, calloused hands traveled up my body. I glanced down and my exhales came out heavier. His hands were masculine yet elegant with his long fingers. His hand was rough and cool to the touch against my smooth skin, and goosebumps erupted wherever he touched.

I licked my lips and tried to warn him again.

"You can't—"

Surge leaned in to run his nose along the crook of my neck.

I froze as he *inhaled* me and memorized my scent.

I never had someone do that before.

My breath hitched.

"I can, and I *will*," he countered in a low, husky voice. "And you will let me."

The deadly promise echoed in my ears.

My breaths came out shallower and my body molded itself against him.

"If you think you can stop me with your weapons, you can go ahead and try. I don't fear bullets but the determination of the person holding that weapon, and I'm sorry to say, Little Assassin, I've already made your resolve weak."

And with that, his hand wandered to my back, trailed up my spine, and tangled itself in my hair. I arched my breasts against him and bit down on my lip. His face was still buried in the crook of my neck as his tongue snaked out to lick across my collarbone before his hand unhooked my bra like an expert.

A tiny gasp escaped my lips and I jerked back. My hands that held the weapons faltered, now resting on his broad and muscled shoulders. I glanced down at my breasts that hung freely under my bra. My gaze dropped lower, and I refused to look up since I didn't want to catch that look in his eyes again.

This was wrong.

So wrong.

I shouldn't even be here. I shouldn't even...

I never finished my sentence, because his calloused hands that were on my back slipped to my front without warning. My gun slipped from my hand as it fell with a clang to the side. I jerked my heavy eyes up at him as he cupped my breasts under my bra. I bit down on my lip, and his equally heavy eyes met mine.

I didn't even know what we were doing.

This was inappropriate and just wrong.

His thumb brushed against my erect nipple, and it hardened under his touch. Tingles shot up my spine as his hands explored my body. Confused, I stared down at them again. His thumbs and forefingers tugged on my little nubs as they stretched them out like they were made of dough. They turned redder and rawer, the more his fingers pulled on them. Bolts of electricity shot through my body like a circuit gone haywire. I whimpered and clung to his shoulders as he continued torturing them.

One of his hands left my sore nipple as it drifted to my back and tugged on my hair. A sweet sting greeted me as a gasp left my lips.

My head lifted and I met his gaze. His eyes had turned stark black again, the irises growing darker until only a black void was staring back at me. His hand jerked on my hair again, forcing me to lift my head and meet his cold, deadly eyes.

"Does it hurt when I pull your hair?" he asked after a moment.

His voice was lower and gruffer than usual as he spoke.

My pulse spiked, and I wondered why he asked.

Our breathing came out hotter and heavier, fogging up the windows around us.

"No," I admitted breathlessly. "Not the way you do it."

He swallowed as he stared into my eyes.

His hand stilled on my breast before it moved away to bury itself in my hair with his other one. In doing so, my body moved against him, and I whimpered when my core hit his groin. He was *hard*. So hard that I could feel him through his jeans, and I wanted to move against him again.

He gave a look like he knew what I was thinking, but what came out of his mouth was something else entirely. "But when someone else does it, it hurts?"

I stilled. How did he know that?

Unease crawled up my spine as the dreadful memories filled my mind.

I exhaled and my breath hit his lips.

Averting my eyes, I looked at anything but him.

His hand jerked my hair back again, and I groaned as I glanced at him with dimmed eyes. I raised a brow, and he ordered, "Answer me, Ana."

Ana. "My name is Anastasia."

"Fuck that. You are *Ana* to me."

He had another nickname for me.

My soul tingled, but I crushed it before it could disobey me again.

"You are such a bossy man," I huffed out, wrinkling my nose.

He looked at me like he wanted to throttle me. I rolled my eyes. As if his hands in my hair weren't enough.

"Obviously. I'm a Don. Now answer my fucking question."

Well, he had a potty mouth… just like *me.*

I shook the last thought away. Even if I cussed like a sailor, that didn't mean I'd tolerate him cussing in my presence. I should've cleaned his dirty mouth with soap. Then again, how could I? I couldn't help but stare at his freckles.

"Did you know your freckles turn dark whenever you're upset?" I said out of the blue. I don't know why I said that out loud… maybe to piss Mr. Ginger off?

He sighed under his breath before pulling his face closer to mine. His warm hands were tangled in my hair like we were one body and not two separate entities.

"Answer. Me."

His lethal command hit right in my soul.

Through dimmed eyes, I replied in a low voice, "It hurts when others do it."

I didn't know why I thought he knew the answer already, but he needed confirmation from me. He growled under his breath. "Kirill?"

I closed my eyes. I didn't want to hear that name.

"When he does it, it hurts."

Even though I could feel dangerous energy boiling inside him, Surge remained quiet. The conversation had changed its course. Blood thumped in my veins and my pulse spiked with each passing second. Tension filled the air between us, and I considered removing myself from his lap, but I remained seated on it.

"I saw him," Surge replied tightly. I flicked my surprised gaze up, but his voice didn't skip a beat as he asked, "Has he done it before?"

My features scrunched up.

"It's none of your business, Mr. Romano."

Surge's grip in my hair tightened and my eyes watered a little. The dampness in my underwear continued, and I hoped he couldn't feel it.

He countered in an even gruffer voice, "You're almost nude in front of me, and you're still saying that? Everything about you is *my* damn business."

My lips parted, and I breathed slowly.

I didn't want to ask him what he meant by that.

"It's the first time he did it," I replied, answering his original question. "When I was a teenager, I was kidnapped and one of the people holding me yanked on my hair." I frowned as my chest heaved, pushing itself against Surge. "They damaged my eye. Although I'm not completely blind in it, I can't see clearly with it."

I had no idea why I'd told him.

I didn't bother to look into his eyes. I moved back to pull myself away from him, but his grip in my hair didn't drop.

"Ana…"

His low voice came out again, laced with conflict.

"What did they do to you?"

I wondered for a second if, by *they,* he meant the Bratva or the kidnappers.

"Surge," I whispered, my voice laced with torment.

I glanced up.

His eyes flared.

"Don," he corrected. "I ordered you to call me Don. You're terrible at following instructions. It's no wonder you keep failing at your latest mission."

Like a wild cannon, I bucked against him, insulted. His hand finally released its grip on my hair, and I glared at him with malice. He only blinked. I still had the blade in my other hand. My gun, on the other hand, was a lost cause as it had disappeared somewhere under the seats. He raised a subtle brow at me, and my eyes only ignored him as I brought my blade to my side. Still holding his gaze, I slammed my blade right into the fleshy part of his thigh.

He grunted in pain, and I laughed.

I *laughed* like I was fucking delirious before flashing him a smug smile.

My eyes widened dramatically as I placed a hand on my chest and twirled a loose tendril of my hair.

"Am I so terrible now?"

I'd stabbed a ruling Don without regretting it.

One more feat to my long list of achievements.

Surge's eyes glared daggers at me.

"You murderous psychopath," he jabbed.

With the way he hissed those words, things wouldn't end well with me at all. I was proud of my handiwork, though. I mean, who got to say they'd stabbed a powerful Don, *twice*? I glanced at my blade still embedded halfway into his skin. Trickles of blood poured out of him like a stream. My car would end up dirty, but it was worth wiping that smirk off his stupid face. I wanted to provoke him some more.

"It's your own fault for wanting to see the psycho in me again." I stared at the red gash pouring out of him in fascination before reaching out a finger to poke him in the bruised spot some more. "It's *your* fault."

He muttered Italian curse words, and I caught him saying, "*Cazzo.*" That one was familiar. I'd heard made men say that before dying. I jabbed a finger deeper into his wound just to torment him some more. His hand shot out, knocking my hand out of the way, as he grabbed the blade's handle and took it out of his skin. My lips parted as he dropped my blade on the floor and kicked it somewhere under the car seats.

Blood continued to gush out of his wound. I hadn't just nicked him. I'd sliced him open. I observed it for a few seconds, but a hand moving in front of me caught my attention. It pulled on the edge of my bra's cup before pulling it off my body. Dumbfounded, I glanced up at his fierce eyes and his cruel sneer. I opened my mouth to yell at him but stopped when his eyes wandered to my now-bare breasts.

Without thinking, I draped my arms around them, but it only sprouted them upward. His hands shot out and pulled my arms apart as I was bared to him again. My breasts heaved and my dark, pink nipples stood to attention like obedient little soldiers. Blood rushed to them the more he stared at them. I snarled as I made a move to shove his hands away again. Now, he gripped my wrists as he pulled me closer until I slammed against him.

Our fuming faces glared at each other, chest against chest, misty eyes locked on to one another, and fingers itching to go for each other's throats.

"You're a pain in my ass," he muttered at last.

I snorted. "I didn't know you liked it in your ass."

He shot me a look of displeasure.

"I've killed people for far lesser crimes compared to what you've done to me. You think you're a tough little girl, huh?" he taunted.

Before I could counter, his hands dropped from my wrists. One of them captured my full breast again before the other reached for the gash on his thigh. He ran four of his fingers over the wound and reached those same fingers on my hardened nipple and smeared blood all over. The rusty scent lingered in the air. I stared, half horrified at the thought of his hand staining my skin with his blood.

God… What was he doing?

"Now you're coated in the same blood you like to shed."

His other hand reached out for his wound again to smear my other pale breast with his bright blood, like he was painting over a blank canvas. The loud thumping in my ears grew by the second. I breathed roughly as the fog of our breaths filled the car.

I jerked out a hand, and it landed on the cold window of my car. Dragging it down, I returned it limply by my side. My body burned everywhere he touched me. Everywhere he touched, he smeared me with my crime. I glanced from one bloody mound to the other before flicking my gaze up. The heat in his eyes made me cower, and I quickly looked away. His firm, bloody hands grabbed and pushed my damp breasts together mercilessly.

I met his vast, forest-like eyes as I lost myself in them slowly.

He tilted his head as he observed me. "Now, every time you look at your body, you'll remember this very moment, Little Assassin. You can't run away from me or escape me. How can you when my very blood is *on* you?"

He pulled my breasts higher, dragging my hips up with them as he lowered me again against his hard shaft. I hissed under my breath as he continued moving me over his clothes. I still had my underwear on, but I could feel him as if we weren't wearing anything. One of his hands slipped from my chest as it wandered down my stomach. It left a wet trail of blood behind as his fingers slipped inside my underwear. I gasped and squeezed my legs shut, caging him in place. He only pried my legs apart as his damp red fingers settled between my core's slit.

My *glistening,* swollen slit.

My cheeks fumed and my neck flushed at the sight.

"This is what you've been hiding from me?" he murmured under his breath. "My, my, is this how a proper, married lady behaves when her husband isn't around?" I heard the taunt in his voice, and my breath hitched. "You're already soaked, Ana. I wonder if you still need my blood as lube."

Not only did his dirty words traumatize my mind, but they made me even wetter.

Surge's blood-coated fingers found my folds as he shoved two of them inside of me. This was so fucking dirty, and damn me for liking it.

I groaned and my eyes became misty. Not long after, his hand covered my mound and his fingers curled on my most sensitive spot.

A treacherous moan escaped my lips before I could clamp my mouth shut. Horrified by what slipped out of me, I looked away. He slipped another finger inside, and I held on to his shoulders for dear life at the foreign intrusion. My muscles clenched around him, wanting him out, but my body continued to ride his hand. It went searching for him whenever he thrust his finger in and out.

"Your little cunt is tight, Ana. Why is that? Your husband doesn't give you a good fuck?" He chuckled like he'd cracked a joke.

My body only stilled at the comment. I stopped gripping his shoulders and stared at the collar of his leather jacket now.

Surge's hand stopped moving in my body. He always said the most inappropriate things and shattered the mood completely. I should plaster his mouth shut with tape. My soul dimmed by the second, and my hopeless eyes continued to bore holes into him. A moment later, his finger slipped into me again, and I gasped.

Surge tilted his head as his green eyes observed me.

"He doesn't?"

My cheeks burned. "I hate you," I muttered under my breath and cast my eyes away.

"How would he feel when he finds out his wife is letting another man fuck her with his fingers? His enemy? Her assignment?" His taunts kept coming, and I glanced up at his smirking face. His smirk faltered a little as he caught the expression on my face.

I didn't think Kirill would care at all who I spent my time with.

I looked away again and moved back to get off, but he pinched my clit.

A yelp left me as I met his heated eyes.

"You look at me with those doe eyes like you're screaming for something, but you cannot say it." I glanced dimly at his jacket again. "Are you happy in your marriage?" When I didn't reply, he leaned in to whisper and answered his own question,

"Because if you were, you wouldn't be here with me. Riding my fingers. Coated in blood like it's your very first night of consummation."

He lifted my hips with one hand and slammed me back on his hand. Only this time, it was four of his fingers. Stars spun around my mind as water filled the edges of my eyes. I hissed at the hard slam before shooting a glare at him. I felt my legs dampen as my pussy clenched on him. If his fingers were enough to hurt me… I didn't want to imagine what it would feel like if he was inside me.

"Do you touch yourself at night, Ana?" Surge continued asking. I didn't answer as my hot cheeks scraped against his rough jawline. "Because late at night, when I'm alone, I think about running my tongue across your clit."

His words left me hot and bothered as my lips trembled with desire.

Not only did I hate this man, I desired him as well.

"I won't fuck you tonight, Ana."

Disappointment settled over my soul before I could scold myself for my absurd thoughts. I glanced up at him, but he only smirked. My breathing was shallow, and something lodged in my throat, making it hard for me to swallow. The tension between us was now mellowing out, but his deep, masculine voice spoke again.

"Although, I won't stop myself from doing this."

His fingers moved inside me again.

An illicit and sinful tension filled the car. I sucked in a sharp breath, and I could feel the heat coming from him. My pulse spiked and my heart hammered through my chest.

The wind's howling continued outside. I turned my head to the side and caught the trees rustling as the dusky atmosphere curled itself around the branches. Although a windstorm was raging outside, nothing could beat the storm brewing between us. I moved my body and it unwound itself around him.

I clutched my hands around his neck as my breathing came out heavier. His own breaths tickled my cheek as his face bent down to breathe on my neck.

His lips were soothing, almost like soft, feather touches as they dotted and dusted my collarbones as they caressed my skin. I shivered against him, afraid he could hear my thudding heart. Although his heartbeat vibrated through me, he remained calm while I was in utter chaos. I released all the air I had been holding in my lungs and focused my eyes on the swirls of ink marked on the side of his neck. Dark ink peeked out from underneath his hair, and I wanted to push it back to see if he had more tattoos pledging allegiance to his cause.

"You know," he continued like we were having a casual conversation and he wasn't currently fingering me. My body still moved against him in slow, rhythmic movements. He took his sweet time like he had all the time in the world.

"I haven't fucked an assassin." The confession came out oh-so-low against my ears. My greedy eyes glanced up from the side of his neck before landing on his sensual pink lips. "Especially not someone hell-bent on killing me."

My lip quirked in a tiny, reluctant smile.

He raised a brow. "I didn't know you were capable of smiling."

I lost my smile immediately and blew out a deep breath.

"I haven't slept with a Don." The words rushed out under my breath. My eyes widened at the confession, and I glued my eyes to his jacket again. The tightening in my core continued. The pleasure his touch gave seemed too much right now. My body grew hotter as our uneven exhales mingled. My sapphires clashed with his emeralds as they battled for control.

Blood rushed to my face as his other hand pressed against my back. My breasts bounced in response, drawing his attention to them. They were pressed against the tight ridges of his muscles. Too much power laid beneath his casual clothes. No one would expect him to be a Don.

I had nowhere to go, and as I tried to move, his fingers curled inside me again as they dragged me toward him. My eyes glazed and my erratic, mad heart thumped over time.

The heat of his breath was warm on my exposed skin, and his scent seduced me into my undoing. His fingers picked up speed and my breaths came out in ragged pants. I practically soaked his fingers with my arousal. A meanness filled his touch. There was also a sense of power and cruelty in it as he snaked his other hand across my back to tug my hair back. I whimpered as my glassy eyes met his.

"Only I can pull your hair like this, Ana. No one else is allowed. Otherwise, they'd end up with a burned head."

There was a grave timbre in his voice, dragging me further into his darkness. My mind spiraled out of control and the sensible part of me disappeared. He dropped it oh-so-casually, but I heard the dangerous wrath in his tone. I stifled a gasp as realization hit me.

Burned head.

How did he know about Kirill's current state? We hadn't told anyone about what had happened to him.

His lip curved as he noticed my baffled face.

"You... You... Y..."

My voice trailed off as he tugged more forcefully on my hair. I choked on my raging thoughts. It was better to pretend that I hadn't heard the truth.

He'd just admitted what he'd done.

This would give me a valid reason, at least in my world, to slaughter him.

But why would he do that, though?

It wasn't his business what another man did in a relationship. Everyone turned a blind eye to other people's marriages. I swallowed as I thought hard about it.

Although I knew my weapons were under the car seats, I didn't reach down to retrieve them. I lost all brain and motor function as I turned into mush before him. My erect nipples brushed against his chest again, and I ached to feel him naked as well.

I stiffened against him when his arousal pushed through his pants. I didn't know why he wasn't taking this a step further. If he did, I didn't think I would be able to tell him *no*. I didn't think I'd want him to stop. His warmness made me want to curl up against him.

"It isn't fair how I'm almost naked, while you still have your clothes on," I accused under my breath. I immediately clamped my mouth shut and looked anywhere but him.

He chuckled in my ear.

"I want you out of my system, so I'll only let this happen just this once."

A thrum of unease beat in my veins.

His words cut through me like a knife.

Repulsed, I shot him a glare for saying such shameless words.

"I'm not even *in* your system yet," I clarified as I glanced down at his bulge.

He leaned in to breathe against my neck, and I shuddered against him. His mouth only nuzzled me as heat filled my core. His thumb stroked my pulsing clit. All the oxygen in my lungs evaporated. His fingers continued to play me like an instrument, and I hated him for teasing me. Every tempting and forbidden touch—I craved every single one of them.

He was draped around me like a second layer of skin. His red fingers traced my silky wetness before slipping back inside roughly. I hissed under my breath and dug my fingers into his shoulder blades. I wanted to stab him again for teasing me. His thumb rubbed small circles against my opening, and I grew moist under him. My slickness coated his fingers, and my breaths came out labored.

"Fuck," he muttered against my collarbone.

My skin tingled at the gruffness in his voice. My tight muscles clenched on his fingers as they pulled him deeper inside. Pleasure replaced the initial pain of his fingers' intrusion as I rode his hand. The world dissolved into ash and mist around me, blurring until the only thing I could see was him. With every dominating touch, wild tremors took over my body.

It was like he'd reined all the power in the world into his very hands.

He snatched my control right from under me.

His mouth licked the pulse on my neck.

I exhaled and rocked my hips against him. As I met his hazy eyes, a deep desire woke up inside me. "I'm still going to stab you"—I yelped as I cried out—"*again.*"

Lust and desire blurred the world before us, and a raging inferno claimed every fiber of my being.

"As long as you don't stab me in the heart, *amore mio.*"

His voice was low against my neck.

Seconds, which felt like an eternity, passed between us when he finished speaking.

He held all my senses captive—his voice, his hands, and his blood. He hadn't even fully touched me, and my body was already at his mercy. We'd crossed a boundary I wasn't sure we could ever come back from.

My body was filled with an urgent need as unfamiliar sensations crawled over me. Adrenaline pumped through my veins as I rubbed my mound against his fingers. I felt like I'd climbed a cliff. His touch only egged me on, filling me with a thrill I hadn't felt before. My body hummed with electricity as it vibrated through my core and limbs. The sensations raging inside me climbed higher and higher with every magical stroke and circle he made against my skin with his trained fingers.

Thud. His fingers pulled out and his hand smacked against my clit.

I shattered on impact.

He smacked it again.

Thud.

Electricity vibrated through my entire body as I collapsed against him. His hand in my hair loosened its grip. My sticky, jelly-like body sagged against his chest as I screamed. I shattered into a million pieces before him.

My body floated into the air, and I lost all the willpower to push him away. My eyes glazed over as I lifted my head. Through my dreary vision, I met his misty eyes. His pupils were still dilated, and he looked like he wasn't done with me yet.

My breaths came out hard and uneven as I tried to catch my breath.

With a blissful sigh, I sagged against him like he was my cocoon.

His fingers emerged from my core, and he held them in front of me. They glistened with my arousal. My cheeks burned like the midsummer's heat. He reached out with his soaked fingers and traced my lower lip, coating it with my treacherous arousal. Then, he took those same fingers and sucked them dry, one by one, until they returned clean from his mouth. My skin flamed under his intense gaze.

He was *tasting* me.

The gesture was too erotic, too forbidden, too illicit, and too *him.*

I inhaled the intoxicating, steamy air surrounding us, and a sudden thought of hidden cameras installed in the car filled my mind. I hoped there weren't any.

I pulled back even though my body protested. It still wanted to rest for a little while longer, but the logical part of me knew I couldn't be caught screwing with this rival Don. My body shivered as it missed his heat. I glanced down at my nude breasts which were still coated in his dry blood. He'd left a permanent mark on me.

I sighed silently before shaking my head fiercely.

A pang of guilt settled into my heart.

What was I even doing here? I hoped Kirill never found out.

I avoided Surge's gaze as I looked aimlessly for my bra. His eyes seemed glued on my breasts every time I moved. His own personal canvas.

"This can't happen again," I mumbled. "Actually, it *never* happened," I declared matter-of-factly. "You are still my target, my assignment, and nothing has changed between us. This means absolutely nothing to me," I rambled on as I finally found my pink bra. "*You* mean absolutely nothing to me."

If I was a normal person, I would be crying in shame for committing adultery, but this didn't feel like adultery at all. I waited for the disgust and guilt to deepen and overwhelm me, but it never came. It was hard to feel guilt for a marriage that had never had a true connection.

A marriage that was only a one-way street.

A marriage that had room for outsiders but not its spouse.

My marriage was a sham from day one. It was as if it had only been done to bind me to my cause.

Without warning, Surge snatched my bra out of my hands and dropped it on the floor. Caught off guard, I flicked my gaze at him with a frown. He reached out and pinched my nipple tightly. I yelped under his touch and threw an accusing glare at him.

"It did happen, Ana." His voice was clear and concise as he spoke.

I only shook my head fiercely.

He raised a brow as his still-wet fingers dropped to my pink underwear. He pulled back the elastic of the plain cotton I wore and let it flick against my thigh with a snap.

"You just had to wear cotton today of all days?"

I frowned, even though tremors ran through me. "Cotton is comfortable."

He pulled the elastic on my thigh, stretching it as much as possible before he snapped it against my skin again. I yelped, jumped, and landed right on his hard groin again.

He. Was. Still. Hard.

"I like lace," he murmured as he trailed his hand along my smooth bikini line. "And silk." My heart leaped out of my chest. I felt his fingers doing another tug, but this time, the fabric pulled tightly against my slit before he let it hit me again as if to punish me. "Wear those next time, or don't wear panties at all," he ordered in his low, smooth voice.

My treacherous heart sped up.

Half of me wanted to scream, *Don't tell me what to do!* But the other sick half of me wanted to tell him to order me some more. I didn't know what was wrong with me. Everything about this encounter was just so wrong, yet *I* let it happen.

My eyes widened and I tried to move away but unintentionally landed on his bruised thigh.

He winced and his fingers went to the gash on his thigh as soon as I shifted away from it.

My eyes followed the movement as he held me in place on his other thigh.

The bleeding had stopped now, but his jeans were still damp from all the blood.

I chewed on my inner cheek, curious to see how deep his wound was. My fingers wanted to reach out and trace his injury. What was even crazier was the fact that I wanted to take out the first-aid kit and bandage him up.

First, I'd hurt him, and now I wanted to mend him.

I was still busy staring at his wound when he sat upright and leaned in to whisper in my ear, "Careful there. Your face almost looks like you care."

My mouth dropped, appalled by the absurd comment. As I turned around to shoot daggers of a glare at him, our lips almost brushed against each other. My breath hitched and I pulled back an inch. "*You* sounded like you cared about me when you went around toasting my husband's head," I countered. My deep, sea-blue eyes challenged his green ones. He practically confessed that it was him for knowing what had happened to Kirill, but he'd never mentioned anyone's name.

Surge shrugged boyishly, making it hard to believe he was a forty-year-old man. He was a grown *man*. Much older and more experienced than I was. He knew more about the world we lived in, and it felt like sometimes, he knew more about me than I did.

"I don't know what you're talking about."

Oh, now he wanted to play dumb?

I threw him a look of annoyance before snatching my bra from the floor to re-dress myself. Surge watched the entire time as I clasped the hook of my bra behind me.

The simple underwire lifted my cleavage, and his eyes went directly to the slopes it made. I followed his gaze, a little annoyed that I'd forgotten about the bloody stain he'd imprinted on me. I hated getting blood on my clothes. I preferred not to get my clothes dirty… but it was his blood.

I kind of didn't mind.

"I'm afraid I must leave now." His deep voice came a moment later.

I scowled in return. "Then get out."

I glanced over my shoulder at my dress in the passenger seat up front.

"I'll be able to leave once you remove yourself from my lap," he countered.

I could hear the smile in his voice.

I glanced down at my legs which were still cradling his arousal. His still hard-as-a-rock erection. I blew out a tired breath as heat pricked my skin. He leaned in until his face was just millimeters away from mine. I avoided his eyes. I didn't know if I could look at him right now.

"I didn't know you were capable of blushing, Ana." He chuckled softly. "I can't wait to leave you pink in other places."

My heart bounced in my chest.

It raced uncontrollably.

I glanced up. "Stop staring at me, you creep," I hissed.

He raised a subtle brow. "Some would say my stare is romantic."

I crossed my arms over my chest as I studied him.

This Don had no romantic bone in his body.

I wondered if he'd been in a relationship before I met him. I didn't know why I even had such absurd thoughts. I couldn't give two shits about him.

"Who's being a creep now?" He said it like it was a fact and not a question.

I wrinkled my nose in response.

When he realized I had no plans of moving, his hands lifted me by the hips and placed me on the seat beside him. When I peeked up at him again, he'd already turned the handle of the door.

He grunted as he stepped outside, and my eyes instantly flew to his injured thigh. I pressed my lips together as I stared at the gash, I'd left on him again.

The frigid wind filtered inside my car and my burning skin shivered. The foggy windows were a telltale sign of what occurred just moments ago. Goosebumps erupted on my skin, and instead of seeking out the rest of my clothes, I continued to stare at his wound as I wrapped my warm arms around my body.

"You care." His voice rumbled with the wind.

Startled, I glanced up at him again.

Surge Romano's lip quirked as he caught me ogling him.

He finished off with, "I should probably let you injure me more often. Maybe then, I could see that tormented and concerned look on your face again." When I didn't say anything, he continued, "You *feel* pain when I feel pain. Who knew the Bratva's assassin cared about Don Sergio?"

He took in the baffled expression on my face before closing the door behind him.

It took me a moment to realize that he'd revealed his true name.

Sergio.

Sergio Romano.

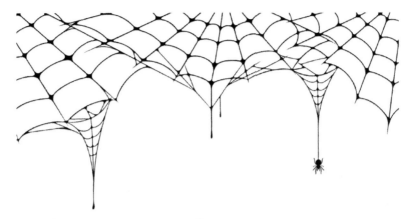

Ana

11

When I returned home, Kirill still laid in bed, sound asleep.

I noticed the supper on the table next to my side of the bed and realized he must have eaten.

I took one look at him before disappearing into the bathroom to clean my sins away. I had deep cleaned the car before returning too. A flutter of guilt filled my soul before I could clear my head, and I vowed it would never happen again. I should've received the Best Wife Award.

Sergio Romano and I were from two different worlds.

He was Italian, and I was Russian.

I was Bratva. He was Cosa Nostra.

The only real exception to our people's norms was *Pakhan's* cousin, Vlad. Otherwise, our people would never mingle with each other. It wasn't allowed. Too forbidden, too illicit, and too wrong.

I stripped off my clothes and let them drop around my ankles before stepping into the shower sill. I turned on the hot faucet, and the icy water immediately burst out from the showerhead above me. With a jump, I stepped back and let it run until it was warm.

I leaned against the bathroom's tiled wall as I stared up at the ceiling. A few moments later, I stretched out a hand and let the water fall on my skin. It had turned warmer now, so I stepped under the showerhead again. I blinked slowly as vivid memories of what had happened earlier this evening flashed through my mind again.

Blood.

Heat.

Him.

Surge's fingers.

Sergio... I savored the name on my tongue.

His real name was Sergio Romano.

I supposed it fit him, since he looked like a Sergio.

Strong. Strict. Disciplined.

I glanced down as the cascading water from above washed his blood away from my breasts. It still left tiny red circles on my skin until I smeared it off with my hands. The clear water now ran in long, red streaks as it surfed its way to the drain. With quick movements, I rinsed my body and washed my hair with shampoo.

I scrubbed on my breasts in an attempt to wipe off the hands that had been there. Despite feeling like I couldn't completely rid myself of Surge's phantom touch, I scrubbed, smeared, and washed until my skin was left raw, pink, and burning under the shower's hot water.

I can't wait to leave you pink in other places.

His words echoed in my mind.

I blinked again as water clung to my long brown eyelashes. My core tightened and I squeezed my legs together to stop the ache forming between them. Licking my lips slowly, I looked around me as if afraid I might get caught doing something *illegal.*

A smile tugged at my lips.

As if I cared about doing anything illegal.

My hand wandered between my thighs to spread my folds apart. I rubbed circles around my clit again. Closing my eyes, I tried to imagine it was Kirill's hand.

He was the right person to imagine, but instead of my husband, a pair of misty emerald eyes flashed in my mind. The image was so vivid that I wished he wouldn't take over my mind as well. It felt like my mind didn't even belong to me anymore when he'd taken over my thoughts.

I picked up the pace and stifled the moan that wanted to burst out of me. I was afraid someone would hear me and punish me for doing something so *forbidden*. I didn't care if my husband was bedridden. Why shouldn't I give in to temptation at this very moment? It wasn't like he cared about me, anyway.

One finger became two as my skin flushed pink under the hot water. I held on to the wall with my other hand as I rubbed my mound for more friction. It throbbed as I slipped another finger in, imagining it was the fingers of the Don instead.

I hated that he brought my forbidden desires to the surface. I was better off when I didn't have to think about these things at all. I had buried them a long time ago, yet I felt like my body had been awakened to feel things I didn't know I was capable of. I didn't remember when the last time I'd even touched myself was. Normal people touched themselves. Sadly, my libido had been dead for years until it was awakened by him. It wasn't just today. I felt it when I met him for the first time.

My mind soared high in the sky as my body sought the same filthy rush I'd felt in the car an hour ago. Adrenaline rushed through my veins as my core pulsed and trembled with an impending release. My sensitive clit pulsated as I came hard.

I closed my eyes as my back sagged against the wet wall behind me. I breathed through my nose as the sweet taste of bliss fell over me. I lingered in the shower for several minutes to savor a few more forbidden moments with myself before I had to return to playing a façade in front of the world again.

In private, I could be just *Ana*.

When I emerged from the shower sill, I stopped by the mirror to stare at my reflection. I ran a hand over the foggy mirror to get a better look at myself. My skin was flushed pink from all the scrubbing. When I looked up to stare at my face, my eyebrows furrowed, and I reached out a hand to touch the roots of my hair.

Blonde.

Dark blonde hair.

I dropped my hand instantly as unease trickled down my spine.

I had black hair.

I rubbed my eyes together, frowning as I wondered if my vision had worsened in one of my eyes. I could still see well in one of them.

I'm surprised that Surge didn't mention anything about my roots. Maybe he hadn't noticed them. I didn't even notice something was amiss with my hair this morning.

I glanced at my eyebrows and eyelashes.

They were a distinct shade of light brown.

Still puzzled, I wrapped a white robe around my body as I exited the bathroom. Stopping by the vanity table, I brushed my hair before slipping into bed.

Kirill was still fast asleep as I laid on my side.

Tired from the night, I fell into a restless sleep with my mind still full of questions.

I knew I'd feel a pinch in the side of my neck a couple of hours later.

A similar pinch I'd always felt when I was younger and woke up in another room.

When I woke up the next morning, I yawned. My eyes felt heavier than usual. Rising slowly, I glanced at Kirill, who still slept. I moved toward the bathroom and switched on the light. My eyes immediately went to my hair. At the roots.

They were now black.

A tiny gasp left me as I took a few steps back until I hit the tiled wall behind me.

I stared at the hollow-eyed woman in the mirror.

Had I imagined my hair being blonde yesterday?

I glanced at the rest of my hair. It did have its occasional blonde tendrils sneaking through, but I had just assumed that was part of my natural hair color since I never dyed it. I thought it was weird I had two tones in my hair, but I just assumed it was a genetic mutation. Now, I was unsure.

I had never seen my roots as blonde before. I blinked slowly as reality sank in. I leaned in closer until I got a better look at myself through the mirror again. My eyes caught a black spot on my robe. A leftover mark of something that hadn't been there.

My finger reached up to touch the spot.

It almost looked like some kind of liquid, and from the angle, it looked like it had been dropped accidentally.

Something awfully like *dye*.

I swallowed thickly as my hand shot out to my neck.

I remembered feeling a prick against my skin.

I remembered feeling those when I was younger too.

I didn't take my suspicions seriously, because I woke up in one piece the next morning.

Afraid, I turned my neck to see what I might find there.

There were no marks on the sides of my neck.

I lifted my hair over my head and turned my back to the mirror.

Through the corner of my eye, my gaze landed on something I knew didn't belong there.

A small red dot on my nape.

I pressed my lips together just so I couldn't cry out in alarm.

It had always been hidden from me.

Invisible.

Most likely to fade away in the next two days.

Dark blonde hair. I'm naturally blonde.

That explained why I had blue eyes.

It was more common in blondes.

As I wrapped my head around my new discovery, more answers began to pour into my mind. It explained the brown eyelashes and eyebrows. They tended to be shades lighter than my black hair. I grew body hair, but it was always light brown. It explained so much more. Someone who had raven hair could never have lighter hair in other body parts. Things I could never explain to myself. Things I had just accepted as a birth defect because I couldn't explain the anomaly to myself.

Who was dyeing my hair in my sleep and *why*?

I peeked out through my bathroom door and my eyes landed right on Kirill.

He'd been injured and unconscious for days… hadn't he?

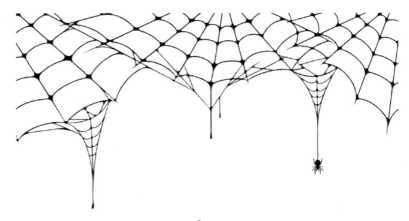

Ana

12

TWO WEEKS LATER

I shouldn't even be here.

This was a terrible mistake.

I mumbled a string of cuss words under my breath as I climbed the Don's balcony again.

These weren't my people.

This wasn't my world.

But why did I want it to be?

I stopped breathing when I peered through the closed window. A shirtless body laid on the satin, white sheets, and I wished it was draped around me instead. I made sure to carry my weapons and wear my black outfit and hood tonight. It wasn't wise to step into his home after what had occurred between us in my car.

He'd only touched me once, and here I was, looking like a sex-crazed fanatic seeking that same rush he gave again. I could only touch myself so many times before craving something greater. Glancing around me, I cracked open the window to slip inside like a ghost of the night. The window made a slight noise, but he didn't stir in his sleep. Heavy breathing bounced off the walls as if he was knocked out like the dead.

He hadn't locked the window.

Was he expecting me to sneak in?

My pulse jittered and my breathing felt labored.

My soundless shoes didn't make the slightest noise as déjà vu hit me again. Quietly, I moved toward him. It would be easy to murder him right now, in his sleep when he didn't expect it.

My eyes slowly adjusted in the dark as the moonlight fell on his golden beauty. God, he resembled Christ when he slept. It was a shame he acted the opposite when he was awake.

His lips parted as he breathed blissfully. As my eyes ventured away from his mouth, I caught sight of the reddish-brown curls clinging to his muscled chest. A memory of my body pressed against it flashed before my eyes, and I swallowed at the thought of me being alone with his shirtless body once again. I'd never seen him like this before. He had a well-built, muscular body.

A body of a man, and not a boy.

As I studied him, I realized that he looked different compared to my leader, who was a lot slimmer and younger.

This Don looked like he was *born* to lead.

Not only that. He was handsome. Beautiful, even.

My eyes narrowed on the blank ink that swirled on his skin. I caught a large tattoo of an animal. Tearing my eyes off his tattoo, I took in the mop of hair on his head. His hair was no longer clean cut and tucked neatly behind his ears. It hung loosely around him like a lion instead. I tiptoed like a mouse as I inched closer. I wanted to hide a smile as I bent down to read the English oath inscribed on his chest.

Honor is power. Those without honor have no power.

My lip twitched. It sounded nice to the ears...

I'd expected to read something much more arrogant. It was different from our oath, where the Bratva wiped out our identities completely and molded us as one of their own.

Isn't that exactly what they did to you? my inner voice hummed.

Startled by my sudden invasive thought, I shook my head and focused on him again.

No point in grieving over the past when I lived in the present.

Now, I only focused on my future.

My misty gaze fell on Romano again.

A tendril fell on his eye, and he twitched. He reached a hand over his face, but he missed it. He grunted like a feral animal in his deep sleep, annoyance etched across his face. I couldn't help but reach out with a hand and smooth the back of it over his forehead.

Big mistake. I shouldn't have done that, because his eyes popped open a second later.

I took a step back, surprised as his large hand shot out and grabbed a hold of me.

His tired emeralds eyed me curiously.

"You have feminine hands," he observed in his deep, sleepy voice.

A second later, his long fingers entwined with mine like two stems meeting for the first time. I hadn't worn my leather gloves today. Clearly, a big mistake, since I always made sure not to leave any evidence behind. I glanced at our entwined hands. I'd never held a man's hand before... It was calloused against my soft one.

A smile tugged at my lips. I was doing that more often around him. I tried to recover and replaced the smile with a resting bitch face instead. I liked the sound of his sleepy voice. It sounded like he was drunk on whiskey and tempting as sin as it rumbled and echoed in the dark. I didn't know why, but he sounded much more attractive now. Men were so much more attractive when they weren't trying to do anything to impress you. His soothing voice was enough to make my knees weak. I wanted to replay his voice in my head.

The Don tilted his head as he observed me.

I wished he would stop looking at me like that.

It didn't help the butterflies swarming in my stomach.

I wanted to stomp on them and crush them under my feet.

"And why the fuck are you wearing a black hood in the middle of the night? What if you traumatized me in my sleep?"

I frowned. Forget that I even wanted to hear his voice on replay. "Well, hello to you too," I muttered.

His lips pressed in a grim line as he reached out to pull my hood off my hair to reveal my face. I yelped before straightening my spine as I stood up. I shot him a look with as much venom as I could manage.

Sergio sat upright on his bed as he leaned against the headrest. He turned on the nightstand lamp, and the light radiating off it illuminated the room. His gaze dragged down my face before it traveled to my body. The look in his eyes as he took me in made my skin crawl, and I wanted to hide under the bed. I wasn't sure where these ridiculous thoughts were coming from.

Since when did I get intimidated by someone's stare?

"What brings you here?" Before I could answer, he murmured, "Don't tell me that you finally decided to kill me." His mocking voice came.

"Keep talking and I just might stab your other thigh."

His lip curved. "Go ahead, you look sexy while doing it."

My mouth dropped.

He.

Thought.

I.

Was.

Sexy?

I wasn't sure if I should take that as a compliment or an insult.

My cheeks flamed, and I wanted to smack him across his head. "You talk too much."

He clasped his hands in front of his lap. "As long as you can play my nurse."

I didn't bother to reply this time.

"So, Ana," he casually said, even though I knew he would follow up his sentence with anything but casual. "You never answered my question. Why are you here?"

I only blinked as I met his haunting gaze.

His invasive gaze burned through my skin.

Without breaking eye contact, I reached below me to remove my boots and black socks. I unzipped my black trench coat and pulled it off my arms.

It dropped on the floor beside me. Surge swallowed thickly as he eyed me. Reaching below, I unzipped my pants and stepped out of them. His hands rested behind him like I was putting on a show for him. I swallowed, because I might as well be. It wasn't just my clothes I was removing. They were my most prized possessions as well. My weapons. Something that made me who I was. I untucked three of my revolvers from my waist and dropped them on the floor. My holster was now gone. My extra bullets were also removed. I removed the hidden blades—all different sizes—from under my sleeves and dropped them on the ground as well.

I still wore a black t-shirt and my underwear as I went to stand by the bed, fluffed one of the pillows, and slipped under his comforter. His bed felt comfortable, more luxurious than mine. It must have been the sheets. I inhaled them deeply. They smelled like him, too.

I peeked an eye at him from the pillow I held hostage, and he stared at me with a puzzled expression. I hated to burst his bubble, but I did it anyway. "I'm tired," I said softly.

I pulled the comforter up to my chin as I eyed him curiously.

His eyes turned amused. "And you came to have a sleepover?"

I didn't smile as I replied, "Would you believe me if I said yes?"

He lost the amusement in his eyes.

"I didn't want to be alone tonight," I admitted under my breath.

Surge looked at me for a few seconds. His jaw clenched and unclenched as he studied me before moving to slip under the comforter with me. He angled his body toward me, and I angled mine toward him. There was still space for another person between us. He didn't move toward me, and I didn't move toward him.

"Where's your toasted husband?" he questioned.

It wasn't a dig but a truth. Still, my lip still quirked before I lost that expression. "He's not home," I admitted.

Surge waited for me to continue as he rested his head on his arm. I eyed the swirling ink on his skin, wanting to trace it with my fingers, but kept my hands to myself. I took a deep breath before replying to the unspoken questions lingering in his eyes. "He's with his mistress. One of the many that are out there. I don't know how many. I think he had them before we were married too."

He told me he would be stepping out for a bit after two weeks of bed rest, but I knew where one of his many stops would be.

Surge was quiet before he spoke again.

"Why did you marry him?"

I looked away from his invasive eyes. "It seemed like the right thing to do at that time. He's all I've ever known since I was young. It just made sense for us to be together."

I didn't tell him a part of me feared my husband now.

A man I once trusted with everything.

A man I knew nothing about.

I hadn't confronted him about anything.

That forbidden secret would stay with me to the grave.

When he didn't reply, I asked something that lingered on the tip of my tongue. "Are you with someone?" It wasn't my business to ask, but my nosy ass needed to know.

I just wanted to come first to someone.

A priority instead of an option.

"No," he replied after a beat.

My erratic soul steadied, seemingly content by his answer. He could be lying, for all I knew.

"Why aren't you married?" I continued pestering him with questions. "Most Dons marry young to secure heirs. Arranged marriages. Alliances happen all the time."

He exhaled. "I haven't found someone worth marrying."

The thumping in my heart returned.

It was the loudest noise in the room.

Slowly, I lifted my gaze to look at him as his eyes focused on me. It was like he was referring to me... but I was already married. Fate couldn't have played a crueler joke on me.

I inhaled tightly. Then, I released it.

"Don't you feel pressure to marry?"

His eyes narrowed. "Other than my step grandmother and my stepsister, I have no one around to dictate who to marry. They both live in Paris."

My soul diminished. "Must be nice to not listen to orders." Then, my eyes brightened. "What's your family like? Are they nice to you?"

I didn't have anything besides Kirill to compare.

Surge chuckled in a low, *sexy* manner.

It sent tingles up my spine.

God... my kind would skin me alive if they saw me in bed with this Italian Don. Granted, we weren't even doing anything illicit, but just speaking to each other like this was forbidden. I was supposed to be murdering him, but here we were, cuddling in bed. Okay, I exaggerated a little. We weren't cuddling, but it was kind of close to it.

He shrugged before replying, "Full of questions today, aren't you?" I frowned. He took in my expression before replying, "They're a handful. My stepfather was killed in prison years ago, and my mother died shortly after. I was twenty-three when my mother remarried my stepfather—they married after my father's death. Annalisa was three around that time."

I nodded, even though I already knew this.

A moment later, his hand reached out and he grazed it across my soft cheek.

My chest hammered against my rib cage.

My face turned into his hand, and he turned it over as he nuzzled my cheek.

"You remind me of someone I once knew," he murmured.

My pulse spiked, and the green-eyed jealousy monster grew in the pit of my belly. I wanted to demand that he tell me everything about his past. I didn't want to imagine him with anyone else. "Who?" I asked, trying to keep the sternness of my voice.

He didn't notice the sharpness in my tone.

Surge's haunting eyes turned hollow for the first time since I'd met him.

I regretted asking him the question now.

Now, he resembled a lost version of himself.

"She died," he revealed after a beat.

Instantly, guilt hit me for being jealous of someone dead.

I wanted to reach out and return the brightness to his eyes.

"Where did you come from, Ana?" he asked after a moment.

Puzzled by the sudden question, the edges around my eyes narrowed.

"I didn't know a female assassin existed in the Bratva until recently," he explained in a low voice. "No one knows about you. Why did they hide you besides the fact that you're a secret weapon?" I pressed my lips together and my eyebrows furrowed. They sloped together toward my slim nose. "Who are you?"

I sighed under my breath as I broke off eye contact. I turned my face and stared at the ceiling, where the golden chandelier hung above us. Glancing down, I lifted the blue necklace I had hidden underneath my shirt in front of my face.

"I only have this left to remind me of my family. I assumed it was a family totem." I glanced at the pendant. It was a blue music box plated with gold. I held it in my grip for a few seconds before I let it drop to my chest. I didn't dare look into Surge's eyes and only continued to stare at the ceiling above. "I have long stopped seeking answers to questions I had as a child. They only hurt." It was the most honest thing I had admitted recently, and I didn't know why I had revealed anything to him.

He was the rival, an enemy, and his blood was ordered to be shed by my hands.

I stared dimly at the ceiling now. I felt worse than when I'd first entered his room. Another reminder that it was a terrible idea coming here in the first place.

"Are you still tired?" His voice came.

The blood in my veins hummed.

"I'm trying to sleep," I replied.

"You look pretty awake to me."

Movement stirred next to me, and the sheets rustled. I wanted to stab him again. Annoyed, I turned to glance at him and pick his brain some more. I was just about to open my mouth, but I paused when I realized how close his looming face was to mine.

Don Romano was like an addictive drug. The kind that hooked you fast and left the most devastating withdrawal signs.

"You didn't just come here because you were tired and wanted to sleep," he began, and his eyes turned into green slits as he spoke. "There was another reason why. Something you weren't planning on telling me, but I know."

I raised a subtle brow and waited for him to continue.

What kind of mind game was he playing now?

Without saying a single thing, he snatched the edge of the comforter and threw it away from my body.

"Hey!" I protested. My body instantly missed the warmth of it. "I'm cold," I whined. I reached out a hand to tug the comforter over my body again, but he only shoved it further away from me and toward my feet.

I frowned as my accusing eyes met his.

He returned my glare before glancing down. His tattooed hand glided toward my thigh, and my heavy-lidded eyes followed it before they rested on the thin fabric still clinging to my skin. The hungry look in his eye intensified as he tugged on the fabric and pulled it away from my body.

"Do you always wear panties for your assignments?" He dropped the question casually.

I swallowed and looked away.

When I glanced down, my eyes landed on my panties.

My red *lace* panties.

He said he liked that color on me.

"No cotton today," he taunted. His breath tickled my ear like a caressing whisper. "Lace," he declared. "You wore lace. Red lace. For *me*."

I opened my mouth to protest but clamped it shut as I stared, mortified by my glaringly red lace panties.

I pretended to play dumb instead. "I don't know what you're talking about, Mr. Romano. I'm colorblind." I slipped in that lie.

He growled like he'd had enough of my charade. "You fucking liar. You knew what you were doing when you came to my bedroom wearing that."

I frowned. "Well, it's not a complete lie. I can't see correctly in one eye, anyway."

I tried to downplay the entire thing and hoped he would take a hint and shut up instead. "I must have lost my way and forgotten that this was *your* bedroom too. Poor me. I'm just a lady who can't see right."

My eyes twinkled, and I couldn't help but slip that in.

Unfortunately, he didn't shut up. He seemed to have had enough of my antics as he grabbed the elastic of my panties with his hand and pulled it tightly against my skin until the thin covering cut into my slit. I gasped as I turned to stare at him through my hooded eyes.

"I really am tired, though," I admitted, and another gasp escaped me when he gave my panties another tug.

His eyes flared. "Too fucking bad."

I sighed restlessly.

"You cuss too much. Is that an old man thing? The more you grow older, the crankier you get?" I teased. He was far from old, but I wanted to push his buttons some more. "Maybe you do need a wife in your life to teach you a thing or two about elegance and manners."

His jaw ticked as he sat upright on his elbow, and with his other hand, he tore apart my panties in one single movement. Appalled by his astonishing strength and rudeness for ripping my panties, I wrinkled my nose. "Those were expensive, and I specifically wore them for you to see and not tear them." My mouth dropped open when I realized what I had just admitted.

Damn me and my big mouth.

Surge paused and his heated gaze flicked up to me.

"You wore them for me?" he repeated the admission.

I bit down on my lip and shook my head fiercely.

I would never admit that a second time.

"You stubborn little thing," he chided under his breath.

The cold air hit my bare sex, and I clamped my legs together tightly. He only reached out and pried them open again. I whined, but he ignored me. He seemed to be lost in his world as he moved to crawl between my legs. The comforter was long gone as we tumbled in the sheets together.

"Surge," I whined again.

I waited for him to correct me to say *Don*, but instead, he said, "Sergio."

His voice was gruff as his eyes met mine.

I glanced up at his looming body. He looked large and intimidating. I swallowed before repeating softly, "Sergio."

It was the first time I'd spoken his name out loud.

Sergio. Sergio. Sergio.

I repeatedly chanted the name silently in my mind.

"You don't want to admit how you wore lace for me, but look how soaked you are for me, Ana." He reached below and swiped a finger across my tingly flesh. It returned wet with my arousal. I wanted to deny that it was mine, but that would be the biggest lie of them all. "You're wearing too many clothes," he grumbled.

I blinked. Too many? I only had my shirt left.

Before I could correct him, his hands gripped the hem of my shirt and pulled it over my head. Bewildered, I sat upright and stared up at him.

Our eyes clashed with each other when they met.

I bit down on my lip.

His eyes followed the tiny action.

I licked my lower lip slowly.

He sucked in a sharp breath.

Tingles shot up my spine.

I had him eating out of my palm.

Well, hello, womanly power.

For as long as I could remember, I'd hidden my true identity and pretended to be a man to the point that I forgot I had other secret powers as well. Adrenaline rushed through my veins as my passion-glazed eyes found his green ones again. He stared at the red bra cupping my breasts. I glanced down at them, appreciating the fact that it made them look larger and fuller. When I met his eyes again, I wasn't surprised to find the growing desire in them. I liked his reaction. It only egged me on.

"You fucking tease," he hissed under his breath.

I frowned as I scolded him, "You told me to wear lace."

He arched a refined brow. "And you listened to me?" I didn't bother to reply. "Why don't you be a good girl and take off your bra for me, then?"

Good girl.

My chest trembled and expanded at the praise.

If I listened to him some more, would he say other things as well?

"Nope," my rebellious mouth replied instead.

I had a death wish.

Untapped wrath radiated off his body as he loomed closer.

I gulped, but I stayed strong as my challenging eyes locked with his.

"Do. It," he gritted.

I only smiled. "Say please. I like it when men beg."

Clearly, he didn't like that last remark. He had enough of me toying with him, because his hands reached out to unhook my bra and pulled it over my head until my breasts tumbled out. Cold air fluttered against my skin and cut into my nipples as I watched him throw my bra over his shoulder. A whimper left my lips as I wrapped my arms around myself to hide them. His hands only pulled them apart and he eyed my breasts appreciatively. When I searched his eyes, only lust and desire swirled and roamed in those cloudy eyes of his.

It left me half thrilled about what was to come and half afraid of what his reaction would be once he saw me naked. I wasn't used to being looked at like that. "You are such a bully," I accused. "You took off all my clothes without my permission."

His eyes tightened, and he looked like he wanted to choke me. "You started it. I'm just finishing it," he replied darkly. The danger in his voice made me think it would be best if I ran.

He was both dangerous territory and a safe haven at the same time. There was no place for me to run off to now, not when he had me right where he wanted me. Still, I wanted to fight some more. Sue me.

I had too much fun with this game of tug of war we often played every time we met. My eyes brightened. A brightness that I had once lost but returned whenever I was around him. I couldn't remember the last time my mind and soul felt the same sense of giddiness this man brought.

His lip quirked again, and I opened my mouth to give him a piece of my mind, but his hand landed on my throat. My eyes widened as he gripped the sides of it. "You will learn to shut up for once. If you can't, I have other uses for that mouth of yours."

Oh? My skin flushed and I wanted to run my mouth some more just to see if he'd follow through with that threat.

As if he caught on with what I had planned, his arm stretched in front of him as he shoved me deeper into the bedsheets—*his* bedsheets. He looked like an untamed, sinister giant towering over me. The outlines and contours of his body were illuminated by the light coming from the nightstand. As the Don loomed over me, his hands were glued to my neck like another part of my body.

There was a confidence about him that reminded me of a predator. A very attractive predator. His fingers tightened on the sides of my throat, and I gasped as he built pressure on my neck. I could feel my soft nipples tightening and turning erect until they started to hurt. The harder he pressed, the more erect my nipples became. His eyes glanced down at them, and my breasts grew heavier under his gaze.

I glanced down at the veins pulsating beneath the fair skin of his bulging arm. The same arm that could snap my neck like a twig. His grip against my throat cut off my air, and a wheezy breath left my lips. My mind free-fell into nothingness and stars circled my mind as my eyes fought to focus. I couldn't see anything through my blurry vision.

"You enjoy hurting me, huh?" he growled, his words dark and deep like the endless ocean. "You just love pulling a knife on me every time you see me. Now, your very life is in my hands. You're at my mercy, Little Assassin. Your life belongs to me now. You only live for *me*."

His hand loosened its grip on my neck, allowing me to breathe for a few seconds before it tightened around it again. My neck pulsed, and his hand tightened with each passing second. Stars spun across my eyes as my eyes rolled back into my head. I breathed a shallow breath as his hand dropped from my neck. I exhaled in relief and glanced up at him again. Heavy and rough pants left my mouth and my chest tightened, aching to replenish the oxygen I was momentarily deprived of. I didn't even get a chance to recover and catch my breath, because his mouth slashed against mine.

A tiny gasp left me as his finger snaked around the back of my head and dug into my mane. He pulled me closer to him until my naked breasts slammed against his nude chest. I could feel him naked for the first time. My femininity clashed with his masculinity as lips only swallowed mine and his strong grip held my hair hostage. He tugged on my lower lip as he silently urged me to open my mouth to him. He was a man on a mission now, as if he wanted me to lower my defenses. He hunted and invaded my mouth. His tongue was hot, rough, and wet.

He nipped my lower lip, and he swallowed my moan. My eyes closed shut as his warm tongue sneaked inside my mouth with a little hesitation, like he was tasting me for the first time. Now a little more confident that I didn't protest, his warm tongue prodded and explored my mouth.

His mouth pressed harder against mine, leaving wild, sloppy kisses in its wake. I sank further into the bedsheets, caged like a helpless animal as he claimed me like a lion claiming his lioness. My shoulders slowly sagged as I returned the forceful kiss.

Fireworks exploded in my head as my mouth moved across his hungrily. Excitement bubbled in my mind as my mouth moved over his harshness and his over mine. As he tugged my hair to pull me toward him, I clung to his shoulders and slammed my mouth against his.

Something cannibalistic spread through me like a wildfire, and it was only then that I realized that that part of me had been drowning all this time until this man brought it to the surface to stand tall, proud, and very much alive. My hands left his shoulders as they moved up and down his chest. I explored his hard muscles and tattooed skin for the first time.

Whimpers and tiny moans left my mouth, only to be swallowed by him. He was all man and hard muscle as my hands roamed the solid ridges of his skin. His hands were still entangled in my hair like they refused to part from me. We were no longer two bodies but one soul.

Heat filled the deep pit of my stomach as his scorching tongue explored every part of my mouth. Slowly, I opened my heavy-lidded eyes and realized he seemed to be watching me the entire time. I was surprised his eyes hadn't been closed.

Then again, it wasn't surprising at all. He was considered off-limits, scandalous, and infamously notorious by my people. Yet I craved him even more as his soothing touch explored my skin. His hands moved from my hair and moved toward my frontal area. His thumbs ran in small circles around my collarbones before they ventured downward.

The ache between my legs intensified. A whimper left my lips when his eyes landed on my face again. My swollen lips throbbed as he dragged his mouth from mine and to the hollow space surrounding my collarbones. The amusement in his eyes was gone now as they focused on my mouth before lowering to my breasts. He licked my neck before dragging his tongue down the slopes of my breasts to the dark valley between them. My breathing came out ragged as he eyed my nipple. No words were exchanged between us. Just primal hunger and *need*.

His head dropped low to capture my nipple in his mouth. Both of his hands smushed my breasts together as he gave my nub a hard and long suckle. Heat erupted inside of me as he gnawed on my skin. I gripped the sheets next to me as I shoved my breast further into his mouth. I'd never felt anything like this before. Ecstasy filled my mouth as a soft moan left my throat.

He lifted his eyes, and our gazes collided, fighting for control. Chaotic tension filled the space between us. I should pull away and end this. I knew that there was no coming back from this, but the pull of this tempting man was too strong. It would be easier to just give in for once and stop fighting.

I stared at his reddish-brown locks as his soft and warm tongue laved over my sensitive skin. His leather smell covered me with his darkness. On the surface, he looked all light, but if I dug deep enough, I would find terrible darkness—kind of like the one that surfaced in my soul whenever I was out on a mission to kill.

He gave my sore nub another slow suck. Dropping the hold I had on the bed sheet, I tugged back harshly on his hair instead. His eyes flared as he glanced up to hold my gaze but didn't stop sucking me. His teeth deliberately grazed my nipple slowly, and I whimpered. My claws dug into his scalp as I pressed his mouth more firmly against my breast. He moved away from it instead, snatching my other neglected breast in his mouth. My now neglected nub wanted his attention as well.

He pulled back just to murmur, "Fuck, I could do this all day long."

My skin flushed at his crude words.

"You are beautiful, perfect, and so pretty…"

He cupped my breasts together as he laved at my flesh again. His smooth tongue swirled around me, and his teeth raked against the tight nub. I let out a moan as my glassy eyes met his. My core trembled and I wanted to push my legs together, but he was wedged between them. He pulled my taut nipple into his mouth as my breaths came out in rough and uneven exhales.

He held my glittering eyes the entire time. I was the first to break off eye contact as blood rushed from my nipples to my core. My arousal trickled down my thighs, and it was clear that I needed more friction. He left my nipple with a pop, and when our eyes met, a glint filled his eyes. He opened his mouth wider as he suckled my breast harder. His stubble scraped against my skin, leaving whiskery pink kisses behind. Without thinking, I ground my sex against the bulge in his boxer briefs.

He hissed, and the sound of it vibrated through me.

I yanked on his hair again and his eyes shot up.

I pleaded with him through my gaze as my hips moved against his.

More. More. More, I mentally screamed.

As if he heard my plea, his mouth left my breast as he crawled lower until his head was between my legs.

Well, I didn't ask for that…

I reached out a hand to pull him back up, but his hands only pried my legs further apart until my glistening sex was exposed to him.

He caught me looking and raised an eyebrow.

"This is the only time I will kneel for you."

Thump. Thump. Thump.

My heartbeat accelerated.

I never imagined the Don kneeling for me until now.

Heat filled my face as blood shimmered in my veins.

He blew on my pussy, and my hand and head dropped on the sheets beneath me. His breath was cool against my ignited flesh, and as his nose brushed against my folds, I wanted to hide my face from him. "This is inappropriate," I squealed as he inhaled my glistening flesh.

Surge's laughter chortled in the air.

My lips parted.

He *laughed.*

It was the first time I'd heard him laugh like that. It was different from his smirks and his chuckles. It was his deep, raw laughter as he threw his head back.

It made a bolt of electricity shoot through my veins, and I itched to hear it again. It was like music to my ears.

It transformed him from Don Sergio Romano to just Sergio.

He gave me a roguish grin before chiding, "I think we already crossed that line the day you wore red lipstick for me."

I pressed my lips together because I didn't want to admit he was right.

He dropped his head between my legs again.

A strange fascination lurked in the deepest shadows of my soul. He blew softly on my flaming skin, and I shuddered underneath him. His tongue gave me a slow lick across my pink swollen pussy. I yelped and tried to tug myself back, but he only gripped my ass firmly before bringing me back underneath his mouth again.

Then, he licked his lips slowly as if savoring my juices. My cheeks burned bright like a raging inferno. He tasted me again as his lethal, hungry tongue licked my slit from top to bottom aggressively, like a starved man who had missed out on dessert.

My heavy eyes stared at him in wonder.

He ravished my achingly tender mound as he explored and devoured everything that made me feminine. His tongue ran in slow circles around my clit, forcing my hot and needy body to demand more. My legs shook as the flat of his tongue ran a straight line across my flesh before he sucked on my clit directly. He consumed me like a raging fire, and my toes curled as he left long licks on my clit with his insanely talented tongue. As raw, animalistic noises erupted from my mouth like a cat in heat, I lifted my hips to meet his mouth.

I was a woman who'd been denied for so long.

He pulled back just to mutter, "Fuck, look at you, starving for my mouth."

Surge eyed me as he sucked on my pussy's lips slowly, and I shoved my mound into his mouth even more. He licked me with a smooth stroke of his tongue before lifting my legs and wrapping them around his shoulders. An idea appeared in my mind. I tightened my grip around him as I pulled his face closer to my pussy like I wanted to suffocate him.

Surge's eyes flashed at me as if he knew what I was doing, and before I could see it coming, he *bit* me in the place.

He. Was. Biting. Me.

"Still wanna kill me?' he taunted, his breath fanning me.

He pulled at one of my folds with his teeth and stretched it to see how far it would go. My vision misted and I cried out. Tears welled up at the corners of my eyes as tormented shouts left me. I tried to pull back, but his hands gripped the back of my ass to hold me in place as his mouth chewed on my sensitive clit. My plan to suffocate him had obviously backfired.

My face twisted with bliss, and estranged cries left my mouth as he continued licking and gnawing on me. The sharp edges of his teeth grazed my skin and I felt myself flush. My body trembled as I arched my back to brace my impending release. He stuck his tongue inside my pussy, and that was when I lost all control and gave my complete surrender to him. The high of all the adrenaline coursing through my veins collected and shimmered in my stomach before climbing up my spine and shattering with my release. My heady breaths and moans filled the atmosphere as a blissful orgasm overtook me

My shoulders sagged as I collapsed on the bed. Surge continued to lick me clean. He popped his head up from wolfing me down, and my juices dripped down his mouth. My glassy, unfocused eyes were one second away from a complete blackout.

"Your pussy is pink and raw, just like I thought it would be. I'm about to make it rawer." I heard the dark promise in his magnetic voice as he moved up to align himself with me.

I didn't know when he had pulled his boxer briefs down and pulled a wrapper over his throbbing length.

His thick bulge brushed against my still trembling and glistening swollen core. My eyes widened as I glanced down at his cock. His pink cock was large and turned borderline purple. My breaths came out in rough little pants as I eyed it.

Could that thing even fit?

I lifted my eyes just in time to see him plunge into me mercilessly, like he wanted to split me in half.

Shit. I hissed like I had been cut open with a knife's edge.

Fuck. That. Hurts.

My back arched against the bed as my breasts smashed against his chest.

Water filled my eyes at the feeling of fullness with him inside me.

"Finally," he murmured.

My ears perked up and my soul smiled at the vulnerability in his tone.

"I've been waiting for this since I pulled that hood off your face the very first time."

My heart hammered in my chest.

My misty eyes met his, and they stared at him. His face was distorted as he replied, "Your cunt is so goddamn tight." A puzzled expression crossed his face as his eyes searched for mine. "I knew you've only been with one dick your entire life, but still, you can't be this tight. What the fuck are you not telling me?" There he went with that potty mouth of his. I couldn't believe he was striking up a conversation with me while he was still inside me the entire time.

My lips trembled as I breathed heavily.

"Once." My voice came out small.

A crease filled Surge's forehead.

"He only touched me once, and then he never touched me again." Shame hit me that I repulsed my husband. That he'd done the part of a husband for one night and then he'd never looked at me again.

Surge's eyebrows shot up, appalled by my revelation.

"You are kidding..."

His cock froze inside me—still thick and hot, though.

My muscles clenched around him as they tried to shove him out.

I shook my head slowly. "I wish I was," I admitted.

Surge's lip curled up in confusion. "Are you sure he doesn't like dick instead?"

A smile broke out across my face, and I giggled.

I fucking *giggled* like a teenager.

Oh my God.

Surge didn't smile as his haunting eyes met mine. He finished with, "Because I know if you were my wife, I would find every moment, every second, every minute, every hour I could, just to touch you." My soul tingled. His voice softened as he said, "Once I'm deeply embedded inside of you, nothing will make me leave unless someone forcibly cuts me away from you."

He thrust into me again and I cried out in pain. My lower lip trembled, and he caught it between his lips with a yank. I whimpered as my growing hunger matched his. He let himself loose as he repeatedly slammed into me. My eyes brimmed with water and a tear rolled down my face. I choked out a breath when he licked the tear from my face like a savage.

"Surge," I whimpered.

He paused to meet my soft eyes.

"It hurts," I admitted in a muffled voice.

Thrust. I cried out, "You're too harsh." *Thrust.* He didn't stop when I protested. I accused him through my glowering eyes. *Thrust.* "Too cruel!"

"Good," he declared. "Now you know how it felt to be stabbed by you both times."

He gave me a knowing look, and I stuck out my tongue in return. His eyes narrowed before he reached down to bite down on it. My eyes widened as I choked out a breath.

His ravenous acts continued their assault against my sore body as he turned menacing and explosive in the blink of an eye. I clawed my nails into his back and dragged them down his back. He grunted when I drew blood.

His thrusts remained intense, and my body slowly grew damper. His violent thrusts continued as his hips smacked against mine with a thud. My breathing came out clogged through my nose and my eyes misted again.

"Slow down," I croaked out.

He eyed me before replying, "Say please. I like it when *women* beg."

He taunted me with my own words.

I frowned as I met his glassy emeralds. "I would rather die than say please."

My heart stuttered as he eyed me intensely, waiting for me to speak. He didn't slow down when I asked, but he pulled to a complete stop when he heard my last comment.

"I want this to be my *real* first time," I admitted. "I want you to give me something since I'm giving you my first time." My hopeful eyes searched his. "Sergio?" I bit my tongue at the fact that his true name slipped out of my mouth.

Sergio held my eyes the entire time as he slowly rocked his hips against mine. His movements slowed down as if he were following a rhythm.

Thrust.

In. And. Out.

My body moved against his.

My eyelashes fluttered, half closed.

Whenever I exhaled, he inhaled.

Whenever I gasped, he watched.

His hands rested on the sides of the bed as his hazy eyes stared down at me.

My inner muscles slowly adjusted to him as they accommodated his size. Thankfully, I was already soaked from our earlier shenanigans. My heat clenched on his cock, pulling him deeper into me until I felt him close to my stomach. It was as if he became a permanent part of my body.

My mind spiraled out of control as he kept on thrusting inside me. As my breasts bounced and slammed against his chest, my glassy eyes focused on his sweaty skin illuminated the moonlight pouring into the room. His girth easily slipped into my opening now as tiny mewls escaped my lips.

Our bodies became one as if they were a perfect fit. He slid easily into my sopping wet mess. We continued like this for a couple of minutes, him thrusting into me as I tried to match his pace with my hips. Slowly lifting my eyes, I met his carnal gaze as my breaths came out in labored pants. He grunted as his face distorted right before my eyes.

"I. Need. To. Move," he gritted.

I laughed, but my smile was immediately wiped out of my face as he slammed into me.

Hard.

He sucked the laughter right out of me.

I glanced up at him in surprise.

"Is this not *moving* to you?" I said in between pants.

Slam. He completely ignored what I'd just said. *Slam.*

"I'm going to ravage your body like I want to kill you."

With every thrust and every slam of his hips, my head shoved back into the fluffy pillow. I breathed hard and nodded, accepting my fate.

A dark glint glimmered in his shimmering eyes. He pulled back just a tad before he slammed into me with all his strength, like he wanted to tear into me. I yelped as his wicked thrusts became harsher as he plunged into my wanton-like body again and again. Bolts of static emerged through me as our bodies connected. His arm stretched above me until it dug under the pillow he once laid on. As he impaled me, I turned my head and blinked at the blade he held. My gaze focused on the silvery tip of the dagger. I hid a smile as I turned to look at him again.

"Is." *Thrust.* "This." *Thrust.* "The." *Thrust.* "Moment." *Thrust.* "Where." *Thrust.* "You." *Thrust.* "Remember." *Thrust.* "Your." *Thrust.* "Vendetta." *Thrust.* "And." *Thrust.* "Slit." *Thrust.* "My." *Thrust.* "Throat?"

He ignored me again as he rested the blade right across my collarbone.

I wrapped my legs around his waist as I pulled him deeper into me. I arched my back as a moan escaped me. My ragged breaths landed on his lips.

"This looks like my blade." I eyed the silver weapon again. "Did you keep it as a souvenir? If I didn't know any better, I'd think you were growing addicted to me, Mr. Romano." Without giving him a chance to reply, I accused, "Ever since you entered my life, I have been losing my knives and my clothes. You *thief.*"

He didn't smile this time as he slid the blade between my breasts as the flat of it glided down the shadowed, dark valley of it. He continued his relentless thrusts, but it was more controlled and slower now. His eyes burned into mine as he grabbed it by the handle and pointed the tip against my pale skin.

I swallowed thickly as I arched my back to drive myself further into the knife.

My breasts rose and I thrust my body forward.

I sucked in sharp and shallow breaths as he dragged the tip of it back up the valley where it came from. As he slashed small and deep lines on my skin, whimpers erupted from my lips, the cuts setting my skin ablaze.

His eyes stayed on me the entire time as he slammed into me, and his hand buried the tip of the blade into my skin. He twisted the knife as if he enjoyed cutting me. Trickles of warm liquid coated my skin as it rolled down. His lip curled in a twisted smile and his eyes darkened like he wanted to hurt me for those times I tried to harm him.

Mission accomplished.

Like a trance, his gaze moved from my face as I laid there, whimpering, tormented, and cut open underneath him. He'd left a carving on my very flesh. My skin stung as the cold air hit my skin, and I hissed under my breath. My eyes glided to the scarlet-covered tip of the knife.

Using the same tip, now he laid the blade now flat against my sensitive and sore nipples, one by one. I stared down at it in fascination as he smeared my blood on my skin like he was performing a satanic ritual. The liquid felt sticky and heavy on my skin, and I wanted to wipe it off. I always rinsed off my body whenever it was bloody.

My hands reached up to clean the blood, but I caught the disapproval etched across his face and I instantly dropped them. Now, they laid limp by my sides. His eyes flared with approval and my soul beamed like it was happier I was letting him butcher me. He dropped the bloody knife on the carpeted floor below us before dropping his face between my breasts. I mewled as his hot tongue left rough strokes on my skin.

I hissed when it made an impact on the bleeding mark he'd left on me. His tongue ran across my skin horizontally as he tasted my blood, and his gaze flicked up at me as my blood coated his lips. My core tightened and grew damper at the sight. I could feel my arousal trickling down my thighs.

He pulled back and blew out cool breaths against the bruises. I shivered and goosebumps erupted on my skin. My nipples turned erect again as his large body hovered over me. He admired his handiwork as his passion-glazed eyes filled with a glint. "The more the savage in me tortures you, the wetter your little hole becomes. Did you know that, Ana?" he crudely remarked casually. A twisted smirk framed his face as he fed on my deprivation. "You don't need flower petals for your first time. You especially don't want me to *make love* to you. You *need* me to take you violently, just like it's always been between us. A ruthless love."

My mouth dropped and before I could counter, he slammed the entirety of his manhood into me again and again, and my body slammed itself further into his bed.

Did he just say, love?

My body jumped with every jostle of his hips as I took every inch of him. He impaled me every time he sank into me, and my breathing intensified in uneven exhales as I forgot his earlier words. His large, tattooed hands smushed my breasts together and he squeezed them so tightly, that I cried out.

My eyes turned into mist and my body dissolved into ash as he molded it just for him. In doing so, the long line of cuts he'd made against my skin opened again as more blood gushed out of them. It might leave a mark for several days. He didn't seem to mind though, since he was lost in his world as his tongue ravished me and his cock plunged into me with lightning speed.

I squirmed and gasped, unsure if my body could take him anymore. Still holding my breasts, he flipped me over and he plummeted deeper into me and more recklessly from behind. This was a new position I wasn't used to, and he felt even thicker. His hands pulled the backs of my thighs closer to him as my ass slammed against him. I couldn't even scream with his never-ending movements behind me. His hand yanked on the hair on the back of my head as he slammed inside of me into my still-soaked sex.

He was planning on turning my pussy pink today.

I groaned and arched my neck backward as he tugged on my black mane. My head was flipped so upside down now that I could see him. A lump formed in my throat. His gaze could swallow me whole.

Breathing hard, I closed my eyes for a second, but he tugged harder on my mane. I groaned as my eyes popped open to meet his mosses.

"Look at me when I'm fucking you. That's an order."

God... He was so demanding with that rumbling voice of his, and my body seemed to like it a little too much.

"Mhmm. I can tell you're having fun," I said drily.

His other hand left my ass to clutch my jawline. He opened it to slip three bloody fingers inside, effectively shutting me up. I gasped and gagged as I choked on his fingers and my own blood, but he didn't stop there.

I couldn't see straight anymore. My misty eyes welled, and salty water leaked from the edges of them. He noticed and triumph filled his green eyes. "You're sore, Ana?"

His voice came out in a panting taunt as he thrust into me again and again.

Flesh slapped against flesh. Hips against hips.

The smell of sex filled the room until we no longer smelled like ourselves.

I would never admit that to him, so I only shook my head since he was too busy smothering my mouth.

"Still so stubborn even when I'm fucking your tight little hole while you lay whimpering under me." He chuckled darkly against my hair. "You look even sexier like this, little girl."

My eyes widened and my inner muscles clenched on his shaft.

My skin flushed at his crude words, but I refused to admit my defeat.

"Admit it. This is a battle you're bound to lose." His thick voice came against my ear again. "Especially with the way your sweet cunt is gripping me."

As if on cue, my hips rocked in sync against his until I was left completely and utterly breathless. "Yes, give me all of you, Ana." His rich voice boomed in the atmosphere.

I remained silent and his cruel thrusts greeted me in return as one hand continued to yank my hair until I felt the sweet, torturous sting on my scalp, while his other hand continued to gag me. Our skin continued to slap against each other, and our breaths fogged the atmosphere in our union. Tingles ran down my spine as my mind grew foggy with pleasure. My saliva was coating his hand at this point, but he didn't care at all. He stayed hell-bent on torturing me and pounding into my body instead.

"This is your real first time. The next time I fuck you, I will come on your face." His throaty grunts filled my ears. "And when I do, I want to see my come coat your pink lips and drip down your chin."

My clit throbbed at his crude yet addictive words. My breathing faltered at the cruelty his mean touches wielded. Malicious intent laid within him as he wrecked me completely. Spit dribbled from my mouth from being open for too long as his fingers reached farther into my mouth and hit the back of my throat. I almost gagged.

Finally, his hands dropped from my hair and mouth.

"I can tell this has been on your bucket list for a while," I murmured tiredly as my utterly spent body sagged against his mattress. "You must be very proud. After all, it's your biggest achievement to still be alive and fuck the person assigned to kill you." The mouthiness in me slipped out again.

He gripped my hands to pin my palms flat against the mattress.

"Don't make me take off my rubber and shoot my load into your mouth."

His voice came out gruffer than usual.

My breath hitched at his dark promise.

"You don't know how to behave, do you? What if I turn your pretty face over and fuck it instead?" I could hear the challenge in his authoritative voice.

My pulse spiked and the blood in my veins thundered with anticipation. I stayed quiet this time, because he just might do it. "These holes are mine. I can do whatever I want with them." His voice was laced with a possessiveness as his breathing came out labored behind me.

Desperation took over him as he tightened his hold on my body and drove into me. My heart thundered at his viciousness and my moans grew louder in the night. As he continued to slam ruthlessly inside me, wrecking me completely, the bed springs creaked loudly beneath us. I had no doubt that he was marking my body as a permanent reminder of himself and tarnishing every part of my body. I was on the brink of insanity at this point, but my body continued to jerk in rhythm with his. My entire body trembled as I neared another orgasm, and my lungs tightened as they craved for air.

Euphoria hit me as I let loose and crumbled before him. My body drained the remaining hot liquid left in me and coated him with my essence. As my release hit me hard like a flood, I breathed roughly.

I gasped as I laid there, sweaty, and well spent underneath him. I sighed restlessly as Surge hovered above me one more time before giving me one last intense thrust. His throaty grunts filled the air as he released inside me.

A second later, he murmured in my ear, "I found a woman worth marrying, but you are already married. Either way, you are mine, Ana."

Surge

13

Another week had gone by, and I hadn't seen Ana.

Ana. She wasn't Anastasia for me.

She was simply Ana.

She hadn't returned lately with her knives flaring and her revolvers spraying bullets. It was like she had almost disappeared.

Vivid images of that single night we spent together flashed in my mind. I reached a hand and grazed my chin. I'd shaved it this morning, but a hint of stubble had already formed again.

The Bratva had an event today.

Man, I was starting to get annoyed with these unnecessary events. I mean, all I had to do was show my face and pay my dues. I always left after ten minutes, but today I stayed more than an hour for a reason. I still hadn't found the assassin I hunted for.

Night had fallen, and the newly wedded couple would soon disappear for some nightly fun. I needed to look like nothing was wrong and pretend like I didn't know that they had tried to assassinate me. At least I wasn't alone.

Nonna Alice and Annalisa were also in attendance. They had flown into town as per my orders and were currently mingling and chatting away with other guests attending the reception. I'd called them over because I had someone I wanted to introduce to them, but the person wasn't here yet.

My wandering eyes searched for that individual around the large venue, but I couldn't find her. Maybe she wasn't here yet. I did find the bride and the groom nearby. Apparently, everyone was getting married except for me. Which was ironic since I was the oldest of them all.

The Bratva had arranged an alliance with the Irish mafia. I'd heard Alexander Nikolaev had turned down the Irish's bride to marry his wife, Ghislaine, so the duties had been extended to one of his cousins instead. The bride was the daughter of Cian Doyle, an Irish mob boss.

I shoved my hand into my silk pants pockets as I approached them. The bride was turned away as she chatted with someone nearby, but the groom kept an eye on me.

Raoul's suit was tailored with the finest satin, and it clung over his well-built, six-foot frame. Below, he wore a pair of custom-made, expensive black leather shoes. Dragging my gaze upward, I took in his Russian features. The rest of his hair was styled neatly over his head, but two locks had fallen on his high and proud forehead.

Russians... I gloated. *Always so damn proud.*

His blue eyes met mine as he assessed me.

Blue...

They reminded me of Ana's sapphire ones. I wished I could stop thinking about her. That girl had been a pain in my ass since her first attempt to assassinate me. I brushed off my thoughts and focused on the young groom again. He was in his early twenties. He'd been promoted to *Sovietnik* a year ago—one of the two internal Bratva spies. And a *lethal* one at that.

I wasn't supposed to know this information, but I did anyway. No wonder his eyes were so cunning as they stayed glued on me. As the *Sovietnik*, he oversaw the *Brigadier*—Kirill— to ensure the foot soldiers' loyalty.

He was kind of like the US government's checks and balances, so the captain didn't grow more powerful than the *Pakhan*, and business was regulated. Underneath the Bratva's *brigadiers* was the working unit, and in this case, it was the assassins. The assassins were part of Kirill's crew.

Raoul spied alongside Dimitri, who was both the Second in Command and the *Obshchak* in charge of Bratva's security. Although the *Obshchak* and the *Sovietnik* were equal in power, Dimitri was more powerful. This was because Dimitri was Alexander's blood brother, and should anything were to happen to their leader, Dimitri would be next in line to rule the Bratva.

Now, Raoul's eyes were reserved like many members of the mafioso. This life turned you into something that you weren't born to become. I wondered if he knew how to smile. I learned how to smile recently, but this kid didn't look like he'd ever crack a smile in this lifetime. I took in his raven hair and blue eyes. Raoul reminded me of an emo kid.

His inky hair fell further onto his face. The sharp contrast between them was astonishing. He could be a carbon copy of Ana, but Ana wasn't naturally raven-headed.

Blonde. Anastasia Volkova was blonde.

An image of her in the car flashed in my mind. The same night I made her come with my fingers. I'd seen her roots.

She was definitely blonde.

As I approached Alexander's young cousin, he nodded his head in hello. That was how it always was when it came to him. His mother was Galina Ivanova. Rumor had it that he couldn't speak, but others said they would sometimes hear his ruthless voice echoing in the middle of the night. No one truly knew the truth but Raoul Zakharov himself.

I didn't know if he couldn't hear, and I didn't know how to use sign language to communicate with him. So, I only said, "Congratulations."

I wasn't sure if he could read lips, but I guessed he did. Raoul extended his inky fingers and thumb. He touched his fingers to his chin before bringing his fingers forward and slightly downward. I thought that one meant to *thank you*. I'd seen it in a movie once.

I nodded and then moved away from him. Not too long after, the newly wedded lovebirds left. More and more guests had left until a few close people had remained. I didn't get far from the venue when I bumped into someone's shoulder. I turned my face to the right and a pair of black-as-an-abyss eyes greeted me.

Alexander.

The colors black always clung to him whenever I saw him. However, instead of wearing his signature purple cuffs, he wore burgundy. Although I was taller than him, he was lankier and leaner than most people. He looked dapper, clean, and elegant, like a mythical storybook character, in his fitted clothes. He wasn't the prince charming, though, but the villain.

I shook my head. He wasn't the only one.

We were all villains. We all had demons.

He grazed a hand through his trimmed black beard as his mischievous eyes landed on me. I didn't know what he thought and imagined most of the time. It was like he smiled to your face, but he'd already executed your death in his mind.

My body grew rigid as if I sensed an unplanned attack from him. My men still lingered around me. Even though they weren't directly with me, I knew they were watching. I should've called a private meeting, but conducting it publicly seemed better for what I was about to do.

Surely, he couldn't assassinate me publicly.

He would be the number-one culprit.

"So, Surge," Alexander spoke in his smooth, suave voice. He shrugged before he continued, "Did you like our wedding?"

I raised a brow. "It was all right. Anyone else planning to get hitched?"

His lip curved in a teasing smirk, and he shook his head.

"No one else for now."

Someone came up next to him to spark a conversation with the *Pakhan.*

"Excuse me," he said to me before turning his attention to the newcomer.

I looked away from him, and my footsteps wandered to one of his soldiers who drank on the job. I had no idea who he was, but if I were Alexander, I would have fired him by now. With a sly smile plastered on my face, I came right in front of him.

"Hello. I'm Don Surge."

I didn't have to introduce myself to him, but I liked how his eyes briefly widened at the mention of my name. Poor fellow looked shit-scared. I liked the rush of adrenaline flowing through my body at the fear I brought him.

Power was a wicked and strange thing. Those that didn't have any power would never understand what it was like. And those that did, didn't know how to make it last.

Perspiration trickled down his forehead, and I wondered if he was one step from pissing in his pants. After all, I only wanted to strike up a conversation with him.

My smile turned sinister.

His mouth parted and he nodded curtly.

"Sir Romano, hello."

I noticed he didn't call me Don.

Other soldiers didn't acknowledge other leaders as their own.

"Shouldn't you be protecting your *Pakhan* instead of drinking?"

His cheeks turned beet red as he spluttered. "Oh… Oh, of course, I will. I mean, I am," he corrected himself. He looked for a place to leave his drink, but there wasn't a table around us.

Like the most perfect gentleman I was, I offered him some assistance. "Allow me."

Before he could protest and disagree, I reached out to withdraw the drink from his hand. His mouth dropped open, stunned by the idea that I was offering my services to him like a waiter. I wasn't. I gave him another one of my charming smiles before turning around. As I lifted the drink in front of me casually, I lifted my other hand with a ring wrapped around my finger like a snake. Staring straight ahead and not at the drink, I turned my finger over it, spraying its contents into the drink.

Still smiling, I turned around slowly to the soldier who hadn't moved from the spot. "On second thought, why don't you take a break? After all, it's a wedding."

My charming smile stretched across my face, and his eyes ate up my sense of approval as I handed the drink to him. I felt no remorse in my soul as he brought the rim of his drink to his lips and drank. A soldier would always be a soldier.

They always obeyed leaders.

He'd let his guard down with me.

With a smile still plastered on my lips, I turned and moved a few steps away. Reaching a hand over my ring finger, I closed the secret compartment of my pillbox ring. Drumming my fingers on it slowly, I counted in my mind up to five. It would only take less than five seconds.

I managed to take one more step away before I heard the clank of something falling behind me.

My soul brightened at the small victory.

My twisted insides were pleased.

I didn't have to turn around to know that the soldier had fallen on the floor, dead.

Every single voice in the hall quieted.

Total silence greeted us until the whispers began once again.

Maybe the guests assumed he'd had too much to drink, but when they noticed me standing there ever so casually near the body, still smiling, their eyes turned accusing as gasps filled the air. They didn't have any proof, but they knew I had done it.

I had poisoned one of their people at their own fucking party.

The poison had rapidly spread, just as easily as my conversation and smile.

I didn't need to pull out a gun when poison was my weapon of choice.

No violence. No guns. No bloodshed involved.

Just death.

They called me Surge for a reason.

I was the reason why people felt sudden overflowing emotions that resulted in their deaths.

The emotions left destruction in their wake.

"Surge, what the fuck is this?" a familiar voice seethed out from behind.

Alexander. I chuckled before turning around.

"Finally caught your attention, huh?"

Alexander's eyes looked at me in disbelief and his pale face fumed. "If my soldier is dead and not just drunk off his ass, this means—"

I cut right to the chase and cut him off. "You have something that doesn't belong to you, Zander."

I looked him dead in the eye as I spoke.

Alexander's eyes narrowed. "Like?" he probed.

Like a lethal predator, my hands shoved into my pants pockets as I slowly began roaming in circles around him. The slow motion caught the eyes of the nearby guests. I didn't give a fuck. There wasn't just the Bratva Brotherhood around me. There were other Families too, other business entities, and other infamous elites. No children were in sight. They must have been somewhere else in the hall or home. I'd heard this place had a playroom.

Although Alexander kept his gaze straight ahead, I could sense his body had turned still as he observed me like a cat assessing his prey. Jerking my eyes away from him, I stared at the hundred-something people around us. The crowd had dropped from the thousands just half an hour ago.

The venue fell startlingly quiet as the people around us watched in anticipation. Everyone had their eyes on us now. It was kind of hard not to stare when a Don was walking in circles around another mob boss.

I eyed Alexander again. His dark eyes analyzed my every movement, as if sensing I might lunge at him any second now. The Russian soldiers roaming around exchanged looks with each other before glancing at their leader for his command. No one pulled their weapons out yet. They were probably aware that I'd used my trick on one of them, but it wasn't on Alexander.

I could see some fidgeting as they waited for instructions. They wouldn't hesitate to put me down if their leader commanded it, even if I was a Don. Other guests, on the other hand, stared with curiosity as they studied us.

I met his dark stare head-on. "Anastasia Volkova."

Alexander lifted a brow. "What about her?"

I smiled coldly. "I'm aware you brought her in to kill me."

Surprise gasps and shouts filled the air. A sense of unease passed through the crowd as everyone glanced at him for his confirmation. If he confirmed it to be true, it would mean war. It would be one or *none* of us walking out of here alive.

Although Alexander's face never gave anything away, he frowned at the accusation.

"Kill you?" he repeated as he stared at me sternly.

Gone was the smile on his face.

I chuckled darkly. "Oh, come on, Zander. Let's not play games now."

Alexander's face looked genuinely puzzled, almost lost. His jaw clenched and unclenched. "I'm not," he replied smoothly. "I'm already at war with the cartel. You think I'm planning on waging another war with you? I don't have a reason to do so." His eyes narrowed in disbelief, as if everything that came out of my mouth was a lie.

He was the liar and not me. "Why don't we bring out Anastasia and ask her why she wants to kill me, then?"

Alexander's frown deepened as he gazed around his surroundings as if to search for her. He couldn't find her, but he did find her husband. The fucker, Kirill, was standing near one of the food tables. The ingrown hairs on his head had grown slowly, but I could still tell he had burn marks. His eyes had widened at the mention of his wife's name, but he kept his mouth shut.

I focused on his leader. The fucker would never admit the truth. Alexander's hand grazed through his beard as he turned to face me. "If you are claiming Anastasia has attacked you, I will find on *whose* orders, because they weren't mine." His edgy voice dropped so low that chills ran through my body.

He didn't lose his cool easily, but I could tell my words had gotten to him. His midnight black irises were like ghastly souls as they stared me dead in the eyes. They were narrowed, as if assessing me, as untapped wrath lurked in them, promising destruction in its wake.

His jaw clenched and unclenched. The chill Alexander took the backseat and the *Pakhan* took over. His pale skin flamed under the artificial light, and he looked close to pulling out his revolver and shooting everyone.

I was just about to speak when the hallway doors creaked open. The silence in the air was so deafening that even the slightest noise alerted everyone. I stared at Alexander the entire time in case he tried to pull a fast one and attack me while I wasn't looking.

Slowly, his dark eyes moved away from me and went toward the door. His eyes narrowed before a puzzled expression filled his face and he lost the wrath he'd been displaying just moments ago. I didn't know what he was looking at, and quite frankly, I didn't give a fuck right now. I wouldn't be distracted. My hand drummed along my waistcoat's belt, ready to pull out my pistol and shoot all my bullets into Alexander's brain. He no longer paid any attention to me as he stared straight ahead.

Footsteps moved toward us until the clack of high heels on tile filled the atmosphere. I kept my focus on Alexander.

He tilted his head as he murmured, "She is here."

She. My body turned rigid, and I stilled.

The fingers that once drummed on my belt froze.

I clenched and unclenched my other fist before sneaking a glance to the ground on my left.

Fuck me for getting distracted.

My soul stirred with something unfamiliar, something I didn't recognize.

My stormy eyes lifted and landed on the floor-length dress with a slit that showed her ankles. I took in the turquoise-colored material that clung to her goddess-like body.

Blue. The color of her eyes.

They were darker than the blue that dominated the sky.

The kind of blue that reminded me of the bottomless sea.

I swallowed thickly.

I only just noticed her thin ankles with nude-colored stockings wrapped around them. I caught the silver blade poking out from under the side slit of her dress as her body swayed.

My breath caught in my throat.

She was always a sight to look at—a wicked temptation.

A woman who was both beautiful and cruel.

My hungry gaze trailed her athletic, shapely legs again. Long and fair, just as I remembered them when she wrapped them around my back. I continued up at her small waist and how that silk dress hugged her hips. She still wore that necklace I'd seen her wearing before. It completed the dress. The gown also had an off-shoulder neckline, revealing her sharp collarbones and strong shoulders. I sucked in a sharp breath.

She had the most porcelain skin I'd ever seen.

Unblemished. Flawless.

She looked more like a fairytale character than a real-life person. With her looks, she *belonged* in books, not reality. I hated how fucking beautiful she was. I hated imagining Kirill every time with her, touching her, defiling her every night. My blood boiled underneath my skin just thinking about it. I had a good night's sleep on the night she'd mentioned he'd only touched her once. Once was more than enough. Heck, it shouldn't have happened at all. She never belonged with him, to begin with …

It was fucked up, what he did. He'd taken her virginity, given her something to remember as her husband, and then snatched it away from her until she craved it again and again.

Ana's stunning face came into my view. A peach-colored lipstick hugged her lush lips, and her dewy skin was radiant, like the brightest of all summer days. It was hard to look at her sometimes. It was hard to *breathe* whenever she was around. All I wanted to do was just look at her. No matter how creepy it was.

Sometimes, I thought about the night we met. If I hadn't snatched that hood from her face the first time she had attacked me, would she still have killed me? If I didn't know she was a girl, would I have killed her? My decision to order the removal of her hood defined everything for us. It altered our paths.

Our destinies collided and led back to each other.

She wore that blue dress like she owned it, like it was meant for her, like she had been born to wear dresses and not hoods. It was different from the black and scarlet clothing I often saw cloaking her. She always blended into the shadows, but today she stood out like the princess she was.

She raked a hand through her long hair hanging in loose waves behind her, and it was only then that I caught the uncovered cobweb tattoo. She'd chosen to reveal it tonight. It was clear that she wasn't planning on playing the role of a ditzy wife anymore.

A few surprised gasps filled in the air, as if they had noticed the black marking on her skin as well, before quiet voices dominated the hall. People spoke over one another until they quieted down to see the scene unfold.

Surprise, surprise, everyone.

The artificial light caught on her blonde hair.

Blonde. I had to do a double take to make sure I wasn't imagining it. I wasn't. It was fully blonde today, like the roots I had seen up close. It was as if her natural hair color had returned. Vibrant and voluminous. It looked supple, like it was woven out of silk, and I wanted to run my fingers through it.

She must have stripped the black out of it completely. The bouncy mane on her reached just past her chest. Surprise filled me, because I'd always wondered if she dyed her hair black on purpose. Now, the black looked like it had never existed.

She resembled a young blonde woman with blue eyes in that gorgeous dress of hers. Hardly dangerous, like an innocent and delicate angel... yet it was clear that those icy eyes of hers were enough to kill people. Her real appearance didn't match her profession at all. Sometimes, I wondered if this was who she was meant to be—looking like royalty. The softness of her hair and dress had returned, but she remained cold as ice. She carried that new change with her like a regal queen. She even had the kind of flair and confidence of a queen.

I wasn't sure if she'd heard the conversation I'd had with Alexander, but I was guessing she hadn't, because her bold, kohled eyes stayed glued on me for a few seconds. Her eyes softened as she held my gaze. When looked away, her gaze landed on Kirill, and the iciness in them returned.

She swallowed as she stared at him, and he looked at her, equally confused, before exchanging looks with some of his soldiers. Nobody would ever think she'd always had black hair. The blonde looked too natural on her not to be in her DNA.

Alexander spoke once she was standing closer to us.

"Anastasia." He spoke low.

Her head jerked in his direction, almost bowing her head before catching herself. She *froze* in a half bow. Then, she straightened her head and looked Alexander right in the eye. Not an ounce of fear was etched across her face. I wasn't even sure if she knew what fear was. This woman was born without fear.

Like me, everyone's eyes were glued on her, like she was a beautiful and ruthless creature that would disappear if we blinked. Nobody could remove their eyes from her as they stared at her in fascination.

"Did you attempt to assassinate Don Surge?"

Alexander went right to the point without beating around the bush.

Surprise flickered in her eyes before she could carefully mask it with a void face. Her icy blues flew to my face, and I could see a million tormented questions going off in her head.

How does he know?

Did you tell him?

Her throat bobbed as she swallowed.

A flicker of hurt slipped through her cold-as-ice eyes.

It was the same vulnerability that she'd revealed so many times when she'd told me about herself. About who she was and what her story was.

My eyes seemed to be telling her a story of their own, too.

It had to be done.

Her lip almost curled downward as if she wanted to frown. I wondered if she was regretting all those times, she'd hesitated on slaying me. "Yes." She exhaled, tilting her head to the side. "I was informed that was my new assignment."

She spoke for the first time in her deep voice.

That. I noticed her choice of words.

Her cold-as-fuck words tore right through my soul.

Not even a *he*. I became a *'that'* to her in an instant.

As if I was some meaningless assignment.

She must have thought I had sold her out to have her killed.

Untapped wrath brewed underneath my skin, and I wanted to grab her by her pretty shoulders and knock some sense into her.

Her eyes moved from Alexander before they landed on her husband. "Kirill gives me my orders. I'm always told that they come from you directly," she continued as her cunning eyes sized her husband up before returning her gaze to Alexander.

Her *Pakhan* only replied with, "I didn't order this hit."

Puzzled by his revelation, she stared at Alexander again. A frown formed on her forehead, and she didn't even bother to hide her distaste anymore when her gaze narrowed on her leader. She pushed her pink lips together before gratingly saying, "Since the truth is now revealed, you're denying it to make me a scapegoat?" The deep blues in her eyes darkened and flared with hostility. Gasps filled the air again, and I almost took a step back at the defiance coming from her. I didn't expect her to show it to her leader too. "I will *not* be a scapegoat. Not for you. And not for anyone else." Her eyes flew to Kirill as she spoke the last line.

Alexander froze next to me.

I could see why …

He'd been publicly defied by one of his own soldiers.

He grazed a hand through his trimmed beard as he studied her again. Instead of reprimanding her, he glanced at Kirill and narrowed his eyes.

"Is this true, cousin? You placed this order?"

Kirill looked like he wanted to soil his pants already. His pale skin fumed red like a volcano, ready to erupt any second now. A sheen of perspiration rolled down the sides of his temples. He opened his treacherous mouth like he wanted to deny it, but then he clamped it shut.

He couldn't even blame Anastasia for acting on her own. She had no personal grudge for wanting to kill me besides the order.

I was another kill for her.

Another assignment.

And he couldn't blame it on Alexander... that is, *if* Alexander was telling the truth about not placing the order.

Kirill was royally fucked in the ass, and don't mind me as the monster in me enjoyed relishing his growing fear for his life. He decided to be smart and not answer at all.

He broke off eye contact with his *Pakhan* and stared at the people surrounding him. Everyone's eyes were now on him, as if he was the new spectacle. I flicked my gaze to Alexander, whose jaw ticked as he narrowed his eyes at his cousin. I could just imagine him connecting the dots in his head until a full picture formed in his mind.

Kirill just stood a few feet away from us.

"Why?" Just a single, deadly word came from Alexander.

That single word vibrated through the entire hall.

Alexander reached behind him, and my shoulders tensed. I also reached for my own weapon as he drew his gun out from the back of his waist. His face had tightened, and alarm flashed in his eyes. "Better start speaking now, Kirill, and tell me this is one big fucking misunderstanding."

Flabbergasted, Kirill cleared his throat as his face turned a deeper shade of red again. Now, he looked like a lobster, and I was tempted to burn his flesh again.

"And also tell everyone why you have been dyeing my natural blonde hair black in my *sleep*?" Anastasia's icy voice had no chill as she spoke.

Puzzled, I glanced at Kirill.

Had he? I'd assumed she'd changed her hair color.

Unease ran down my spine as I stared at the asshole. I should've done more than burn his head. I should've slashed his fingers off.

The crowd around us gathered. Although, some people slipped off and left, as if they sensed a wrath that would leave bodies in its wake.

Ana's face was beautiful and calm, but the inferno that flared in her eyes shone fiercely. She wasn't done speaking. "As well as why you always drug me in my sleep. Why are you doing this, Kirill?" The edges of his eyes narrowed at her accusation. "What don't you want people to find out? What are you trying to hide?" Her voice raised as she shot question after question at her treacherous husband.

Her eyes searched through his, maybe for the man she once thought she knew and trusted. However, I didn't see a husband when I looked at him. I saw a poor excuse for a man.

Perspiration trickled down Kirill's pale face as Alexander continued watching him. He still wore a puzzled look on his face, as if he hadn't been made aware of what he'd been doing to her. Maybe he wasn't, but...

I stared at Kirill's side profile. This man knew everything, yet he stayed mute. He wasn't giving them answers on purpose. My fist clenched and unclenched, and as much as I wanted to knock him into next week, I had to force myself to look away from him. My hatred burned stronger with each passing second, and before I could do something insane, my eyes glided to Ana.

Finally, the cheating piece of shit spoke.

"Anastasia—"

My teeth ground, and I interrupted, *"Annalisa."*

My heart rate thumped.

Dead silence trickled in the air.

I'd stunned everyone at the wedding.

A few painful moments later, the voices began.

Ignoring the shocked gasps, I met blue eyes in front of me.

Those blue eyes of hers looked lost.

She was *so* lost... and I hated that I would be the one telling her this.

I swallowed before I continued, "Your father waited until his last breath for your return. He always believed you were alive, and he searched for you every day."

Her feet faltered and her eyes widened in alarm.

I would be crushing her perfectly constructed world, but it was the right thing to do. She didn't belong here in the Bratva syndicate. She never did. She belonged with *me*, and damn anyone who would dare take her away again.

"Your birth name is Annalisa Romano, the *daughter* of the Romano Family and... you were stolen from us seven years ago."

Surge

14

PAST
FIFTEEN YEARS OLD

It was days after my father passed away before my mother came down with a high fever.

I didn't know what was wrong with her until we had taken her to the hospital. Turns out, she was diagnosed with meningitis.

I stared at the hospital bill in my hand.

Ten grand.

It had only been a two-night stay. Sometimes, I wondered if hospitals saved lives more, or if they overbilled more for profit. I saw a charge on the bill for television and observation.

Were they seriously kidding?

The television wasn't even on the entire time, and they were going to charge us for simply watching her? There wasn't a nurse in her room the entire time, nor a doctor. It was just me. I didn't know how I was going to pay it off. They had diagnosed her and given her a prescription for some expensive antibiotics. I didn't have any money for it. The hospital couldn't deny us when we went into the emergency room, but now we were on our own with the medications. What was I going to do with a diagnosis alone?

I needed money, and I needed it now.

Shit…

When Papa died, he left nothing behind but a house over our head with a roof that leaked during rainy and snowy weather. The fridge was empty most of the time. The bathroom was often left unclean to the point where mold grew on the walls. I stared down at my shirt and looked at the holes in the hem of it. I couldn't even sell it to gain money.

Blood whooshed past my ears, and I cussed at fate and my life. I sat down on the couch, and, after a long, silent moment, my ears perked up at the sound of my mother's vomiting. There was a trash can next to her, and my soul went out to her.

I gripped my locks into my hand and tugged on them fiercely, hoping I could draw blood instead. Earlier in the day, she'd had a severe headache and a stiff neck. From what I could gather, her body ached every time she moved. Chills and fatigue ran through her body day and night, and I just felt so powerless to only be able to watch over her. I didn't know what to do.

Fuck, I cussed my Papa too for dying young and leaving us in a life of poverty.

My mother's vomiting intensified, and I wanted to shut my ears from her pain. Her hurling came violently, and I didn't know what to do for her.

I was fifteen, and I wondered if I could get a job so that I could buy antibiotics for her. We didn't have medical insurance.

Even if I got a job at a café or a restaurant, I wouldn't be getting paid until two weeks later. My mother didn't have two weeks. The doctors warned us that she should be placed on antibiotics right away to fight her illness.

Disappointment settled over my soul.

Slowly I rose, and I asked one of the neighbors to watch over her and alert me if anything went wrong. I stepped outside on a hunt for something that could help her. I didn't have any siblings or living family. I was an only child.

We mainly relied on the government and food benefits. As I left my home, I wandered over to the city side. I needed about ten grand or something, and if I needed to start begging for money, I was ready to do so.

I couldn't have my only living parent dying on me yet. I wandered through the late city until my feet began to hurt. My sneakers had holes between my toes. Tired and frustrated, I sat down on one of the bus stops benches next to a stranger who smoked.

I inhaled tightly.

Then, I exhaled. I did this for about two minutes until my mind became calmer and my breaths steady. The more I stayed calm, the more I could think rationally.

Stay calm.

Stay. Calm.

Fuck it.

How the fuck was I supposed to stay calm like this?

A grunt left my mouth, and it caught the attention of the stranger next to me.

I didn't bother giving him a spare glance.

"What's going on with you, boy?" His older voice came.

I sighed and rubbed the back of my head.

"Mind your fucking business."

I had no interest in being friendly right now.

"Sounds like you've had a rough day."

I stayed silent and stared at the ground instead.

"You need a new pair of sneakers," the unfamiliar voice said.

I sighed before snapping my head up. He wore all black and his brown eyes stared right at me. He was a large and tall man with broad shoulders. A deep scar ran down his face. I wouldn't let him intimidate me, though.

"Size ten?" he questioned.

I scoffed under my breath before snapping, "Twelve. And leave me the fuck alone and take your shitty, privileged ass somewhere else."

The man was quiet for a second before he spoke again.

"I'm not privileged. I've worked for everything I have today."

If he was expecting an apology, he wasn't receiving one.

At last, he finally rose on his feet and disappeared.

I let out a sigh of relief as I closed my eyes momentarily and sagged onto the bench. I rested my head on top of it and tried to sleep before I could figure out my next move.

A few moments later, a movement stirred next to me, and I scowled.

I was moody today. Sue me.

I opened my eyes to glare at the person and realized it was the same man I had met earlier. He was walking away now. I glanced down at the orange box on the bench. With my jaw ticking, I studied it. I wondered if he'd left it accidentally.

Curious, I reached out my fumbling hands and opened it. My mouth dropped open as I stared at the new pair of black sneakers inside. My hands snatched one of them to glance at the size number.

12.

Size 12.

My pulse spiked and the blood in my veins thundered.

I didn't understand why he had bought me any at all.

"Hey!" I called out to him as I rose on my feet and chased after him.

The man in black paused and glanced over his shoulder.

"What is this?" I gritted out.

He raised a refined brow. "You needed new shoes."

I sucked in a sharp breath as I stared at him suspiciously.

No one truly bought an expensive gift for a stranger without anything in return.

I eyed him up and down before lifting my gaze to his face again. "What's the catch? I ain't sucking your dick."

I was ready to throw the sneakers right at his face, but he replied, "I'm not asking you to. Keep them. You need them."

My cheeks turned hot at the reminder of my poorness.

"You need a job?" the stranger questioned.

I sighed and chewed on the inside of my lip.

After a brief moment, I nodded. "Fast," I muttered. "Something that pays within the same day." I rolled my eyes in disbelief. Like that would ever happen.

"Oh, so you need money?" I nodded vigorously. "How much?"

I stared questioningly at the stranger again.

"Fifteen grand or something."

The man whistled low before he looked at me. "What for?"

"*Madre,*" I mumbled, and I doubted he understood Italian.

"Your mom?" he replied without missing a beat.

I took a step back, surprised.

Just who was this guy?

"Italian?" he questioned.

I nodded.

"I have a job for you," he continued. The edges of my greens narrowed. "If you can do it, my Boss will pay you for it."

Boss? What was he recruiting me for?

I still didn't believe him. It sounded like some kind of scam.

"Why would you pay me? I'm only fifteen."

He only looked at me. "Fifteen is the age we start."

Puzzled, I threw the sneakers right into his chest before turning away. It sounded too good to be true, and I had no idea what he was talking about.

His voice came a moment later. "I can ask the Boss to pay half right now. The rest once the job is complete."

My footsteps paused. I could buy my mother's antibiotics.

I still had my mother's prescription right in my pocket.

It would stop the fever, the fatigue, the headache, and the vomiting. Her sickness would be managed, and maybe she could be cured.

Desperation kicked through my soul.

I turned around slowly.

"What kind of job is it?" I questioned carefully under my tongue.

The stranger smiled widely.

"Depends on how comfortable you feel using a gun."

That night, I made my first kill.

I was desperate enough to do it.

And I would do it again, because it saved my mother's life.

The stranger I'd met was a made man of the Romano Family.

The week afterward, I was initiated.

They called themselves the Romanos.

The kills added up, and so did the payments.

It brought a better roof over my head, and food, and it also paid my bills.

The Romanos protected me.

And in return, I served them.

I'd kill for them.

❖

TWENTY-THREE YEARS OLD

My mother Ginevra was remarrying again. I couldn't say I was surprised. She was young and beautiful. Don Angelo Romano had seen my mother recently at an event and gave her a grand marriage proposal.

She'd accepted it, and here we are.

Post-marriage.

Our first day settling here at the Romano estate.

I drummed my fingers against the pistol still clipped on my waistline, and my eyes glided across the lavish display of wealth in front of me. I came from humble beginnings. Never in a million years did I think I would be living here one day.

"You look like a carrot."

My body stilled.

I glanced down at my cotton black shirt which still had a ketchup stain from yesterday's dinner. I hadn't bothered washing it. Removing my gaze from the stain, I glanced at the culprit who'd called me out in her tiny voice.

I looked at the small child in front of me. She couldn't have been older than three.

My lip twitched at the smile on her face.

Carrot. Well, it wasn't original.

My favorite one was, *Are you red down there too?*

Although I had tamed, light brown hair that looked somewhat red, I was still lumped in the same category as redheads. "Are you planning to eat me, then?" I joked in a low voice.

She grinned at me as if that was her answer.

"Papa says you are my brother. Is that true?" she questioned softly.

Her voice was high-pitched and laced with curiosity.

I realized who I was staring at.

Annalisa Romano.

The only biological child of my stepfather.

I was an only child, so I wasn't too happy about having a replacement so soon.

I eyed her quickly. She didn't even reach my knee. It was my first time meeting her. Children were kept at a distance from the mob life, especially girls. Her wide blue eyes peered up at me, and her long, golden blonde hair was in a loose braid behind her. It reminded me of buttermilk. Smooth and silky. Some tendrils had fallen out in wisps. Bangs covered her forehead and her neck glistened with sweat like she'd run.

I glanced behind her and saw the nanny a few feet away. Annalisa must have run a marathon just to escape her. I don't know where children gained the infinite amount of speed to outrun most adults. It was as if they were running for their life. The nanny placed her hands on her hips as she blew out exhales as if she was tired and out of breath. She noticed me standing there and I nodded politely.

I glanced at Don Romano's daughter again.

She wore a baby blue frock that ended at her chubby knees. Her ample cheeks were pink as she smiled up at me like I was her new favorite doll.

Kid was cute, though.

"I'm Surge," I corrected her.

I was way too old to have a sibling her age.

She tilted her head as she observed me. The same way children did when they were deciding if they liked someone or not. She clasped her hands in front of her before lifting them slowly. My breath faltered, and I wondered how I should get out of this situation. I didn't have any experience with other children. My teenage life had been about guns and violence ever since I'd been a member of the Romano empire.

I grazed a finger over my chin as I studied her.

I thought it was best to walk away, but I knew those big-ass tears would come if I did, and my stepfather might whip my ass for making his precious princess cry.

I would risk it, though. I moved to leave and only managed to take a few steps before hearing the girl whine in the background. I sighed as I sensed her tantrum coming.

I was just about to turn around, but something launched on my leg, holding it hostage. I raised my leg to shake it off. When I glanced down, I realized it was Annalisa. I wasn't sure if I should laugh or be horrified. She'd clung to my knee like a monkey, and by the looks of it, she had no plans to let me go.

She rested her chin on my pants and glanced up with accusing eyes. "Papa says I have a new mommy... and brother."

Her hopeful eyes stared up at me.

I almost felt bad for the kid.

Her mother had been killed, and she had no idea how.

She was better off not knowing.

I tried to shake her off from my leg, but she refused to budge.

"You are a mean carrot!" she whined in her babyish voice.

Ouch.

She apparently didn't understand boundaries like the rest of us fucked-up soldiers. Then again, it was no surprise. She was her father's daughter, after all.

"Ana," I chided under my breath. The nickname rolled off my tongue before I could stop it. "You can call me Surge, and I will look out for you as Don Angelo's daughter."

Her little, pert nose wrinkled as she blissfully sighed.

She seemed to make my leg her new home.

"That's okay." She admitted defeat.

Her eyes beamed up at me, the blue in them bright as the clear skies.

"You will call me sister soon, big brother," she declared as if she was challenging me.

I chuckled and attempted to shake her grip off my leg again.

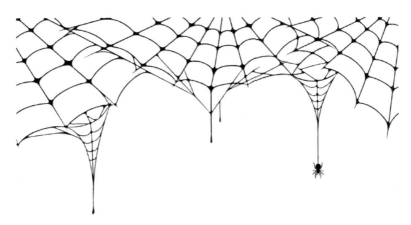

Ana

15

PRESENT

Annalisa Romano.

Time froze for a second.

My body turned rigid.

I simply blinked, like my soul had left my body.

Bile singed at the back of my throat.

My entire world came crashing to the ground.

I refused to believe it.

My astonished eyes met *Sergio's*, and I tried to search for a sign that he was lying, but only dimness lurked in his eyes. My lips parted as I shook my head in disbelief.

No. Never in a million years could that be true.

Your father waited until his last breath for your return.

My father had been looking for me this whole time?

He always believed you were alive. He searched for you every day.

I ground my teeth until my jaw began to hurt.

Why had I even come here?

I'd only wanted to get answers from Kirill, but now I was the one left stumped.

Noises dominated the air as the words, "Princess Annalisa," were tossed around. I was sure it came from some members of the Romano family and guests who were present. My eyes turned misty as I stared at the floor in despair.

No… I couldn't be a princess. It was impossible.

"I'm *Anastasia* Volkova," I corrected Surge, shaking my head. "I don't know what you're talking about."

Your birth name is Annalisa Romano, the daughter of the Romano Family. You were stolen from us seven years ago.

"But you do know, Ana." Surge's voice came a beat later.

I squeezed my misty eyes shut, hoping I could block out everyone.

"You are lying!" I seethed under my breath. I hated how my voice cracked as I said that.

It fucking cracked.

"No!" My accusing eyes flared.

They met his emeralds again.

Only sorrow filled them now. For *me*.

"You were on a train with two of your bodyguards. A crowd came, and you fell and lost unconsciousness. You were only a teenager when you were separated from them. Someone must have found you. Someone other than *us*," he revealed.

A lump grew and clogged my throat.

I couldn't swallow it down.

I couldn't remember any of this at all.

But I did remember waking up with a bump on my head.

Someone else had found me.

The black market.

I shook my head fiercely and clenched my fists.

"We didn't want anyone to find out that you were missing. We didn't want our enemies looking for you too…" His breath faltered. "But it turns out they had already found you and kept you away this entire time. You are the real Annalisa. Our mafia princess. We had someone else stand in your place for the time being while our family searched for you. The Bratva made you live a lie for half of your life. You are Italian and—"

It was too much information to process all at once.

I was still processing the first revelation.

I bent forward and snatched the two blades strapped to my ankles. My chest heaved and my breaths came out in rushed exhales. "I am Russian," I hissed. "If you spread more misinformation, I will kill you this time, *Don*."

Surge's eyes were hopeless as he stared at me.

I was a lost cause to him right now.

My hopeful eyes went to Kirill.

He still hadn't spoken one word at all.

I waited for him to deny the truth.

He looked like he'd seen a ghost as he unclipped his pistol from his belt. My face fumed and my soul ached for him to clear the confusion up, but he said nothing.

Nothing at all.

I could feel a piece of me diminishing as I looked away from him and met two pools of blackness instead. My *Pakhan*, my *leader*, stared right at me. He hadn't said one word either.

His lips were parted, and he looked just as stunned. I'd never seen him wear that expression before.

Speechless. At a loss for words.

Finally, Kirill spoke up.

"Who do you think you are, coming to our wedding and spreading lies about my wife? Her name is Anastasia!"

Surge didn't miss a beat.

"You mean, the name you have renamed her as?"

"A-A..." *I stuttered.* "Ana... Ana..."

My voice trailed off before I could finish. I couldn't remember the rest of my name as I looked away from him and wiped my eyes with my bloody hand. I groaned at the mess I was making.

"Anastasia?" *the stranger probed.*

My eyes flew to Kirill again before they landed on Surge.

He looked like he had aged overnight with this admission.

A tear trickled down my face.

For the first time since I was a child, I could feel my eyes welling up.

He sighed softly before he spoke.

"Why do you think I call you Ana and not Anastasia?" I closed my eyes and hoped I could shut him out again. A painful throb formed on the back of my eye. My pulse spiked with every new revelation. "You said it yourself. Your husband has been changing your natural hair color. He's been drugging you in your sleep. He has altered your appearance and has forced you to live a life as an ethnicity you are *not*." He growled out the last sentence and chills ran down my spine.

My body shivered as adrenaline ran through it.

My hand that still gripped my blade went to my blonde head. I had stopped by a salon, and after a couple of washes, the semi-permanent color had faded. I was baffled by the results. My thoughts were burst by Surge's voice again.

"He didn't even spare your eyes, Ana," Surge hissed.

I could imagine him throwing glares at Kirill. I pleaded silently for him to stop speaking. Back then, I liked listening to that low, rumbling, and magnetic voice of Surge's. Now, I prayed it would be quiet instead. My life couldn't be that much of a lie, but he continued to shatter my hope that what he was saying wasn't true.

"One of your eyes was damaged because of something he put you through as a child. You really think someone else besides your husband ordered that to be done to you? He planned that abduction. He damaged your eye. And then he ultimately got your undying devotion because he saved you in a bullshit heroic act later. What other lies has he fed you?"

No one can ever find out who she is. Her people are still looking for her, I remembered one of those masked men saying.

If a dead heart could crack, it did today.

"What did he tell you of those kidnappers? Are they dead?"

He showed me a video.

"Do you have any proof? Have you seen it for yourself?"

A video. I wasn't there.

Surge continued, "Those were his own men. He took you because that's what his kind do. *Take.* Instead of killing you when he found you, he created a plan to train you just to use you." Each of his vicious words sent invisible daggers to my soul. I didn't know it was possible to assassinate an assassin until now. "He manipulated you with your trust. He said you were his secret weapon, but why did you need to be secret in the first place?" The tension in his voice grew thicker. "It wasn't just because you were a female. It was because you are a *Romano!*"

No. I still wanted to protest.

My eyes slowly opened, and I couldn't see anything through my blurred vision. Kohl and mascara stung my eyes, and everything seemed chaotic around me.

"I don't even speak I-Italian," I mumbled under my breath.

I'd officially lost my mind.

Surge sighed. When he spoke again, his voice was soft. "That's because you don't remember. They taught you a different language. I don't even know how the fuck they could get away with this for so long and not get caught."

My limbs trembled, and I released a shuddering breath.

He finished with, "If Alexander didn't place the hit on me, then Kirill sure did, because he knows exactly who the fuck you are to me. He *didn't* want me to find you, but that fucking idiot led you right to me."

I wanted to stomp my feet on the ground and scream no.

My eyes landed on Kirill.

My husband. My mentor...

"Y-You," I stammered. I'd never fucking stammered in my life. "You saved me, didn't you?" I hated the hope that still lingered in my voice.

His black eyes disappeared for a moment as he blinked, and he swallowed. "Of course, I did, Anastasia. He is fucking lying to you with his theatrics! He just wants to cause a war," he protested.

"Call me a liar again, and I will cut off your hairy balls and feed them to you."

I could hear the threat loud and clear in Surge's voice.

Voices bounced around in the air as they dominated for control and to be heard. For a moment, they all forgot whose voice mattered the most. Mine.

They had stolen my voice right out of me.

Blood whooshed past my ears as I swallowed thickly.

"For seven long years, I have associated myself with this organization. I-I have dedicated myself to the syndicate, this cause, killing for them, supporting them, and I have considered these people my people. And now you..." My hopeless eyes fell on Surge again. "You are saying I am not one of *them* anymore?"

The voices around me fell quiet.

I tried to clear my throat, but it still came out too raw and hoarse. "You cannot take someone like me, someone whose first memory was being on the streets about to be devoured by vultures," I accused Surge. I decided to be most upset with him for now. "And say that all of these new memories are based on a lie! They gave me a home, a shelter, and now you want to snatch it away from me? I don't remember anything from the fall, but this world gave me new memories when I had none and a *family*."

My voice cracked.

It cracked again and again.

Surge raked a hand through his hair as he stared into my eyes. "What memories has this world ever given you besides guns, violence, and..." His gaze flicked to Kirill. "Cheating?"

I pressed my lips together to stop the trembling. Surge returned his intense gaze to me and moved a step toward me, but I raised my blade in front of me.

"Whether those memories are good or bad, they are mine!" I seethed out.

His footsteps faltered and he swallowed as he glanced at the weapon I was holding.

"Why do you think you couldn't kill me this entire time, Ana? Your subconscious memory always knew who I was. I was your only mission left unaccomplished. You still can't kill me..." I could hear the faint smile in his voice. "They trained you to work like a man and you believed yourself a part of them. You molded yourself into someone you're not. You changed yourself. When was the last time you smiled before you met me?"

I still wanted to deny it.

Never. I'd always hated smiling until I learned how to—until I met *him*.

The blood in my veins thundered.

My heart only hammered harder as time moved on.

I blew out a shaky breath. "Why...?" I choked out. "Why didn't you tell me sooner?"

My dim eyes stared into his.

I'd slept with him. Once. I still thought about it.

"I wasn't sure in the beginning," he admitted. "You looked familiar, but you were older, and your hair and eyes were different now. The Annalisa I knew didn't know how to use weapons. She carried all the softness in the world, and when you appeared again, Anastasia had taken over with all the ruthlessness this world could offer."

He shrugged, and when I met his eyes, they softened. "I couldn't kill you either, because you are my family." My breath hitched at the word 'family.' "We are not blood-related, but you are still my *family*. You grew up in front of me. I have watched you transform. You are the Romano family's heir, the only descendant of Don Angelo Romano, and the people you still want to believe in wanted to destroy that."

I opened my mouth to speak, but I clamped it shut.

The edges around Surge's eyes narrowed.

"They found you and never returned you. Instead, they took you to use you."

The bitter words stabbed my soul.

"Your husband used marriage to cage you to him, so you would never leave. He manipulated you into thinking he was your new family, but you already have one. You have *me*." The last word came out as a plea, like he desperately needed me to believe him. "You're not alone, Ana. This is not your world." He sighed restlessly as his eyes landed on the pendant around my neck. The same blue pendant I wore as a kid. "That necklace was given to you by your grandmother, Alice."

Grandmother?

I opened my mouth to speak, but a voice spoke over me.

"Ana."

The voice was unrecognizable, hoarser than anything I'd ever heard, and belonged to someone I presumed was elderly.

Puzzled, I glanced in the direction of where that voice had come from.

An older woman in her late seventies stood a few feet away from me with tears streaming down her cheeks. Her hair had wisps of gray in them, and I could only imagine they were once blonde. She was Surge's grandmother.

I waited for recognition to fill my mind, but it never came. It was still vacant, hollow, and utterly useless. Even with all the so-called evidence right in front of me, I had no way to confirm it with my mind. Coming up speechless, I stared at her with parted lips. Her blues were so similar to my own.

Curious, I stepped closer to her. Her skin had deeper and finer wrinkles on them, but those eyes… They looked even older than her age, like she had spent the previous years of her life grieving. An unfamiliar sensation filled my soul.

A sense of restlessness took over as I lowered my weapons, and with hesitant footsteps, I took baby steps toward her. I tilted my head as I looked at her in her white dress. The more I stepped closer, the more the blue in her eyes resembled mine. They weren't the sky blue like many blue eyes. They were darker and deeper, like the bottomless sea. My footsteps faltered and the restlessness in my soul intensified.

She looked familiar. She *felt* familiar.

But I still couldn't recognize her.

I'd heard of her before.

Alice Romano.

Her footsteps rushed toward me until they stopped right before me. She was a couple of inches shorter as her eyes beamed up at me. For a moment, the grief in her eyes diminished completely. Now, she looked like she cried from happiness.

I didn't know I could be the source of anyone's happiness.

"I knew it was you the second you walked through that door in that dress. I've always told you turquoise was your color!" Her hoarse voice came again.

It sounded raw, like she'd been crying. She had a slight accent, the graveness lurking in it when she pronounced the *th's*. I swallowed thickly and my hungry eyes ached to hear it again. It sounded different from the Slavic accents I'd listened to before, where the *R's* were rolled, and the natural pitch was lower.

It sounded like… *home.*

Home. What a strange word.

I didn't even know my permanent home.

I didn't know why I'd chosen to wear this dress. I thought it would look nice with my blonde hair. Her footsteps filled the space between us, and her trembling hands reached up to cup my cheeks. My body wanted to pull away, but my mind willed me to stay still. Her hands were soft and fragile against my face, like she would crack at any second.

"We've looked everywhere for you," she whispered. "I prayed day and night for you to return to us." Her hands were warm against my skin, and I let her hold me for a few moments. "One of the servants had seen you outside your school once but you had quickly left. You have no idea how much happiness it has brought me to see you alive, princess."

There went that nickname again.

The princess has distinct and healthy eyes. No one can recognize them now.

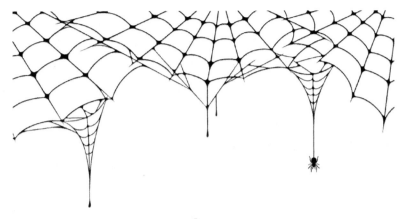

Ana

16

I broke away from her hold as those words hit me again.

I gripped the handles of my blades so tightly that without looking at them, I knew my knuckles had turned white.

"Anastasia," a familiar voice came from behind me. It belonged to Kirill. "These people are trying to fill your thoughts with lies and deceit. I'm your husband! Would I ever lie to you? Do you actually believe these strangers?" He gave a dry chuckle, as if everything that had been said was completely ridiculous.

My throat tightened, and I exhaled a ragged breath.

My jaw clenched as I turned around to glare at him.

His blacks widened as he shook his head, as if he were in denial that his wife could stand up against him.

Lifting my eyes, they landed on the scars on the top of his head. His hair had grown out in uneven patches, but I could still see deep, burgundy wounds on it. I almost felt guilty for him the same night he pulled my hair.

The punishment of burning his head seemed cruel.

Almost too cruel.

I glanced over at Surge, who still stared at me with those intense eyes of his. The mosses of them were dimmed, as if they were losing their sparkle. He wasn't sure if I believed him.

Clearing my throat and squaring my shoulders, I looked away from him to focus my attention on *Pakhan*. Alexander had remained quiet the entire time as his eyes met mine. He was still studying me as if he was also unsure of what was fact from fiction. He hadn't passed his judgment yet. It was actually smart of him to actually think all of this through and not act irrationally.

If he spoke in support of Kirill, he'd risk a war with the Romano Family.

If he spoke against Kirill, he'd lose all his allies from his mother's side of his family.

Either way, he had to make a choice, and it was time for him to do so.

"*Pakhan*," I began slowly, bowing my head slightly. He was still my leader. He was a good leader, and I would always obey him and follow him, no matter what anyone said. I exhaled as I continued, "When I first met Kirill, your father—" I glanced at the previous *Pakhan*, Daniel Nikolaev, who now hovered right behind Alexander. "He was present. He mentioned that I looked familiar. I specifically remember him saying this ..."

Pakhan's eyes widened, as if he hadn't expected that. Slowly, he glanced to his right as his father made himself visible. For a few seconds, he didn't say anything. Alexander remained silent as he glanced at his mother, Natasha Zaitseva, lingering just a few feet away before he returned his gaze to his father again. I could only imagine what was going through his mind right now. Maybe I'd made things much worse for him by involving his father, but it had to be done.

"Is this true, Father?" He finally spoke. His voice came out smooth, but there was uncertainty that laid in his raw voice. I was sure this wasn't how he'd imagined the wedding to end.

His father's jaw clenched as his gaze briefly landed on Kirill before returning to Alexander again.

"She looked familiar, but I didn't know who she was exactly."

That sounded like a lie to my ears.

His father opened his mouth to speak again, but another voice interrupted us.

"Your people altered her appearance, but you cannot alter a simple DNA test."

Surge. My heart wanted to sing.

"Quite frankly, I have had enough of this shit. You steal the girl from my family, and now you are fucking lying about it when your petty asses have been exposed?" His voice was tight as he spoke, and it looked like the emotions coiling inside him were too powerful to be restrained. They practically ached to be unleashed. Time seemed to stop as we all waited for the shoe to drop. Then, as if a dam had exploded, Surge pulled out his revolver from his waist and pointed it at *Pakhan.*

My footsteps faltered when *Pakhan's vors* pulled out their weapons and pointed them at Surge. In return, Surge's made men aimed theirs at him. As if on cue, more of Romano's soldiers filled the massive hallway, increasing in number by the second.

I wondered if they were waiting outside this whole time for a signal.

Clearly, Surge had planned this all along.

Tingles ran down my spine.

Pakhan didn't pull out his weapon, though.

Maybe because the second he tried, Surge would press the trigger.

Surge's beautiful jaw ticked as he stared at *Pakhan's* cold eyes. The mischievous devil in him was gone today. He breathed hard through his nose as he moved his pistol from *Pakhan's* face to my husband. It rested on Kirill's face now.

Pakhan was never the target. It was always Kirill.

My darling husband's eyes flared wildly, and he stormed past me to stand just a couple of feet away from Surge, holding his own gun out in front of him.

Surge hadn't fired yet.

I thought he should fire at this point, because Kirill was a highly trained and advanced killer. He didn't go on missions himself, but he trained others—which made him even more deadly, since he trained his best assassins himself.

Two of Surge's men stepped in front of him, ready to die for their leader if Kirill pressed the trigger. My heart worked overtime as my poor mind struggled to digest all this new information. It was too much, and I wanted to leave already.

Bright green eyes met mine.

The dimness in Surge's eyes was gone now.

"You're one of us. Open your eyes, little sister."

My footsteps faltered.

A throb formed in the back of my head as bolts of electricity attacked my brain.

I could feel a headache coming now.

Too much strain on my forgetful mind.

I squeezed my eyes shut before opening them.

You will call me sister soon.

A faint memory filled my mind.

It started with a slow tingle before growing louder until it began to roar.

My hands trembled violently.

I remembered saying that again and again as I grew older to someone with light reddish-brown locks…

As a child, I remembered feeling hopeful he'd one day call me that.

To hear Surge call *me* that.

But he never had, until now.

I was like a deer caught in headlights, frozen in place as the familiar words played in my mind.

It was something I'd hoped for as a child, but I couldn't relate to my younger self as an adult.

As the memory unfolded itself in my mind, I repeated the faint chant. "Big brother."

Surge glanced at me in surprise.

His eyes lit up at the fact that I recognized him.

My legs turned to jelly under me, and my body turned into mush. I wanted to grab onto something to keep me steady, but there was nothing near me to hold on to.

I didn't know if we counted as a family anymore, since we weren't related by blood.

My father, who was the only person that bonded us to each other, was dead.

My father.

A dead father I would never meet again.

A flood of memories filled my mind.

My father braided my hair as I sat on his lap.

I chased after my stepbrother and tried to get him to play with me.

I didn't remember my mother, because I was only three when she died.

Nonna Alice's sweet smile flashed before my eyes as she wrapped the blue pendant around my neck. Instinctively, I reached up to touch the music box pendant.

My chest heaved and I dropped forward, holding onto my knees for balance.

Oh dio moi.

The unfamiliar words left my mouth before I could stop them.

Oh my God.

My body stilled at the foreign words pouring out of me.

They were not foreign to me at all.

I *knew* Italian.

I spoke a language I didn't even remember speaking until now.

A voice interrupted my thoughts.

"Now look at what you have done. You are messing with her mind. She is nothing to you. She belongs to me!" Kirill's deep shouts filled the hall.

"She belongs *with* me," Surge countered in a low voice.

It's strange how both sounded similar to each other but both had different meanings.

"Oh, get the fuck out of here!"

Kirill shouted some Russian cuss words in the air as he continued yelling at the top of his lungs. My ears began to hurt from all his shouting, and I wanted to shut him up.

"Be quiet, Kirill. You have done enough damage already."

A distinct voice had spoken.

It was low, smooth, and coiled with tension.

Pakhan.

Alexander.

At last, he spoke.

The side he'd chosen was clear as day.

He believed in Surge.

I was beginning to believe the Don as well.

Everything just added up.

Buying me at the black market...

She looks familiar... Is that...?

The alterations in my hair and my eyes.

The princess has distinct and healthy eyes. No one can recognize them now.

Kirill was never loyal to me.

He'd cheated on me at every opportunity he'd had.

He'd planned my kidnapping both times.

Once at the market and the second one was when I was sleeping.

She belongs to me.

Lies... I never belonged to him. I never did.

He never loved me.

Kirill had constructed an intricate world of lies to cage me.

A web of lies.

It wasn't the rest of the Bratva members that sought to kidnap me.

It wasn't the Spiders. It was just two individuals.

Kirill and *Pakhan's* father.

Pakhan would never harm a child.

"Anastasia is my wife!" Kirill continued to yell, and it almost came out as ear-shattering shrills.

But you never treated me like your wife, I wanted to scream.

"She is loyal to me!"

No, I broke my loyalties to you a long time ago.

The night I decided not to kill Surge Romano.

I just never realized it until now.

My eyes flared as I stepped behind Kirill, who hovered in front of me like he was shielding me from the Romanos.

Who would shield him from *me*, though?

"Kirill," I spoke his name softly.

He stopped yelling almost instantly. When he turned to look at me, his eyes widened hopefully. "Anastasia, you believe me, right?" he rushed out. When I didn't answer, he continued, "I would never harm you in a such a way and—"

I looked him dead in the eye with no remorse in my heart for what I was about to say, and he shut up. I leaned in, and he inched closer to me like he thought I was about to kiss him.

Instead, I said in a voice so low, like it was only meant for his ears, "I let Don Romano go the first time I saw him. And again... and again..." A cruel smile played on my lips and his eyes bugged out, looking ready to burst out of their sockets. "He touched me. I *let* him, and I would let him do it again." Then, as if to add some icing on top of my poisonous cake, I murmured in Italian, "*Vaffanculo.*"

Go fuck yourself.

The word settled on the tip of my tongue like it had always belonged there. I'd heard my father say it once.

My soul filled with a glint, and he choked on his breath in surprise.

Cheaters get cheated on.

Before he could open his mouth to counter, I pressed the side button on the handle of the blade I held, and it extended the stainless steel to a forearm's size. I pulled up the silver that glinted under the lights above and slashed it through the air forcefully until it landed right through his neck.

I didn't even look down when his head detached itself from his body.

I didn't even look when it dropped on the floor and rolled off.

And assassins get assassinated.

His body sank and crumbled onto the floor.

Surprise, surprise.

Looks like we'd be ending tonight with a bloody wedding.

Screams and shouts filled the hall, but I didn't focus on them at all.

Only steady breaths came out of me.

Whooshes of blood roared past my ears.

I was a married woman a few seconds ago.

Now, I'd become a widow.

I'd *made* myself a widow.

No one could decide how I punished my husband.

My eyes fell on my blade that I still gripped in my hands. The tip of it was stained with scarlet and coated with his blood. My attention glided to my tattooed hand.

The cobweb stared right back at me.

It didn't take long for a married woman to transform into a black widow.

Footsteps rushed toward me, and guns clicked in the air like they were ready to apprehend or behead me for the biggest sin I'd just committed. Instincts kicked in, and I pressed the button on my weapon's handle and my other blade extended to a forearm's size. Without looking up, I jerked my hand up in the air and stabbed whoever it was right in the center of their neck. He gurgled, choking on his blood, before falling near my feet.

I was the most dangerous female in this place right now.

To be a female was both beautiful and terrible.

No one expected them to be killers, and here I was, a living proof of it.

A female could be ruthless too, and those that dared step in her way would taste her hidden fury once provoked.

Adrenaline pumped through my veins at the rush of the two kills. It felt like a comeback after failing to kill the notorious Don as of late. It made me wonder—would I have been an assassin if I hadn't been lost and then taken? Probably not.

My hollow eyes stared down at the Bratva member on the floor. He laid in a pool of his blood. One of Kirill's crew. I'd just killed one of my own...

Then again, they were never my people to begin with, right?

They could easily press the trigger and shoot me with bullets, but no one fired at me. I wondered if *Pakhan* had something to do with it. I'd just killed his cousin, and everyone knew the punishment for treason was death. *Pakhan* didn't like traitors, but I wasn't a traitor. I'd supported them for years. I'd been loyal to them until I found out I was betrayed.

The voices and chants around me grew louder and dominated my brimming thoughts. Maybe they planned on killing me for what I'd done. I didn't care, though. I would take at least dozens of bodies down with me.

I didn't recognize anyone right now in my chaos. The cruelest parts of me came out of their cage. The same parts that I had barricaded and kept hidden this entire time. A deadly sense of recklessness gleamed inside my twisted soul. It diminished as it sank deeper into the pit of a black abyss, until there was no escape. The sickness that the Bratva had inflicted and plagued me was here to stay, no matter who I was.

A killer could never stop being a killer.

Some killers were born and some were made.

I was made.

Kirill had altered my destiny.

He had stolen my fate from me.

A couple more movements jerked from my left and right.

With my gaze still on the floor, I lifted my blades, slashed them across the air, and struck my attackers again. My loose locks flew with it, and little droplets of some sticky substance clung to my hairline, slowly dripping down my forehead.

My body took a fighting stance. The pointy ends of my blades caught on flesh, and I jammed right into it, piercing through it. I didn't have to look at them to know from their gurgling mouths that they would end up dying soon. It would be better if no one came near me right now.

I didn't recognize myself anymore, let alone know who I was.

I just became what I'd been taught to become.

A lethal killing machine.

They'd made me into this, and they would feel my wrath as well.

Hesitant footsteps moved toward me.

"Ana," the low voice said.

It sounded familiar and distinct, but right now, I couldn't place a face to it. It struck a chord in the back of my mind, but I refused to listen.

Lifting my blades, I turned my body and aimed the sharp knife's edge right at eye level as I readied myself to strike again. Rapid breaths came out of my mouth as I held the blades apart at an arm's length and slammed them right down on whoever was near me. He grunted under me as he choked on his own breath.

"You always like stabbing me."

The voice became muffled, and at last, my narrowed eyes lifted and met his.

A pair of green orbs stared right at me.

Those green orbs always reminded me of wet mosses.

The entire forest laid in those magical eyes of his.

Never changing before me.

Puzzled, I stared down at each of the two blades I had jammed into his broad shoulders. The handles poked right out of them as déjà vu hit me. It reminded me of the night we first met.

I didn't think and only reacted as I pulled those blades right out of his shoulders. I didn't see Surge anymore. His pain didn't hurt me today. His face distorted as his features scrunched in pain. However, his eyes glowed like he was proud that I had managed to stab him again, like he was proud of the woman I had somehow turned out to be. Even though I wasn't around the Romanos, I'd managed to take care of myself without their protection. Before I became a long-lost princess, I was always sheltered like any other mafia princess. However, I wasn't lost anymore. I could see the future clearly now.

I exhaled tightly as I narrowed my unblinking eyes at Surge. My heart flipflopped when I caught the burgundy metallic liquid soaking his suit. He would probably need a new wardrobe after I was done with him.

A gasp escaped my lips. The hysterical thought left me baffled. My eyes blazed, but a piece of me urged me to stop my rampant descent into madness. I tried to bury that feeling, but it came out madder than ever. I was like a storm unleashing its wrath on everything in its way. The rush of killing still roamed deep within my soul. My soul grew colder, like the oceanic waves in the middle of the night. Even though Surge had peeled back the layers I had wrapped tightly around myself, it had hardened itself once again.

I desperately sought vengeance against everyone, even though I had already killed the main culprit of my rage. I still wanted to punish others. I still needed to kill because I didn't know what else to do with my hands other than do what I'd been taught all my life—to take a life.

Surge's eyes focused on the blood-stained blade in my hands.

I lifted the blade. I wasn't sure what I was about to do... yet.

His eyes softened.

"You're going to hurt me again, Little Assassin?"

Those words sliced right through me.

I choked out a breath, and my hand stilled in the air.

I hurt him.

His hands gripped his bleeding shoulders.

His eyes were so empty as he stared at me.

They were vacant like... *mine.*

The fastest way to die from a stab wound was to withdraw the blade.

I'd taken them right out of him, and now he was bleeding out in front of me.

My eyes dropped with heaviness, and the madness in me simmered down. A sense of emptiness filled my body.

Surge was always calm and rational, whereas I was chaotic and impulsive.

He was the calm to my storm.

Both Hell and Heaven.

Light and darkness.

Sanity and insanity.

It made me wonder—would I still have wanted him if I had been with the Romano family all along?

I remembered considering him as my stepbrother, but I didn't see that person in front of me anymore.

I just saw Sergio Romano.

Times had changed. *I* had changed.

We weren't meant to live a fairytale together.

Tragedy had struck us when I was taken away from my real family, but we managed to find each other again.

We were stuck here now. With each other.

That would never change.

"Nobody will ever harm you again."

Surge spoke in that alluring voice of his, drawing my ears to the bass of it. I thought of his voice as a temptation that always convinced me to stay. In truth, it was a never-ending cycle. I couldn't kill him, and I couldn't stay away from him either.

"I watched you grow up in front of me. At that time, I just thought of you as Angelo Romano's daughter, as a kid. You were thirteen when you disappeared, and when you came across me again, you looked familiar, but I couldn't recognize you. You were older. You looked different... and you had that damn blade in your hand like you wanted to murder me in my sleep." His lip quirked, even though he bled in front of me.

"It looks similar to our situation right now. You hardly looked like the young girl you had left behind. I had an idea how you'd look, but I didn't know for sure. Maybe I should have told you sooner, because I realized who you were the moment, I saw the pendant on your neck for the first time. I wanted to know more about you, and I couldn't kill you, so I let you walk away the first time, and I let you walk free again and again shortly thereafter." He licked his lips slowly before he continued. "To kill you would be killing a part of myself too, Ana."

I blinked back the water stinging my eyes. My mind swirled around me, and a hysterical noise wanted to leave my mouth.

Inhale. Exhale.

The tremor in my legs grew, and my feet felt like they were ready to give out under me. His words had shattered me.

A cry hurled out of my mouth before I clamped my mouth shut again. My pulse thudded against my skin as I took in his eyes. They were so intense that perspiration trickled down the back of my neck and in between the slopes of my chest. The sweat slipped right under the pendant I wore, and the pounding in my ears roared.

Come closer. I could hear the silent promise under his breath. *I won't hurt you.*

I'd forgotten how to speak now, and I was afraid I might have tachycardia. My heart beat faster than a drummer with its irregular rhythms. I was too young to have a heart attack. I didn't want to die yet, not when he was saying all these things to me.

"You've been a part of me, my life, my family since you were only three, and nothing could replace that. You're a survivor. You made it this far without the help and protection of the Romano Family. You held on your own this entire time, and I am so damn proud of you," he continued and pressed his hand against one of his bleeding shoulders. My misty eyes flew to his wound before they landed on his face again. Like wine, he had aged smoothly. As I studied him closely, I noticed that the wrinkles around his eyes deepened as his lip twitched up to a weak smile.

It was impossible not to fall in love with that smile.

Love? What did I ever know about that?

My ears starved for him to speak again.

No one has ever told me how much I meant to them before.

My heart felt too full right now.

His eyes stayed focused on me while my nerves tumbled, and my body tightened under his gaze.

They were bright, beautiful, and bold. They were priceless, like the dew drops that fall on leaves after heavy rainfall. An unveiled algae hung over his eyes as he continued staring at me. A stark rawness lingered in them, and his eyes showed everything he felt for me. The same kind of feelings I felt for him too.

His long eyelashes reined me in and made it a little too difficult to escape. My heartbeats quickened as his soul was bared out to me.

"You have an empire awaiting your return. Your legacy will continue. You are everything our empire needs. You have faced many losses. I know you have. I can't ever bring the seven years of your life you have lost, but we can make new memories. We can replace these bad ones…" My heart hammered in my chest, wanting to fall out any second now. "I don't give a damn about anyone but you. If you return with us, the unapologetic way you deal with death does not need to change. Every dark, fractured part of you will remain. I would never try to tame it. If you find solace in your shadows, I'll find solace in them too."

He swallowed again and his Adam's apple bobbed.

His promises brought a splurge of adrenaline through my body.

I felt like an alien in my own mind.

Come with me, his voice silently beckoned.

His eyes looked into mine with longing.

The same kind of longing I felt deep in my bones.

"Maybe fate picked the name Anastasia to symbolize your resurrection. You were the missing girl to some, the lost to others, and the dead girl to many. However, your essence can never die. No one can hide you away from this world ever again. You are not a secret weapon. You will not be molded into a weapon for anyone's profit ever again. You can let go now, Ana. You are the strongest person I know, and you don't have to be so strong anymore. We can be strong together."

He looked at me like I was the most incredible thing in the world.

My lips quivered and my shoulders sagged at the resignation in his voice. My blood rumbled and jostled me like thunder had struck me. A lump clogged my throat as I tried to swallow my tears. A soundless look passed between us, and the rest of the world blurred, like we were the only two people in this world.

As I studied him, trailing and committing every divine feature into my memory, he broke eye contact with me to stare at his bleeding shoulders. He winced, and his skin only paled in color even more. He was losing color, resembling the sickly whiteness of a blank wall and a translucent ghost. I had caused him pain. I had hurt him. And he hadn't even defended himself even once. I glanced down at my cruel hands and stared at the blades—the same ones I had used to slash into him mercilessly—before letting them go. I didn't want to hurt him anymore.

They fell to the floor with a clank.

Surge sighed with relief as his knees gave out right from under him. He crumpled to the floor with the two gashes inflicted on his body.

"S-Sergio," I began, but my voice wavered.

A tormented whine wanted to rise to the surface and scream at him. Our eyes locked for several seconds as the world faded away around us. I didn't see anyone else besides him. His mosses shimmered and then pierced through my insides.

Moving on wobbling legs, I reached out to help the poor, injured man before me. I wanted to hold his beautiful face in my hands and apologize for stabbing him.

I wasn't sure how one did that, though, since I was used to killing without remorse. My fingers itched to trail his handsome features. I tried to breathe through my nose, but I couldn't. It was like I lost the ability to breathe.

His lip quirked at me wobbling like a penguin toward him. Amusement ticked at the edge of his mouth as his cheekbones rose with an amused smile.

My dead soul warmed as water clung to my eyelashes. I swiped my arm across my eyes before he could catch anything, but I knew he did. His smile faltered for a second before his glassy emeralds searched through mine. The black circle on his iris only accentuated them.

My manicured nails dug into the skin on my palm as I moved my jelly-like body toward him. I couldn't believe I'd actually done my nails for once. I let out a ragged breath when I was near him.

I reached out a hand to touch his bleeding shoulder, but a hoarse scream came from him, *"No!"*

His voice boomed loud enough to turn glass into shards.

My fingers froze in the air and my pulse picked up speed.

My heart wanted to splinter into pieces as I glanced at his face.

He looked directly over my shoulder with fire in his eyes.

Instincts kicked in, and I turned around quickly, but it was too late.

A punch greeted the back of my head, on the same spot I had been injured once as a teenager. From time to time, it still tingled, as if it had never fully healed. It brought back memories of the day Kirill had yanked on my locks. His fingers had tugged on my sore scalp so hard that he'd pulled out a patch of my hair and left a bald spot there. The hair never grew on that damaged area.

The strong hand slammed down on my scalp, and I winced as I lost my balance and my vision turned black.

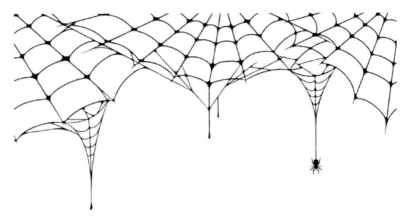

Ana

17

My groggy eyes burst open the second the artificial light hit them. I groaned and smacked a hand right across them. Grunting like a madwoman, I stared up at the silver chandelier hanging above my head. It wasn't golden like the one in Surge's room.

Using my stiff elbows, I sat upright and fluffed the pillow behind me. Leaning back, I rested my back against the bed's headboard as I glanced at my surroundings. One the Russian *vors* must have attacked me before I fainted. I studied the room. My instincts didn't kick in because this place wasn't unknown to me.

I recognized it deep in my soul.

It was my childhood bedroom.

The same bedroom I'd slept in as a child at the Romano mansion.

My eyes blinked back water as I took in the familiar bedroom. It was painted an azure color like the sky outside. I glanced at the window to see the sun streaming through the curtains. December was finally gone, and March was almost here. The first ray of sunlight landed on my cheekbones. The air was still chilly, but I relished in the warmth that it also brought with it. I stared at the walls where my family's portraits hung at eye level and caught a picture of my parents.

My biological parents, who were no longer here…

My soul briefly descended to a dark place, but then I realized I wasn't completely an orphan. I still had a grandmother and Surge. I still had a *family*. I might have forgotten them over the years, but they hadn't. I wasn't sure how to move forward from here, but I had hope that Surge would help me like he had promised me.

Together.

He promised me we'd figure everything out *together*.

After everything that had happened thus far, was I still the same person?

I still felt the same inside, but I felt different somehow.

More aware and more alert about who I was.

I wasn't left in the dark anymore.

Just yesterday, I was Anastasia Volkova, and now I was Annalisa Romano.

What a damn mess.

A hysterical laugh wanted to burst out of me.

My ears perked up when someone emerged from the doorway. Whoever it was hadn't bothered to knock.

I wondered if it was Surge. I hadn't seen him for hours. My tired eyes lifted as I glanced at my room's entrance for the familiar ginger but caught a full head of black hair instead. My breathing faltered as I stared up at *Pakhan*.

What was *Pakhan* doing here?

Well, he wasn't truly my *Pakhan* anymore, and it would take time for my tongue to remember not to call Alexander Nikolaev that. One of his soldiers must have knocked me out.

The edges of my eyes narrowed at him.

"Have you finally come to kill me for my crime?" Before he could counter, I added, "It shouldn't be considered a crime, though. Your cousin, Kirill Volkov, deserved it. I want to bring him back to life just to slaughter him all over again." I didn't even know where I got the balls to speak to him that way. Never in my life had I been bold and sassy with him ever before.

His thick, black eyebrows shot up, but I continued, "Your father also deserves to be punished. You should consider yourself lucky that I didn't get to kill him."

Alexander tilted his head as his black eyes studied me. Then, he crossed his arms over the fitted black blazer he wore. Next to him were three men standing guard. They weren't the *Vors*. I caught the sight of a lion's mane tattooed on their hands. *Cosa Nostra*. He was here with them. More like they had brought him to my room, and based on their body language, they looked reluctant to leave the room.

Realization dawned on me.

They were protecting their princess.

Me.

Alexander's face didn't even miss a beat as his eyes turned amused. "Anastasia..." He paused before correcting himself. "*Annalisa*, I am here because I thought we could have a lovely chat." He said this like we were ready to have a cup of tea. In reality, we were far from friends for such theatrics. "I'm not planning to kill you." I still eyed him cautiously like he would attack me at any second. The Bratva always attacked when people least expected it. Those who worked for them knew that was how they rolled. "I thought it would be best to see you one last time before we part ways."

I blinked and sagged against my pillow.

For a second, I thought I had heard him wrong.

A twinkle appeared in his black eyes, and he almost resembled a human for once and not a mythical creature of the night. There was something about him that reminded me of a fairy. I heard he was the type to give you mischievous smiles, offer a hand, and then stab you in the back with the other. I wasn't sure how true that rumor was.

I averted my gaze from his eyes. They reminded me too much of Kirill, and I'd rather not think about him at all.

"As for Kirill and my father, they had never told me about your roots. I was told they found you at the market before recruiting you. You were a part of us before I even came into leadership. I won't apologize to you, because I'm not the one who's done you wrong." Although his deep voice flowed smoothly like honey, the ruthlessness in it was clear as day as he spoke. In a way, it made sense. Just because I worked for him, didn't mean he owed me an apology.

A leader rarely did. Apologizing was a sign of weakness. It meant you were admitting a mistake you had committed.

I scoffed under my breath and glanced at his face, hoping he hadn't noticed me scoffing.

"The only woman I have ever apologized to is my wife."

My eyes shot up at him in surprise.

I hadn't expected that from him.

He continued to look at me. "What I *can* do for you is that you are free to live your life as you will, without harm, and as for my father... he's been exiled."

My eyes widened. I knew what he meant by that.

Stripped from his title and tattoos and publicly branded as *banished.*

It was something worse than death in our world.

To have your identity taken away from you was hell compared to death.

One would live with the humiliation for the rest of their life, and he would *always* have a target on his back as a traitor.

"I'm leaving now, Anastasia." Alexander paused before muttering inaudible cuss words once he realized he'd spoken the incorrect name again. "Anna—" He paused again before resigning to a sigh. "Whoever the hell you are. My brain is starting to hurt now, and that doesn't help the growing headache from last night. Goodbye."

He turned around to leave just as quickly as he came.

I stared after his back as he moved to leave, but he paused again and gazed right at me. My shoulders tensed, and I wanted to look away from his black abyss-filled eyes that looked too much like my deceased husband's.

They were different from Kirill's now.

They lit up, especially around his wife. I'd seen them.

More mischievous and approachable, unlike someone I knew... He wasn't his cousin.

The tension in my body left and my shoulders sagged.

He shoved his hands into his pockets as he took one last look at me. "You were a good soldier."

My chest expanded at his praise.

It was as if I had served him well.

Although he was the enemy now, it felt nice to be appreciated. And with that, Alexander Nikolaev left me alone in the room.

Moments after he left, a maid came in to bring breakfast, but I only said one word.

"Don."

The maid blinked.

"Don Surge. Where is he?"

My restless soul trembled violently, and I longed to see him again.

"He's in his room, sleeping from his injuries," the brown-eyed maid offered in a soft voice.

I winced like she'd slapped me.

I had caused those cruel injuries to his body.

"Where is his room?" I asked quietly.

West wing. "On the opposite side of the mansion, in the west wing."

I hid the smile at the memory.

I remembered where his room was.

Shortly after the maid left, I rose on my feet. Someone had changed me into a silky gray nightgown that ended at my calves. Probably one of the maids had changed me, since Surge was passed out like the dead.

Finding a robe and some slippers in the room that were much too large for my feet, I slipped into them and rushed out of the room, famished.

Famished for something other than food.

I'd been in this mansion before, but I hadn't been in this part of the mansion in a long time. I headed toward the west wing, and as I moved, I took note of the gilded portraits hanging on the walls. Familiar faces that were only alive in my memories flashed before my eyes. My heart worked overtime to pump blood through my jittery veins as the cold floor left peppered kisses on the soles of my feet. A few guards were stationed at some corners as I walked down the endless hallway.

They bowed their heads and murmured, "Princess," as I walked by.

Princess.

I guessed that title was here to stay.

At last, I stood before a familiar room heavily decorated with gold.

Without knocking, I turned the doorknob and slowly popped my head in. My jittery veins thundered, and my pulse spiked in anticipation. The curtains were drawn and pulled tightly together, casting the room in utter darkness, as if Surge had wanted to block out any sign of sunlight.

A body in the satin, white sheets stirred, and my footsteps paused. Tiptoeing like a mouse, I crept toward his bedside. He laid on his back. He probably couldn't rest on his shoulders. Guilt stabbed through my tormented soul as I stared down at his bandages. At some point, the sheet covering his body had come undone and his slick, freckled chest greeted me. I glanced at his face again. His light locks were tousled and his beautiful eyes that I desperately wanted to see remained shut. His face held so much peace, like he didn't have a care in the world that the person who had caused his injuries was standing before him.

In my frenzied state, I crawled onto his bed. His body stirred as if he was attempting to rise, but I threw my legs on each side of his body and rested my head against his heart. I could feel his heartbeat. It drummed against my ear, and I wrapped myself like a snake around him. I wasn't sure what to do right now. I just knew I didn't want to be without him. Maybe he would wake up. Maybe my tight hug would awaken him.

"What the fuck..." His cussing mouth spoke a beat later.

Surge stirred underneath me as he yawned.

I hid a smile as I rested my chin against his chest and peered up at him.

His groggy eyes blinked slowly. "What are you doing here?"

His voice came out even lower than usual, and his sexy voice had returned. I sighed happily on top of his chest. I could listen to him for hours. I turned my face from him and pressed my ear against his chest again.

"Listening to your heartbeat," I replied with sheer honesty.

Thump. Thump.

Dead silence greeted me.

My cheeks flushed, and I hoped he couldn't see my cheeks turning pink.

His heartbeat quickened, and the giddiness in me grew.

Thump. Thump. Thump.

"Are you blushing?" His voice came a second later.

Miffed, I glanced up and lied through my teeth. "No."

His eyes softened as he reached a hand and trailed it across my cheek.

Shivers ran up my spine at his cool touch.

"I'm so glad to see that you're doing all right," I confessed.

I laid with my head against his heart so he couldn't see my face anymore.

His finger moved down and continued to stroke my cheek.

"For a minute there, I thought I'd lost you. I thought I'd lose you a second time."

He was quiet before asking in his sleepy voice, "When was the first? When you stabbed me the first time?"

I would shake my head if I could.

"No. When I had gotten lost in the crowd..." I closed my eyes as the rush of the memory hit me. "It rained at the time. I remember being separated from my bodyguards, and in my head, I remembered thinking, I would never see Papa, *Nonna,* and… *you* again."

He stopped stroking my cheek, and I felt his heart beat wildly in his chest.

Thump. Thump. Thump.

I was sure mine beats the same way.

These memories still felt foreign to me, like they had happened to a separate entity. "When I stabbed you at the wedding, I thought I would be the cause of your death. I didn't think I could see you ever again," I continued in a low voice. "While it was fun stabbing you, I didn't like the actual part where you bled right before me." His chest moved under my face, and I realized he was chuckling. I only wrapped my arms tightly around him. "When you bleed, I bleed with you," I whispered against his chest.

He sucked in a sharp breath and my eyes misted.

I was saying all the things I had longed to say to him.

To kill you would be killing a part of myself too, Ana.

I remembered his words.

They were now my most favorite and painful memory.

"One day, my bleeding heart won't be able to take it anymore. It frightens me whenever I see you hurt. I've never been so afraid in my entire life. It's like if I blink, someone will snatch you away from me again. That if I close my eyes, you'll never be here by my side. I can't believe I'm home with you now."

Surge sighed under me as he reached down and pressed his mouth against my head. My eyes flared with desire and my soul tightened with need.

I sighed blissfully like a cat as I snuggled closer to him. Snuggling was something entirely different for me. I'd never done it before, but I wanted to wrap myself around him like we were one body and not two.

I peered up at him and without thinking, I brought his handsome face down to mine and pressed my mouth against his.

Time stilled as my lips met his soft ones.

I closed my eyes and wrapped my palms over his nape. I sighed against his warm mouth as we connected once again.

He tasted like sandalwood, musk, and home. Riots exploded as our mouths swirled against each other, battling one another and demanding for control. The stubble against his cheeks rubbed against my soft ones.

He groaned against my mouth as he sucked my bottom lip and gave it a sharp nip. I let out a small mewl, and he growled against my mouth. The sound vibrated down to my core as he pressed one bruising kiss after another on my lips.

We were heart against heart now.

Chest to chest.

Our exhales mingled together until they became the same.

Quivers ran down my spine as we unraveled before each other.

Like the two stems in a rose bush, our lips intertwined.

I kissed him like he was the last kiss I would ever have.

He kissed me like I was the first kiss he always craved.

He was the sun to my moon, and the stars in my sky.

I wasn't sure when I'd started to become obsessed with him.

Nor did I know when he became something greater in my life.

I needed him the way I needed air to breathe.

His darkness played well with mine.

It understood me. Even cared for me.

Instead of taming it, he challenged it.

Once we pulled away from each other, his misty eyes met mine.

"Welcome home, Ana."

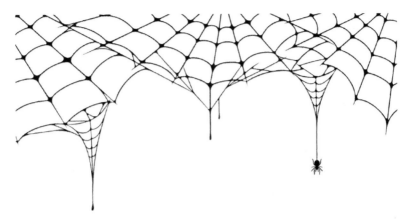

Ana

Epilogue

ONCE UPON A DECEMBER...

I was a wanderess, hungry and homeless.

And then... bought, conditioned, and trained as a lethal assassin.

I didn't remember who I was. I only remembered my name.

Anastasia.

To claim my life as a killing machine, I had to destroy others, and it became my violent destiny.

I was a silent predator underneath my hood.

No one was aware I was a woman until I come across *him*—Sergio Romano.

Meeting him altered my fate then and there.

My duty collided with desire for the first time.

It was risky, falling for my assignment, but I did it, anyway.

I forgot I was born as a woman until I felt my heart beat for him.

Turns out, I'd been living a lie.

With him, I found the truth.

Sergio Romano, my Surge, was seated at the table.

He didn't wear his leather clothing today, but a black suit clung to his tight muscles. Although he'd shaved his jaw clean, he already sported a shadow on his face. His light reddish locks were slicked back and polished behind his ears, touching his nape. His beauty was divine.

Sometimes, I forgot he was the Antichrist. My thoughts burst when his magnetic voice pulled me toward it.

"I wanted to speak to you about something, since I think you have had enough time to adjust to our life as *our* assassin."

A wide smile flashed on his face.

A hysterical laugh wanted to bubble out of me.

"You sound proud, big brother," I teased, remembering how he always hated it when I called him that.

He shot me a look of annoyance before scrunching his face in disgust. "Don't call me that," he commanded.

I grinned. "Why not? It's all right to tell the world you're secretly fucking your stepsister in your imagination." I couldn't help but push his buttons some more.

He glared at me before muttering something inaudible under his voice.

He seemed just about done with me.

Pinching the bridge of his nose, he sighed. "That only happened because I was under the impression that you were Anastasia," he corrected. "Like I was saying before I was rudely interrupted, I think it's time."

Sometimes, I wondered if he was right.

If I had never been lost and taken away from my family, would Surge and I still had happened? My father would've never allowed it. Drifting from my thoughts, I noticed his eyes glided from me to *our* people mingling in the crowd before us. I followed his gaze and stared at the people.

Our people. I'd finally found my way back home.

It'd been tough. Some days, I still remembered the crimes Kirill had done to me. I didn't return to the Bratva anymore after *Pakhan's* last visit. I would always respect him, but I didn't think we were close enough to visit each other's houses.

I still thought about the Bratva often, but I hadn't spoken to them in almost a year. I wasn't close to the rest of the females in the Bratva, since I didn't know how to make friends. I'd always kept to myself. Always been secluded and alone in my world.

I glanced down at the cobweb tattoo engraved on my hand.

The ink glowed on my pale skin, and the web's edges disappeared toward the back of my palm. I hadn't removed it yet. Surge hadn't asked me to have it surgically removed either. My previous *Pakhan* hadn't executed an order to have me stripped of my title and tattoo. No one could ever leave a syndicate unless maybe, they were the leader, but I had.

I'd left the Bratva, and it blew my mind that I was still alive to tell the tale. If someone wanted to leave a syndicate, one was either killed or had to be stripped of their identity completely. Their tattoos would be covered and branded with iron.

A permanent black mark would forever be branded on their bodies. They did that under extreme conditions when someone was exiled. Maybe it was because this identity wasn't really mine, to begin with, so there was nothing to be taken away.

It felt weird to remove myself from something I'd thought I belonged to, just to be part of something else. No matter what anyone would say, I would keep this tattoo.

Ten long months had passed. Time, seasons, and people had changed over time. I'd changed over the past few months, but still, I couldn't part with my tattoo. I couldn't turn off being Anastasia and return to being Annalisa.

It wasn't easy. It was a work in progress.

Some days I failed. Some days I succeeded.

Sometimes I still itched to speak Russian to people, but everyone around me either spoke Italian or some Russian. I'd tried teaching Surge, but he was a terrible learner. Many non-Russian Dons learned it when they were young and Surge couldn't.

Was it wrong for me to consider myself Russian even though I wasn't?

I'd been raised by them.

For the most of my life, I'd identified with them as well.

Why couldn't I be both?

I stared down at my other hand and smiled.

The tattoo of a lion was engraved on it.

The Romano symbol.

I had two symbols marked on me, and I knew I belonged to both.

The Bratva would never attack me or the Romano Family.

I'd served them. I'd fought for them. I'd made too many sacrifices for them.

Alexander Nikolaev had promised.

You are free to live your life as you will, without harm.

He'd let me live after killing his cousin Kirill. I was sure he would face even more enemies. I sighed silently as I stared at the thousands of guests at the Romano mansion. Many drank, many danced, and others simply talked, and they were all here to see me. Surge had arranged this while I'd mainly stayed home and completed my assignments. I was ready to face the real world and the people I once knew.

Although I was still lost in my thoughts, I managed to catch Surge saying, "…I want you to meet someone."

Puzzled, I turned to look at him.

He tilted his head and only gave me a soundless look.

My breath caught in my throat.

"I want you to meet someone.," he repeated, after taking in my lost expression before nodding in front of him.

I turned my head before I lifted my eyes. An expensive cologne and the scent of woodsmoke filled my nose. Mischievous sapphire eyes clashed into mine as I stared at a man wearing a navy-blue suit. My eyes crawled from his fair skin to his slicked blond hair. His angelic gaze held mine as his lips curved in teasing smile.

I held in a breath as recognition hit me.

"Hey there, princess."

A suave and deep voice I hadn't heard before, but I'd seen this man before at previous Bratva events years ago. The man with the angelic eyes and the devilish soul. The Devil reincarnated. The man stood in front of me, and I remained seated. Next to me, Surge spoke.

"This is one of my closest friends."

He didn't bother mentioning his name. It wasn't needed.

Don Salvi Moretti stood next to a woman who was equally beautiful with emerald eyes and midnight hair.

Ehva Moretti gave me a friendly smile as she said, "It's lovely to meet you."

I politely returned a tiny smile. "You too."

I peeked a glance at Don Salvi next to her who now looked at Surge. "You have your family reunited now."

I held in a beaming smile as I stared at Surge's handsome face. They continued chatting and I only added input when needed. The couple walked away later, and I still stared dreamingly at my Surge.

My Surge.

He caught me looking and bluntly spoke.

"I'm stepping down as Don"

I blinked. "Your Second is going to rule now?"

Surge's lip twitched. "No. *You* will."

I stared up at him, stunned.

Me?

He couldn't be serious. I searched for his teasing eyes again, but they remained calm and serene.

"W-why?" I stammered. I cleared my throat. "You don't want to rule?"

Surge shrugged. "I'm retiring. Forty years isn't bad to retire. I had a good run. Seventeen years. I can live peacefully while relaxing in a jacuzzi and riding my Bentleys while you make all the hard decisions for this empire." He lifted his champagne glass to his mouth. "I'll drink to that."

I giggled.

Oh my God.

I never giggled.

"You sound like a girl right now."

I rolled my eyes and resisted the urge to stab him.

"Truthfully, this empire wasn't mine. I helped build it with Angelo Romano."

He sighed as he remembered our father. *Our* father. He wasn't Surge's biological father, but he'd given him everything he had and called him his son.

His eyes glided to me, and that familiar smirk played on his lips again. "Maybe I was meant to keep it stable until you returned to us."

He drank his champagne, and I glanced at the crowd before meeting his eyes again. "And the soldiers would accept a *Donna* as their ruler?" It still sounded too good to be true. Before he could answer, I continued, "There hasn't been a Donna around in..." I paused before mumbling, "Never. Females can't rule in our world." It was a sad reality in our life.

The *Pakhan's* wife was an exception, but for the most part, he handled everything.

There wasn't a Donna who ruled alone.

"And it's fine to make them assassins but not the other?" he remarked.

"I don't think the soldiers would accept me. Most men won't bow to a woman."

I sighed as I took a sip of my own champagne.

"Says who? I bow to you every night when I eat your pussy."

I choked on the drink I'd been sipping, baffled by his absurd words. I glanced around us, and sure enough, some people had heard his crude words.

They coughed and chuckled like he'd cracked a joke. On the other hand, my cheeks flamed brighter than a tomato. He might as well have stabbed me than saying that publicly.

Before I could scold him, he flashed me a triumphant smile. His entire face lit up, and my heart skipped a beat. It was difficult to be upset with him sometimes when he was just so... *him*. Heck, it was difficult to just breathe around him. He consumed my entire being. And apparently, I was the grumpy one in our relationship.

I opened my mouth to speak, but his eyes glided down my adorned face to my breasts tightly snug in the scarlet gown I wore. It rested right below my stomach, and I didn't want to think about what naughty thoughts were traveling in his mind.

My core tightened and grew damper under his gaze, so I crossed my legs tightly. Surge gave me a knowing smile, and I was tempted to throw my champagne at his face.

He raised a refined brow. "The Romano empire is already familiar with you. They know who you are. You're their princess, and it is your right to rule. Not mine," he declared. My heart warmed. "I am not greedy for power, because I have grown up with nothing, Little Assassin."

I chewed on the inside of my cheek.

"They wouldn't trust me to be strong enough for them."

Surge looked me dead in the eye.

"You were strong enough for the Bratva to recruit you. Strong enough for them to not see you as a common whore and make you their assassin instead. Their only *female* assassin. You were strong enough to publicly behead Kirill Volkov."

He punched out that name like it was venom.

I didn't like to think about that name anymore.

After all, it didn't mean anything to me anymore.

Surge spoke again. "I never killed him the first time I set his head on fire because he should have been punished by you instead. You killed your *husband*, and to many, that is ruthlessness at its finest. A leader needs to be intelligent, but they also need to be ruthless, and you have that ruthlessness inside you. After all, you're the angel of death. You are a creature far more dangerous than most humans could ever imagine.

"He's always been your kill and not mine. You killed your trainer, your mentor, the captain of the syndicate that stole you. The assassin of all assassins. Not only that, but you also killed two more Russian *vors* after that, and you stabbed me twice. *Me,* a ruling Don." He waved two fingers in front of him as he listed my *accomplishments.* It wasn't something I would put on a resume. He glared at me for a second before he finished off with, "I almost bled out, but I survived. Thank God."

My face warmed and I tried to apologize through my eyes again.

He glanced around and moved closer to me. His eyes grew brighter, larger, and liquid-like as only inches remained between our faces. "Everyone has already seen your capabilities. I made sure of it that night."

Taken aback by his revelation, I searched his eyes for more answers.

His eyes glinted. "Why do you think I brought so many soldiers with me that night? To see you as their fucking queen, basking in the souls of the people she's killed."

My heart thudded and my mouth dropped open.

Wait... What?

"Y-you planned all of that?"

He shrugged innocently, but his eyes still gleamed with mischief.

"Well, I didn't know you would behead one of their leaders, but I can't say I hadn't expected it. I hoped you would. Let's put it that way," he replied.

I still stared at him, half fascinated and the other half in disbelief.

He reached out and closed my mouth.

My eyes flared and I reached down to pinch him right on his hip.

Hard.

His laughing eyes returned.

"You're the heir of the Romano empire. The only biological heir of Angelo Romano. If you ever have kids one day, they would be next in line to rule. It doesn't matter what you have between your legs. What really matters is what's in your mind and if you have what it takes to rule, and you do." His words came out fierce and protective, like he believed in me when I didn't know whether I was really capable or not.

I sighed happily before fluttering my eyelashes at him.

"You think differently."

His lip quirked. "Obviously. I wasn't born into the mob like every other fucker. They value physical strength. I value skills and lineage."

I frowned. "You cuss too much."

He shrugged. "Poverty will do that to you."

I reached across and patted him on his shoulder. I couldn't believe I'd just patted him like he was a dog. I hoped he didn't notice. Thankfully, he didn't, because he said, "I just want to take a step back while you burn the world to the ground and stomp on their bones. I like the villainous side of you."

I held in my laughter as I averted my eyes from him and stared straight ahead.

I caught a glimpse of a couple of Italian made men, and they bowed their heads to me. My eyes lit up as I murmured, "I would make a good queen?"

"Yes. They would die for you, just as I would."

My throat felt clogged, like it was lodged with rocks.

I lost my voice, like he'd stolen the words right out of me.

My heart stuttered and I sneaked a peek at him.

He hadn't said that to me before.

Well, it was kind of obvious, knowing how I stabbed him every time.

His emeralds looked intensely at mine, and I looked away.

I sucked in a sharp breath through my constricted throat.

"You are my home, Sergio," I mumbled under my breath.

Sergio. I liked saying his name.

I glanced down and clasped my hands in my lap.

He leaned in close and whispered against my ear, "And you are mine."

My soul cheered happily.

Just yesterday I was Anastasia Volkova, and today I was Annalisa Romano.

What a damn mess.

A hysterical laugh wanted to burst out of me.

"I'm sure you must be confused on what name to go by," Surge said slowly, like he was speaking to a child. I flashed a lopsided smile at him. I was doing that more often now. I was smiling. I was happy. Happier than I had ever been before.

Remembering his question, I blinked at him.

He observed me often, noticing my reactions, my small intakes of breath, and my nervousness around new people. He noticed every single damn thing about me. The man had the eyes of a hawk, and I just wanted to stab his pretty ones with a fork.

I thought about what he said.

Donna Annalisa.

The Donna of the fourth ruling Family of New York.

How did one return to being called a name I hadn't been called in years?

I remembered being Annalisa, but I'd always remember being Anastasia.

Donna Anastasia.

If I used that name, it would be a denial to Annalisa.

To who I used to be, to the name my family chose for me.

I couldn't keep the Russian name anymore, but I couldn't relate to my Italian name either. I was placed in a situation where I was stuck, so I did what any sensible person would do. I renamed myself.

"Donna Ana."

The name left my lips before I could stop it.

I could choose my identity.

Ana... I liked being called Ana.

I could be Anastasia and Annalisa.

A representation of *both.*

I liked being both, and I wanted to be accepted as both versions of myself.

Surge's eyes twinkled, and for some reason, I wanted to eat them.

"It rhymes," he murmured as if pleased.

I was pretty sure he was secretly proud I'd picked that name, because he called me that as well. His cool hand reached under the table, and he placed it on top of mine.

It shot tingles and bolts of electricity through me.

I turned my hand and entwined my fingers through his.

The warmth of his fingers wrapped itself around my soul and squeezed tightly. I looked up and my eyes glided across his.

"You don't think a Donna might want a Don one day?"

Surge's grip tightened on my hand, and his eyes shot up with hope. I knew what that hope stood for. Not because I'd asked him to be Don, but because I'd asked him to be with me, forever. We'd always be united as one.

I shrugged innocently, mocking him now. "I mean, not that a Donna needs a Don," I said casually. "And I don't mean anytime soon, but maybe one day?"

I hoped he would say yes.

"I will look into my schedule and think about it."

My mouth dropped open, and I wanted to reach out and throttle him.

His familiar smirk returned, and his teasing eyes gave his answer away.

Yes.

His alpha complemented mine.

His calm burned my fire.

He'd never be the storm in my life but the deep, calm sea.

His light feathers to my darker ones.

My shadows to his.

My once broken soul soared into the sky.

I chose to create a new beginning for myself.

My life had just begun.

Anastasia.

Annalisa.

Ana.

Ghislaine

Extended Epilogue: Ghislaine

TWO YEARS LATER

Marriage.

It was a simple eight-letter word.

I never knew I could be married again.

Times and seasons had come and gone, but I still couldn't believe that a new beginning was possible for me. I didn't know I could fall in love again after the death of my first husband, especially not with a notorious gang leader.

Our seven-year-old daughter Noura climbed onto my lap, even though she was much too big for me to carry. I still loved having her on my lap, though. She liked sitting on my lap and touching my soft belly. It grew bigger every month.

I covered her small hand with mine, and her beautiful brown eyes peeked up at me. She sighed blissfully against me, and her little yellow frock crumpled up at her knees. She always liked wearing those. I hoped she never grew out of it.

My heart felt so full that it might burst as I played with the soft bangs that covered her forehead. Her hair was pulled back in a loose ponytail.

"Mommy!" Noura's tiny voice came. I took in her features again. The sunlight poured onto her light brown locks, accentuating my brown-eyed beauty.

I paused. "Yes, baby?"

She scoffed. "Why doesth everyone keep calling me baby? I am going to school now."

Her lisp had slowly improved over the years, but sometimes it still slipped through. Although she went to speech therapy twice a week to improve her speech, her therapist mentioned that Noura often didn't make an effort to improve.

I reached down and pinched her soft, golden cheeks. She mewled like a small kitten under me. "You will always be a baby to me," I said proudly.

She stuck out her little tongue at me and I gave her a look.

Noura quickly snuck it back in her mouth

"Thome of the kids tease me at school."

I frowned and waited for her to continue.

"They thay my lisp is weird."

A bolt of electricity ran through my spine. My heartbeat thundered and my pulse spiked. My eyes flared and I was just about to open my mouth to demand who these kids were, but a smooth voice beat me to it.

"Who's teasing you, *detskoye solnysko*?"

Baby sun.

My heart flipflopped at the familiar sound.

Immediately, Noura climbed off my lap and ran to the owner of that voice.

"Daddy!" her chirpy voice exclaimed before she wrapped herself around her father's leg.

I stayed seated, even though my heartbeat quickened at the sound of his voice. It still affected me till this day. Gliding my eyes from Noura, I glanced up at her father.

A pair of dark eyes and a sly, sinister smile stared right at me. He always left me breathless. My lips parted as I took him in, even though I'd seen his handsome face just this morning. My husband, Alexander Nikolaev, eyed me like a hawk through his black eyes as he reached up a hand and grazed it through his trimmed, immaculate beard that covered his prominent cheekbones. His other tattooed hand flicked Noura's ponytail as he did so. He winked at me playfully before he reached down and carried Noura like she only weighed a feather.

"Now tell me, who dares to tease my baby girl?" His voice boomed, but I could hear the affection in it. Noura giggled as she wrapped her arms around him. "Some kidth at school. I told them my daddy will hurt them, but they still do it."

Alexander raised a black eyebrow before seating himself across from me with Noura on his lap. "I can take care of that," he murmured assuredly.

I reached out and pinched his shoulder.

His body didn't even react as his glassy midnight eyes met mine. *Stars.* They reminded me of the stars that hugged the night. Starry, dark, and velvety, like a million stars had exploded in them. I tried to shoot him a look.

"No hurting children."

His lip curved. "I'll just have a nice, lovely chat with their fathers," he said slowly. "Communication is always the key, right, Noura?" His teasing voice returned as he turned to look at our golden sunshine of a daughter.

I tried not to roll my eyes.

Murder was clearly on his mind, and here he was, teaching Noura communication skills. A giggle bubbled inside of me before slipping through my mouth. I clamped my hand over my mouth and pretended to avert my eyes.

"Now go play," Alexander said, brushing his soft lips against Noura's forehead. She sighed happily before climbing off his lap and bouncing away. Probably to find Ilya.

He turned toward me, and his misty eyes held me in place for a few seconds. Reaching a hand below, he let it rest on our growing baby.

"In five months, Nikita will be here."

Nikita Nikolaev.

Our son.

My soul beamed. "Can we call him Nick for short?"

Alexander's handsome features scrunched up. "That is not Russian. I prefer Kita."

Before I could say anything, my body jerked as I felt a push through my stomach. Alexander froze and glanced down at his hand still covering my belly. My eyes misted as I breathed. It was the first time our baby had kicked. I sniffled and mumbled, "I think he approves of Kita."

Alexander didn't reply as his large, pale hand traced circles around my belly as if longing for that kick again. I had a child from my previous marriage. I was still excited for the second, but nothing could beat the happiness of having the first.

It was his first biological child.

He didn't get to see the process with Noura.

It hit differently.

His curious eyes jerked up at me before he said, "Why is he not kicking again? Tell him to kick again."

My laughter rang in the air. "I can't order him to kick on command."

He raised a refined brow. "He likes to kick people."

I reached over and pinched his cheek, and Alexander squirmed like a kitten.

He was adorable, and I wanted to eat him up.

"Obviously, he takes after his notorious father," I joked.

Alexander's lip twitched as his eyes met mine again. He sighed under his breath before leaning his head back on the couch to stare at the ceiling. "Our family will be complete soon." My heart smiled. Without turning his head, his eyes glided toward me and the haunting look in his eyes made my breath hitch. "You've made me the luckiest man by marrying me, Little Bird."

Little Bird... I smiled at the nickname.

"It's almost a pity I have to share you with someone else now. I already share you with Noura." His voice dropped low, and his eyes dimmed.

"Are you seriously jealous of our baby?"

He smirked. "Maybe."

"You knew Noura and I were a package when we got married."

His midnight eyes glowed with mischief. "Yes, I was aware. I just can't help but be a selfish bastard when it comes to you. I love Noura to death, and I already love our son. Just some days, I just want you all to myself. *Mine*." The last word rumbled out of his mouth. "Mine to love, mine to care for. Just mine."

I reached over and rested my hand on his.

"When the children are older and married, it'll just be you and me then," I promised.

Alexander's eyes twinkled. "I'm not letting Noura go anywhere away from us," he vowed under his breath. "I don't trust anyone to be worthy of her." His voice was laced with such a deep protectiveness and possessiveness that it was difficult to tell which was what.

I grinned. "Oh boy, I already feel terrible for her future partner."

Alexander turned his head and his long fingers entwined with mine.

He glanced down at our tattoos. I didn't have the cobweb tattoo like the other soldiers. A tattoo of a large black widow with tints of red was engraved on his hand. I had the same on mine.

A reflection of each other.

"You are my world, Ghislaine, and I can't stomach the thought of losing you or Noura. Some days, I wake up in the morning and check you and Noura to see if you're both still there." He almost sounded like a lost boy, and my heart went out for him. "We have buried the past, but if Noura finds out the truth one day... I'm 'fraid..." His voice trailed off. He exhaled before continuing, "That she might leave me one day like you did."

I wanted to take all of his dark memories and consume them. I crawled where he sat and rested my head against his shoulder.

"We'll all still be here, I promise. I promise, Zander," I vowed fiercely under my breath. "Tragedies don't last forever."

Alexander's eyes peered down at me as his lips brushed a kiss against my nose.

He wrapped his arm around me as we sat there in silence.

"You and Noura are the reason I breathe. If I don't see either of you in my world, how will I breathe without you two?"

I didn't doubt his words for a second.

"I love you," I breathed.

Alexander's breath hitched. "As do I."

We'd created a new beginning for ourselves.

We rewrote our love story with a new ending.

He was my dark knight.

My defender.

His touch was poisonous.

And my cure.

Nine

Extended Epilogue: Nine

Blue stared into my eyes.

Tonight, I was trying to teach him how to smile more.

Obviously, I was doing a terrible job at it, because his face remained permanently stoic. I wrinkled my nose at him and stared at the bluish-black sky above.

Every day, I stared at him unapologetically, hoping he would smile at me some more. Sometimes, his full mouth twitched. Other times, it quirked. Once in a blue moon, he would greet me with a full smile.

My heart ached every time to see him smile, but I would never tell him to smile more. It would just look forced, and it wouldn't rest well on his face. My husband, Dimitri Nikolaev, and I laid under the stars on the grass. Our son Ilya was home with his grandmother. We had sneaked out of the mansion to spend some time alone.

At night was the only time I could go out.

My mother-in-law understood why, and I appreciated her so much.

A black, starry night greeted us from above. I sighed blissfully, and my *Blue* pulled me closer to him, right under his broad and muscled arm. The night deepened and expanded like black wings. Shadows of the dark coated us and sucked us into its darkness. Each star in the sky glowed bright like a brilliant pearl. The cool wind fluttered against my chilled skin. I liked the darkness. Most people were afraid of it, but it had become my friend. It held me close like a friend.

My eyes searched through the moonlight and rested on the beautiful moon. It stood out in the pure black of the night. The wind tousled my hair, blowing some tendrils across my face.

I closed my eyes when Blue reached a large hand and brushed them from my face. My breath hitched when his calloused fingers trailed down my nose and rested on my lips. His finger dragged my lower lip down and dropped it with a pop. My breath came out in puffs in the breezy air as he hovered above me like my personal cocoon. His weight settled over me and his lips brushed against mine, but I turned my face.

"No smile, no kiss."

I could hear a low growl coming from him.

I hid in a smile.

He moved and tried to kiss me again. I stayed still like a statue, and he sighed, because I wasn't kissing him back. "Kiss back," he demanded in his cold and harsh voice. It sent shivers down my spine. "Come on, Goldie, I need more kisses."

This came from a brute who'd never liked the idea of kissing before.

I popped open an eye, and, with a smile, I countered, "Smile."

His face remained frozen instead.

A crease filled his eyebrows and he shot me a look of disapproval. I only continued to smile and hoped I could infect him with it as well. I took in his face. A few midnight-colored tendrils fell on his beautiful face. His pale skin glowed under the moonlight while I was hidden in the shadows. When I took in his eyes, his deep, sapphire eyes were staring dryly at me.

The more I continued to smile, the more his prominent jaw ticked.

"I don't know what I was thinking when I married you," he replied instead. His voice grew thicker and harsher with each word, like the wind blowing around us.

My lips parted and then I grinned.

I couldn't help but smile at him.

His eyes softened as he stared down at me.

A real *emotion*.

I loved it when he showed me this side of him.

"You fell in love with me, Blue," I replied easily.

His lip twitched. Almost smiled!

"I can't deny that now." He leaned in and his heavy weight fell on me again. I breathed and my breath landed on his lips. His throat bobbed as he swallowed thickly. He stared into my hazel eyes before leaning down and brushing his mouth against me. "Kiss back," he mumbled while trying to move his lips with mine.

I squealed under him. "Do you mind, you brute? We came here to watch the stars."

His large hand reached up and captured my jaw within his grasp.

Now, I couldn't move at all.

I stilled.

"I came here to watch you," he murmured. "You're my sun and stars."

My breath hitched.

I pouted. "I wanted to see the shooting stars."

His eyes darkened, and he leaned down and sucked on my lower lip. I gasped into his mouth, and he pulled back.

"My mouth is already swollen from your previous kisses," I whined in a small voice. Blue stared down at me, and I bit down on my bruised lips. "You are on a kissing ban from now on," I huffed under my breath.

Blue raised a brow, propping an elbow on the grass and leaning his head on it.

"You truly want to see the stars?"

I nodded fiercely.

He reached out a finger and brushed it against my eyelid. I closed my eyes in response and let him trail them for a few seconds. I breathed under him, soaking in the nice breeze and his warm touch. "Your eye color shines more than any other star, and yet you still want to see the stars?" His voice came low and husky near me. "There is more light in your eyes than the stars themselves."

My soul tingled, and I popped open my eyes.

He stared right at me.

"I'm not sure why you crave to see the day sometimes, when the setting sun is in your hazel eyes." My heart soared in the night sky. "Ilya has your eyes. Our son carries a part of you with him."

I swallowed.

"You never told me how much you adore my eyes."

Blue averted his eyes now that I'd called him out on it.

After a brief moment, his gaze locked on to mine like I was his everything.

We just kept looking at each other like our eyes could never be separated from one another. He lit a flame in me. It felt right in all the wrong ways, and I wanted to come undone before him.

"The first time I met you, I noticed how your eyes fell on me—you weren't afraid at all," he continued.

He'd never confessed these things to me before.

Blue rarely ever talked, but he'd improved in the area of communication over the years.

My hungry ears starved for his voice to continue. Even though it was cold enough to cut through ice, I still wanted to hear it. It was exquisite enough to devour my entire being.

"I see my future every time I look into them."

My gaze softened as I reached up and pressed my swollen mouth against his. He growled against me before wrapping both of his rough hands in my hair and pulling me closer to him. My eyes closed swiftly as I matched his movements. My mouth slashed across his, and he took my lower lip into his mouth before nipping on it. I yelped under him, and he continued kissing me like he wanted to consume me completely. I could feel the stroke of his tongue sliding inside my mouth.

Shivers ran through me. A carnal need rolled off him as he peppered kisses on my mouth. I sighed blissfully and tried to turn my head to catch my breath, but his hand tugged at my hair and pulled me close to him again. He had no intention of letting me go now that I had given him an opening.

He trailed kisses against my cheeks, my jawline, and my collarbones. I let out tiny gasps as he left wet, whiskery kisses across my soft skin. His body crawled on top of me again.

"It was supposed to be one kiss," I mumbled against his mouth. My words came out muffled as his hungry mouth ate them up.

Blue's lips were on my collarbone now, finally deciding to give my chapped lips a break. I wrapped my arms around his solid shoulders as I stared up at the black skies above. I could still watch the stars like this.

Blissful sighs left me as he continued leaving whiskery kisses and touches as he ravaged me. On the inside. On the outside.

Long, sinful moments passed, and he was still there in the darkness.

His magnificent soul connected to mine.

He was the blood within my veins.

If I slit them, he would pour out of them.

"Moya." His voice rumbled against my skin like the silky caress of the wind.

Mine.

My chest arched against his.

My heart pounded, and I was sure he could hear it.

The frenzy I could feel brewing in my stomach exploded.

His soul had wrapped around my heart and squeezed it tightly.

It pulsated in every cell and molecule of my body. I couldn't fathom living without this man. I didn't want to claw my way out of his life. Rather, I wanted to drown myself in the midst of his blue sea.

My heart almost stopped, and my body was conscious of his every move.

My soul remained content yet chaotic every time he was near.

He was both my death and destruction.

He was my ruin, and I was his.

Heartbeats raced.

Breaths accelerated.

Silent promises were made.

Our souls locked with each other.

"Tvoy," I whispered in the dark.

Yours.

I was a tragic beauty with thorns and broken petals.

<u>Order here.</u>

A lethal man.
A ruthless killer, who I have loved since we were children.

Magic cannot turn him into a prince, as he is only my *bodyguard.*

A bodyguard *can't* fall in love with his mafia princess, but we broke all the rules. Kazimir swore an oath, but my protector became the biggest *threat* to me.

My name is Galina Ivanova, daughter of the *Pakhan,* and this is my story.

Available in <u>Italian</u> too.

Afterword

I do hope you enjoyed reading this novel. If you did like it, feel free to leave a review on <u>Goodreads</u>, <u>Amazon</u>, and <u>Bookbub</u> even if it is just two words. I would love to read your thoughts.

This was Ana's and Surge's story. My last books have been filled with emotional and angsty romance, and I needed a break kind of like when I finished *A King of Beasts.* This story is more fast-paced that focused on a woman finding her identity in a mafia world. Sometimes, as writers we need a break from our usual angst. The *Black Widow* series is now complete, and I hoped you readers like the reunion of the previous characters. It's sad to say goodbye to these characters but on the bright side, that means, another series will begin soon. These characters will appear in future books again.

If this is your first book by me, check out the Beauty & The Beast original series, the first book being *A Beauty So Cruel.* The *Black Widow* series is a spin-off series that focuses on the Bratva.

Until next time,

Beena

UPCOMING RELEASES

A Terrible Villain
A Hades & Persephone Romance
Featuring Valerius Vitalli.
A standalone releasing September 15, 2022.
Order here.
Add to Goodreads TBR

A.P.O.A
A Cinderella Dark Mafia Romance
Featuring Gabriele Vitalli.
Release date TBA. 2023.
Add to Goodreads TBR

Thank you to my family and close friends for always encouraging me. Thank you to my team behind creating this novel — the amazing book cover artist Ms. Betty, the beta readers, the editors L.L. Lily, Evelyn, and Zainab.

Instagram: @Beenaxkhan
Twitter: @Beenaxkhan
Facebook @Beenaxkhan
Goodreads: @Beena_khan

Want to join my Reading Group?
Facebook Beena's Beastlys

Feedback or new book suggestions?
Email me ideas at beenaxkhan@gmail.com

Want to be part of upcoming releases, excerpts, and cover reveals? Sign up for my newsletter below. I don't spam and email 2-3 times a month.

Beena Khan Newsletter

Read the first chapter of <u>Book #1: *A Beauty So Cruel*</u>
of the original *Beauty & The Beast* **mafia series....**

ONCE UPON A TIME...

It was Valentine's Day.

More like Death's Day.

Vlad had a deal at the masquerade ball.

It was safer since everyone's face was hidden. No one could recognize him in his black and silver mask. He reached up a hand to rake it through his thick, black hair, but then stopped when he realized it was polished and heavily made up.

Holding in a sigh, he was annoyed. He hated dressing up and was itching to loosen the tie that felt like a noose around his neck. He wanted to take off his suit jacket already, but he had to blend in and not stand out right now.

Vlad sipped his scotch, surrounded by two of his men at the bar area. The laughter was loud, and voices chattered around him, rising above the light background music. Each conversation tried to dominate the other, voices raised to be heard. His ears soaked in the laughter around him. Some people sat in groups of five or more while others danced and swayed on the dance floor like a moving mass around the venue.

Just then, a woman caught his eyes.

She was young, perhaps in her early twenties. Something about her made him watch her. She was tall, maybe five-feet-seven with a willowy frame. She wore a golden masquerade mask, hiding her face. The golden feathers accentuated her silky black hair that flowed behind her in thick, long curls.

The beauty wore a long-sleeve velvet black dress that ended at her knees. His eyes narrowed in on her. The front of the dress had a slit up to her thigh, exposing her nicely shaped athletic legs. She carried a matching small clutch in her hand. Her neckline plunged deep toward her ribs. It had gold sequins adorning it that glittered under the silver and golden lights above them.

Something stirred inside of him, a beast hunting for its prey. Now, a sense of adrenaline rushed through him, and his muscles tightened. He swore his pupils dilated.

He hadn't even seen her face yet. Vlad swallowed hard, keeping his gaze on her, and studied her curiously.

The beauty didn't seem to fit in with the filthy rich people around her. She seemed guarded, curious, and nervous like an innocent gazelle.

A man was with her, maybe her date. He wore a mask, and Vlad couldn't recognize him. The tall man with slicked dark brown hair leaned in and whispered something in her ear. Then, he laid a possessive hand against her waist. The beauty flinched, even though she tried to hide it from the man.

Then, the man walked away.

Vlad waited.

One beat, two beats, three beats.

She glanced in Vlad's direction.

He leaned against the bar and sipped quietly as someone made conversation with him, but he didn't pay attention.

The beauty in black stood still, unmoving. She didn't approach him and neither did he make a move toward her. He wondered who would make the first move. Then, he thought, *screw it.* He might as well walk over.

His cousin, Gabriele caught him looking.

"What is that *thing*?" Gabriele eyed the beauty Vlad was staring at and whistled low.

Amused, Vlad turned to look at him. "Look away."

He carried his drink with him and slipped seamlessly through the crowd like smoke, catching the stares of many women around him. A sharp smell of drinks from the surrounding waiters wafted toward him. He sauntered casually over to the girl, liking how her eyes appraised him. Her gaze traveled from his expensive black suit before resting on his face again. She looked cautiously to the right as if fearing her date would return.

A smirk broke out on his face.

Time to play.

He grabbed a drink from a waiter's tray. He had to bring something to offer her at least.

He stood a couple of feet away from her when her heavily made-up kohled eyes glanced up at him again. Her light perfume lingered in the air. It was sweet and not overdone. She fixed him with a sharp look that would've made anyone else shrivel but not him. It was as if she were trying to gauge him under his mask.

Amber colored eyes.

Hello, beauty.

Then, he spoke.

"Your date ditched you?"

He meant to tease her.

Smooth. Really smooth Vlad.

He was direct and he liked it that way. What was he supposed to say? Hi? In his world, there was no time for casual conversations. No point in getting to know her. He knew what he wanted. He hoped she did too. She seemed shy and more reserved now that he'd approached her. He was doubting that she would agree to fuck now.

Her pink, full lips lifted in a smile.

She's mine.

He knew it before she did.

"I'm glad you came. I didn't like him at all," the beauty replied.

Her voice was deep and raspy. He was surprised since there was no lightness about that voice. It belonged to an older woman, but she looked so young. He'd expected a soft, angelic voice, but her voice was nothing like one. It was nice though.

He wondered how his name would sound when he buried himself inside her.

He studied the dress on her. It was low, hugging her form. His eyes lingered on her curves before he brought them up again.

He offered the drink he held in his other hand.

"Thank you," she said before taking the drink.

She tucked a tendril behind her ear in uneasiness. Was she nervous or did she know who he was? His face was hidden though.

"You come here a lot?" he asked casually.

He didn't really care. He had zero interest in making a conversation, but he wanted her to loosen up. She seemed too cold, too icy. He needed to try with this one.

You're an asshole, Vlad.

Good. Not that he cared. Assholes hurt less.

"No," she said, a small laugh slipping out of her. "It's my first time."

"Who's your date?" he asked.

Small talk. He could do this. Was he supposed to ask her name? Usually, he did that only after he was done screwing their brains out.

"Emilio Valentino."

His eyebrows shot up. He knew Emilio. He was sleazy and often visited one of his brothels. One of his best paying clients. He also knew the kind of sick shit he was into.

Her eyes met his again. They were like two massive amber pools. He liked looking into her eyes. There was something about her that piqued his curiosity.

Maybe it was the fact that she was here, but she didn't seem to belong.

She didn't fit in.

Some women were comfortable and cheerful, and others tried to throw themselves at him. He wasn't surprised, he knew his clothes were expensive and oozed of wealth.

He was just about to ask her name, but then her date returned.

Emilio didn't recognize Vlad in his mask and looked at him warily.

"Who are you?"

There was obvious jealousy in his voice.

Vlad didn't answer.

Emilio's eyes darted from the girl to him, before he asked the girl, "You know him?"

"No. She's all yours," Vlad said, at last even though he didn't mean it.

Emilio's eyes widened.

Vlad tried not to give him a cold smile.

"Oh. Don Vlad… I'm so sorry. I apologize. I didn't recognize you. Please forgive m-me," Emilio stammered, his cheeks flushing red like a tomato.

Vlad only nodded.

The amber-eyed girl looked on with a mixture of confusion and curiosity. He knew she wanted to ask him questions, but she stayed silent, perhaps because of her date.

Vlad walked away.

He could feel the girl's stare burning into his back, but he didn't bother to look. He couldn't cave in and see her face again.

Shaking off his thoughts of her, he focused on the task he came here to do. There was enough mingling now, so he wouldn't stand out so much.

Throughout the night, his eyes came across the beauty multiple times, but he didn't approach her.

He had things to do.

Vlad left with his men and headed to the car. He sat in the backseat in the parking lot while his men conducted the transition from the opposite party. He rarely ever came out. It wasn't safe, so he kept himself hidden in the bulletproof car. He simply ordered, and his men obeyed, handling his deals. He only stepped out when necessary.

There were shouts in the background from his men.

His phone rang, and he answered, "Hello?"

It was Gabriele.

"He's making excuses on why he's short."

That's all he said. They couldn't communicate messages on the phone. He knew their phones could always be tapped.

"You already know," Vlad replied simply.

He knew Gabriele was smart. He knew the code.

He hung up.

Kill him. That was the message.

That was the rule for betrayal.

Taking in the surroundings, he had his window opened an inch so he could hear the conversation.

"Where's Vlad? I want to talk to *him*," he heard the dealer say.

"No," Gabriele said.

"Leo, bring Vlad Vitalli," the same dealer said.

The sound of the heels caught his attention. As footsteps approached, the rhythm was hesitant, and then it stopped.

He saw her first before she could see him.

She stood in front of his window, but she couldn't see him. The back windows were tinted and black.

He was momentarily surprised.

It was the same girl he'd been speaking to earlier.

The beauty.

Amber eyes.

There was a silenced shot in the air.

Then, he sighed when she screamed.

Having a witness was always messy.

PREVIOUS MAFIA BOOKS:
BEAUTY AND THE BEAST SERIES

Book #1: *A Beauty So Cruel*

I was a beauty, a stray orphan until the beast took me as his hostage. Dahlia was the wrong person at the wrong time. To save her life, she made a deal with the beast the mafia don. He didn't know by taking her, he sealed his own fate.

Book #2: *A Beast So Cold*
(Sequel)

Vlad made Dahlia his queen. The reason behind his smile. Then, she set his world on fire. Nobody takes away what he wants. A beast is no man, and he's going to prove it by dragging her from hell.

Book#3: *A King Of Beasts*
(Interconnected Standalone)

A rival Italian mob set my world on fire by destroying everything I love. The people around me look away as my innocence is shed by the Mad King until one stare lingers. Bodyguards are meant to be protectors, not lovers.

Book #4: *A Beauty So Cursed*
(Interconnected Standalone)

Lada Sokolova, a noble Bratva Princess was supposed to be betrothed to my family. I'm twelve years her senior so I reject her. Now, she's getting married to a brutal *Vor* who's more than *twice* her age. I do the one thing I shouldn't have, causing my life on the line. I take her. I kidnap a bride in her wedding dress.

BLACK WIDOW SERIES

Book #1: A Kiss Of Venom
(Complete Standalone)

I've been in a coma for the past three years after an accident has left me unconscious and widowed. I'm in a sleep so deep, it cannot be broken until feel a brush of soft lips against mine. In my groggy state, I wake up to a pair of dark eyes and a sinister smile. As an agent, I revisit one of the most treacherous cases of the most dangerous man in New York City, Alexander Nikolaev, the *Pakhan* of the Russian Bratva.

Book #2: A Lock Of Death
(Complete Standalone)

I was locked in a skyscraper in New York City with eight other girls. I can't belong to a single man because I've belonged to *all*. No identity, no friends, and no life outside the gilded door of this tower. One day, the Bratva Brotherhood comes for me. Imagine my surprise when Dimitri Nikolaev says," You're being delivered."

DEVIL'S LAIR SERIES

Book #1: The Blue-Eyed Devil
(Salvi & Ehva)

I'm a wealthy and privileged Catholic girl who's returned from studying law abroad. It was a night out with my boyfriend, Adamo, when everything descended into chaos at the casino. He lost and gambled me away. Years ago, I took a vow of celibacy, but now a sadistic man tempts me with the dark side.

Book#2: The Fallen Angel

(The Sequel)

I considered Salvi Moretti my God, but he turned out to be the Devil in disguise. He can break my wings, but he may have forgotten my claws will always come out.

Book #3: The Night Thief
(Complete Standalone)

I'm a woman on a run. A con artist, scamming my way into the rich. I set my eyes on one of the most popular casinos in New York posing as a royal princess. Everything was going well until a pair of harsh blue eyes catch me red-handed.

HADES & PERSEPHONE DUET

Book #1: A Beautiful Liar

As a geeky scholarship student at the ancient and prestigious Saint Eudora Academy, I craved freedom, so, I sneaked out into the nightlife. It was a single night. He said, I have six months before he returns. In my drunk state, I agreed, and he declared us as *betrothed*. The next morning, I ghosted him. Imagine my surprise when I see him at my academy six months later. He's returned like a raging inferno to claim me.

MEET THE AUTHOR

Beena Khan is a storyteller based in NYC where she brings dark fairytales and myths to life. She writes mafia crime romance, new adult, and edgy contemporary fiction that gives you a book hangover. Her books are painful, messy, dangerous, and raw. She has a master's degree in Developmental Psychology and a minor in Arabic studies. She often explores the human psyche. She published her first book, *The Name of Red* when she was 26.

She loves hearing from people, and you can find her on her website, Twitter, Facebook, BookBub, and Instagram @beenaxkhan for upcoming releases and further book news.

Beena Khan

Printed in Great Britain
by Amazon